E. J. McGILL

Immaculate in Black

ASBURY PARK PUBLIC LIBRARY
ASBURY PARK, NEW JERSEY

A THOMAS DUNNE BOOK

St. Martin's Press   New York

IMMACULATE IN BLACK. Copyright © 1991 by E. J. McGill. All rights reserved. Printed in the United States of America. No part of this book may be used or reproduced in any manner whatsoever without written permission except in the case of brief quotations embodied in critical articles or reviews. For information, address St. Martin's Press, 175 Fifth Avenue, New York, N.Y. 10010.

Design by Judith A. Stagnitto

Library of Congress Cataloging-in-Publication Data

McGill, E. J.
    Immaculate in black / E. J. McGill.
      p.   cm.
    "A Thomas Dunne book."
    ISBN 0-312-05484-X
    I. Title.
PS3563.C36389I46   1991
813'.54—dc20   90-19458
                                                            CIP

First Edition: April 1991

10 9 8 7 6 5 4 3 2 1

To Ellie

Prologue: Alter Egos

Her head hurt, but Sarah could not stop laughing in that peculiar manner that seemed to imply everyone and everything were fair game. Finally, she asked who was next.

Shelly ran her finger down the list. "How about President Bush?"

Sarah laughed even harder. "No, I don't think we want the FBI after us."

"Then how about somebody local, maybe the sheriff?"

Shelly selected the Channel 5 news disc and found the sheriff on the track menu. "It'll take a few minutes," she said.

"Who's he gonna call?"

Shelly checked the screen. Lisa Conitti, anchorwoman, was the sheriff's opposite number on the interview. "Her."

"What's he gonna tell her?"

"Oh . . . how about some really gross crime with lots of gory details?"

They talked through what would happen, chattering separately but together in unbroken dialogue: Conitti getting into her tight jeans and makeup, camera crews lugging and loading equipment, all of them piling into their vans and roaring off to film a nonexistent cadaver.

"A little girl . . . who's been raped . . . and strangled . . . with her panties . . . trunked outta town . . . dumped in the desert . . . where she's eaten by coyotes."

This would be the best one, they agreed, laughing until they cried.

Isolated in the dark house along the dry riverbed, Shelly and Sarah practiced their pranks on the world and loved one another as one loves oneself, shamelessly, without fear of what the other might think because they were, to each other, only one. Yet they were the same only in their oneness.

Perhaps that is why they loved each other so much. Two bodies in one, half heiress, half gamin; genius and joker, soon to be none.

1

9-1-1

He carried out his visit to the enemy camp in the same measured style as in the old days, wearing his gray, short-sleeved jersey bearing the faded thirty-four, red-striped white shorts, and green Nikes. It was an outfit certain to disarm the impeccably dressed Glidden, who would probably treat him as the last living veteran of an ancient and forgotten war, a treatment he did not necessarily approve of, but appreciated the advantage it offered. Anything the prosecutor had, Sherm was welcome to, a courtesy not usually extended to the firm's junior partners.

When he entered the prosecutor's office, Glidden got up, shook his hand, and expressed genuine delight at having Sherm back on the job, particularly on this case. Bruner was guilty, he said, and there was no sense in tying up the court with irrelevant and endless testimony.

Sherm asked to hear the tape.

Glidden snapped the cassette into the recorder. The woman's voice, he said, belonged to Shelly Eagan, the other to the officer on duty.

OFFICER: Nine-one-one, emergency.
SHELLY: Someone's breaking in!

OFFICER: Name and address?
SHELLY: He's breaking in!
OFFICER: Name and address, please!
SHELLY: He's at the back door trying to break in—Twelve-twenty Rio Verde.
OFFICER: Stay on the phone; a patrol car will be right there.

Glidden stopped the tape. "A few minutes later the victim speaks again."

"A few?"

"Three minutes, six seconds later." He pressed the button.

SHELLY: I'm sorry . . . it's my uncle . . . that's all . . . he's drunk . . . that's all . . . I'm sorry.

"When the patrol car got there seven minutes later, at ten twenty-three, the front door was open and the girl's nude body was on the bed."

"Strangled."

"Antenna cable still looped around her neck."

"Raped."

"Absolutely."

"We're lucky." Glidden opened the folder on his desk. "Before the Monroe case we could never get money for recording equipment."

The paramedics, Sherm remembered, had gone to the wrong address, Monroe died, and his widow and her attorney became wealthy. He asked if they'd verified the address.

The automatic call tracer, Glidden explained, was in next year's budget.

"During those three minutes, six seconds, weren't there other sounds?"

"The victim apparently depressed the mute button. It was one of those electronic phones."

"Doesn't that seem a bit implausible? Her home was being broken into."

"Probably accidental."

Sherm nodded. "Unfortunate."

"Yes, it wouldn't hurt to have Bruner's voice on the tape."

"You're sure the voice is Shelly Eagan's?"

"Positive ID: aunt, workers at AZTECH Micronetics, and, oh yes—" Glidden put on his smuggest expression. "Bruner himself."

"How did you manage that?"

"We let him listen to the tape and after the first line asked whose voice it was."

"Clever—which aunt?"

"His sister, Wilma Bruner. She works for Mothers of the Moon."

"Mothers of the Moon?"

"Religious cult up in Vegas."

Sherm had never heard of them. "What about a voiceprint?"

"We haven't found anything to compare it with."

"May I have a copy?"

"You can have this one. And take a look at this color Polaroid of Shelly Eagan." Glidden placed the photograph on top of the cassette and handed them across the desk. "We found it in Bruner's wallet."

The girl was on a rock, hands and feet flat to keep from sliding into the stream, a pose considerably less than erotic even though, except for a silver cord around her waist with a waferlike medallion attached, she was naked. She had an inquisitive, childlike look, blond braids, a pretty mouth but little jaw, tiny breasts, a roll of baby fat beneath the medallion, thin legs, and small feet. The photo had either been taken with a cheap camera or improperly focused. Its composition was terrible, the girl stuck up in one corner, most of the picture taken up by rocks and water. The scrawl on the back read "Hatch's Pool, 1987."

"You're sure this is Shelly Eagan?"

"The girl in the photo is definitely the victim."

"And you're equally certain the victim is Shelly Eagan?"

"The dead girl, the one in the photo, *and* the taped voice have all been positively identified."

He handed back the photo. Framed in the spacious window behind the prosecutor, above the downtown skyline, were the mountains with the first clouds of today's edition of the chubasco beginning to form above the dark line of pines along Hatch Canyon.

Sherm asked about Bruner's alibi witnesses.

"Can you believe even after identifying his niece's voice and hearing the tape he insists there are two people who can vouch for his being elsewhere? But he won't give out the names. Maybe he hasn't dreamed them up yet." Glidden faked a laugh, then gravely told what they found in Bruner's apartment: hundreds of smut videos. Which proved he was a *first-class pervert.*

Though curious as to Glidden's definition of first-class pervert, Sherm instead asked, "What do you collect?"

The prosecutor grinned. "I have a fairly decent gun collection."

"Guns are interesting. Are those murder weapons?"

"Sporting firearms." Glidden frowned. "You should see Bruner's tapes. Disgusting!"

"I've got a jog to finish." Sherm got to his feet. "Could I have a key to the Eagan house, in case our investigators want to look around?"

"Sure." Glidden took the key from his middle desk drawer. "This opens the sheriff's lockbox by the front door. House key's inside." He swiveled toward the window, motioned to the electric 99° moving across the marquee at the top of the high-rise bank, and suggested that he take it easy.

Sherm nodded. "I seldom do anything at too fast a pace, whether jogging or reaching a conclusion."

"Not much doubt about this conclusion, right? I mean, even if we didn't have the tape, there's also the matter of prints on an empty beer bottle."

"Fingerprints?"

"Seemed hardly worth mentioning."

He thanked Glidden and waved so-long, walking, then jogging down the deserted corridor. It was Sunday and he rode the elevator down to the parking garage alone. Glidden couldn't have been more confident. There'd been none of the usual patronizing palaver. No airplanes or war, just hard evidence and dirty videos.

Too good to be true?

It didn't seem likely. Marc Glidden was interested in locking up criminals, killing them if necessary, the type who'd be genuinely disturbed if he even suspected the real killer was at large.

Serious investigation was in order. The nine-one-one tape was almost certain to be authentic, leaving the defense, and Sherm in particular, with the impossible task of proving "my uncle" was some sort of mistaken identity. The remaining option was to go out and find the real murderer—except that the real murderer was probably already in jail.

He ran the length of the parking bay, sweating away his resolve for further jogging, squeezed into the X1/9, and listened with a small sense of sorrow to the throaty midengined growl echoing in the concrete labyrinth. He knew he and the Fiat were too old for each other, and without air-conditioning it was sheer hell to drive in the summer; still, he couldn't give it up. Vic had loved his yellow toy car and, well—that was enough.

Becky didn't encourage his buzzing about, cautioning him, as she had Vic, to watch out for inattentive truck drivers, but she understood his affection for the little car, and said it probably saved gas, tending always to search out the good in any situation or person.

In Bruner she might have difficulty.

Because Bruner would not leave his cell, their first meeting had been there. The ex-Army sergeant sat on the edge of his cot, ramrod straight, shiny black shoes planted flat, staring at a chipped spot high on the concrete wall, conversing entirely in "Yes, sirs" and "No, sirs."

"Raymond, the court appointed our firm to represent you, but in order for us to do so, you must—"

"Yes, sir."

A hot bubble burst inside. "Damn it, man, don't you know they have a fancy new electric chair up in, up in—" Sherm waved his arm in the general direction of the state prison and was going to tell Bruner about the picture he'd seen of this sophisticated new chair; but Bruner turned his head sharply and glared.

"I don't want you, Mr. Sherman. I don't want you or any other lawyer because I got two witnesses who can prove that tape's phony and you and everybody else knows it."

Angered that Bruner connected him to an imagined conspiracy, Sherm had left the cell swiftly. Now, racing in the outside lane of the city's only freeway, whatever anger had possessed him melted in the heat.

It hadn't been a total waste. From the arrest sheet he learned that after Bruner was picked up at his apartment, where he lived alone, his blood-alcohol level showed he'd consumed about a six-pack of beer but wasn't legally drunk. And he got a good look at the forty-year-old, unemployed Vietnam vet: thin, hard muscled, firm featured, and hair shaved as close as an inmate's, which contributed to a look Sherm found disturbing, that and the eyes Bruner wasn't able to control. He was like a fly frozen on a wall, aware something was after him but not sure what—a look too easily interpreted as guilt.

In his time, Sherm had defended too many who'd been guilty, yet there was a serious difference here. The fever of execution was rampant. Bruner's candidacy for the electric chair had been suggested on the editorial page of the Saturday edition of the *Desert Star* that headlined his arrest—UNCLE SLAYS HEIRESS. The story quoted the county sheriff as saying they had "irrefutable evidence against the accused." *Irrefutable* was correct, but Sherm doubted Kline ever used the word.

Sherm also knew that the publisher of the *Star* was a reactionary who played no small part in returning capital punishment to a state that hadn't had an official killing in thirty years, and never an electrocution.

Good for circulation, bad for Bruner; but as hopeless as it seemed, Sherm wasn't about to let them pull the switch yet. The tape was the kind of evidence Professor Jeremiah Bedford used to say fell in the too-good-to-be-true category, in this case too good for the prosecution.

2

Upstart

Becky was on the wicker couch combing Beau, a daily chore, for the white fluff of Persian that filled her lap put out a cloud of hair that was everywhere on everything.

"Don't wear dark colors to our house," Becky warned almost everyone, "if you want to keep them that way."

So the cushions were white, "Off," Becky said. So were the drapes and most of her dresses. What hadn't been, was now, all because of Beau.

Sherm kissed his wife, but the cat, not wishing to be kissed, jumped from her lap onto the rug and did a turn to show off his coat before sinking his nose into one of his mistress's old open-toed leather shoes.

She gathered the wad of discarded silver-white hair so Sherm could sit beside her and asked how it had gone.

"Glidden's got an ironclad case, is all." He told her about the tape and the rest. "Bruner thinks we're all out to get him."

"If he's innocent, no wonder. You know, to him it must sound like some sort of conspiracy."

"Several people, himself included, identified his niece's voice. Also, it makes no sense that someone else would force the victim to say he's her uncle when a patrol car could arrive at any moment. As it happened, one got there in seven minutes."

"But it makes sense that Mr. Bruner could get in, drink a beer, rape, strangle, and drive away in seven minutes?"

"The tape seems to prove so."

"Also in this age of cheap tape recorders and such, isn't the assertion that there's not a single voice recording available for comparison somewhat questionable?"

He frowned. "We know Glidden isn't out to frame Bruner."

"I'm only trying to look at it from Mr. Bruner's viewpoint."

No matter how reasonable to the troubled Bruner, Sherm argued, a frame-up would have required planning far too elaborate.

"It's an elaborate world, sweetie."

Indeed. What, for example, was Bruner's relationship with his niece? What did he think of her? She of him? How did they get along? There is a complexity in every relationship. And how was Shelly Eagan able to tell that the drunk barking at her back door was her uncle? If she called from the bedroom, wouldn't that place them at opposite ends of the house? He should've been less piqued by Bruner's behavior, Sherm realized, and more concerned with why he'd acted the way he did.

"I'd better call Charlie."

"And I'd better get rid of this cat hair."

Charlie Applegate wasn't in, Ace Investigations' sexy voice recording said, so please leave your message after the tone. Sherm reviewed the evidence and placed an order for information: reasons why Bruner might believe he was framed, possible interests served by his conviction, a full dossier on the murdered girl, names of AZTECH employees, relatives, et cetera who'd recognized her voice, and/or were in for a piece of the inheritance. He concluded with a promise to make a list and, after hanging up, complained that it was a helluva way to run a friendship.

"I talk to his tape machine and he talks to mine."

Rid of the hair, Becky knelt to inspect the stack of VHS recordings they had accumulated. "Those were the best times, weren't they, you and Charlie investigating and all of us so terribly young?"

It was certainly nice to be young, Sherm agreed.

"You know, not being cooped up in an office or courtroom. Dancing, playing tennis, skiing—I'm sorry; I wasn't . . ."

"I know you weren't." But he knew she was really pleading for an end to this limbo of drifting and waiting. "We jog," he said, "and you play pretty good bridge."

"*We* play good bridge." She found the tape she was looking

for, a Pavarotti, inserted it into the VCR and pressed PLAY. "And we are gonna knock their socks off."

Sherm knew better. He dreaded the bridge tournament for the same reason he dreaded taking Bruner to court: losing.

He hadn't always felt this way. For a couple of years after he was first dragged to the club by Becky, who'd played duplicate bridge since college, he really enjoyed the game and the immense popularity he shared because of her. They lost a lot but he hadn't minded because he was learning. Suddenly they were no longer losers and just as suddenly not so popular. It grated on him that he, in particular, was being treated as a parvenu. Imagine, an upstart at fifty-nine!

Not that they were unpopular because they were the winners. Those were, always, Najib and Majida Ammar, the Algerian brother and sister twins who intimidated the defense and slaughtered the offense, often in situations where Sherm felt they must read each other's minds.

Becky chided him for his suspicious nature, asserting that they couldn't possibly have cheated in the qualification round because the hands came from a computer. That was not logic, he argued, but faith. Besides, her assertion was out of hand because the bridge computer was consistently diabolic: Whatever was right by the book always turned out wrong when the computer dealt.

"Now that is really out of hand."

It shouldn't have, but cheating at cards really bothered Sherm. He could understand murder under unusual circumstances, but for the life of him he could not fathom why anyone would cheat when the stakes were numbers on a piece of paper. Especially when the cheaters were intelligent people like Najib and Majida who, like so many of the new smart folks in town who had emigrated from Silicon Valley to join AZTECH, worked in the research lab. They were also good-looking people, Majida in particular: beautiful in an orthodox way, with clear olive skin, and hair that at a distance might appear to be a nun's veil. Both always wore black clothing and stern missionary faces. They were cold perfectionists who won no matter what.

What particularly bugged him was an impossible twenty-two-point small slam made by Majida, and only Majida, in a field of God-knows how many players in the qualification round. To begin with, there was no reasonable way to bid slam. Secondly, her play of the hand violated all the laws of probability. She'd dropped a doubleton queen in the diamond suit, then made an uncanny finesse to the nine spot in spades. Thousands of ways existed to play the hand and not make twelve tricks, yet Majida chose the only combination that made fulfillment of the contract possible. Two plays out of thousands—what were the odds?

But Becky was essentially correct. After being duplicated at another table, computer-dealt hands were placed facedown inside slotted metal boards and handled only by tournament directors and caddies. Other rules restricted movement and made it a virtual impossibility that the hands could be viewed beforehand.

Afterward, when Sherm complained, Becky answered with a gesture peculiar to her, an upward turn of the right hand as though checking for raindrops, loosely translated, "Only God knows." If any human could know, Becky would be the first.

Early in their marriage, Sherm mistakenly attributed her extraordinary ability to associate things that seemed unrelated to intuition. He soon found out it wasn't intuition. She was an extremely fast thinker, quick to make valid comparisons, remarkable in picking out main elements. She'd always been a thinker: high school valedictorian, graduate of Wells with high distinction in English literature. It was hard for him to believe she married a guy who always wound up in the middle of traffic jams while she was seeing the way straight through like a bullet: zip, in and out, in the clear, straightaway! She could have driven at Indy like Janet Guthrie, only

Becky would have won. When he saw trees she was seeing forest. At the bridge table she was able to discern marginal games and bid them, and to stop bidding and collect part score when a hand looked suspicious. Bidding was his weakness, but when he played a hand he knew where the cards were. His brain was more like a memory bank, able to call up hands played weeks before.

Donegan, Charlie's computer whiz, called it accurately when he said Sherm had good RAM, Becky good ROM.

However, the deathblow slam by the twins gave them an absolute top score and the Shermans an absolute zero on the board. Ammars first, Shermans second.

Becky shrugged it off. "At least we qualified." He became depressed. They were right; he was an upstart. In the tournament he'd blow it for sure, except that Becky probably wouldn't let him.

Still as good-looking and smarter than ever, she was the winner in the family, the one who carried the partnership and just might make it unbeatable. She'd done it before; she'd proven herself. Her strength had held them together while he, like a madman, had nearly thrown away all that remained in the futile search for their son.

Becky located the VCR remote control on the coffee table and held down FAST FORWARD. Pavarotti had been put on hold for telephone pledges.

"This case isn't going to keep us from the tournament, is it?" she asked.

"We play," he promised, "hell or high water."

"Hell we have, every summer. As for high water, with the chubasco there's always the possibility." She held up a finger for him to listen to the rattle of thunder rolling in from the mountain.

If it didn't rain, the temperature was certain to hit 112°, but halfway through *"Una furtiva lagrima"* the first sharp tattoo of raindrops pecked the foam roof, increasing steadily until the sound of the downpour drowned the voice of the great tenor. Almost as quickly, the storm passed.

When the pledge segment came back on, Sherm stepped out onto the deck. The desert air was thirty degrees cooler and fresh with the smell of rain. Distant gray streamers evaporated before reaching the ground and weak cloud lightning generated only low rumbles of thunder. But lights were beginning to pop on around the city earlier than nightfall dictated. Becky joined him, held onto his arm, and wondered if it would rain again.

"I don't think so," he said, thinking that with him on the team they stood no chance of winning, that with him Bruner stood no chance either. Still, with Becky for a partner there was hope, however slim, of winning the tournament. As for Bruner, her point about the seven minutes was beginning to gnaw at his curiosity.

"Let's drop by the scene of the crime," he said.

3

Shifting Scenes

Serpentine Rio Verde Road was swathed with gravel and sand, and twigs blown from the trees by the previous night's storm. It was scraggly bottomland, hard caliche and dry sand along a riverbed that sometimes went three years without a flow, a land that grew mesquite, creosote, and catclaw, much of it atop mounds that in the dark resembled an army of giant Medusas poking up in phantasmagoric disarray.

Becky switched on the Buick's headlights and they saw it up ahead, leaning and slightly battered, like some long abandoned mailbox. No name, only numbers—1220.

"That's it," Sherm said.

There was still enough light to see that the chain-link fence was topped by strands of barbed wire canted outward, but the twisted gate was ajar enough for them to coast on through, onto the severely eroded driveway. The house was a ways beyond. Becky tapped the gas pedal to stay on top of the ruts, pulling up to the front.

Sherm got the flashlight from the glove compartment. Together, they walked to the arched entranceway. He played the light along the side of the house, over the washed adobe, a window with wrought iron grating and tiled valance, up to a beam protruding below the flat roof. Painted to blend with the beam, a small TV camera pointed its muzzle over their heads. He brought the light down, searching around the carved Mexican door for the lockbox. The light glinted off the brass knocker plate. Above the plate was the lockbox. He inserted Glidden's key. It turned but the door wouldn't open. He banged on it and a drumroll of distant thunder answered, then the slide of a dead bolt and squeaking hinges.

Becky grabbed his arm.

"Romero!" Sherm cried out.

The graying deputy smiled sheepishly. "Oh, it's you."

"Good God Almighty, did you have to open the door like Bela Lugosi?"

"Sorry." Romero motioned them inside. "Sheriff Kline had me dropped off to look after things. There's been some vandalism in the area and—well, I'll tell you, this place gets to you after a while."

It was hard for Sherm to imagine this burly old friend being gotten to by anything short of King Kong.

The house was larger than it looked from the outside. Many square feet, many bucks. The furniture was Southwest leather, wood, and dust. The lighting was poor and there was a lot of ceiling timber. The walls were thick adobe cluttered with paintings of horses, bronzed men and women, and mesas. The floors were red Spanish tile and Indian rugs.

"Real Navajo," Becky whispered, pointing them out. "Look, a Two Grey Hills, Burnt Water—a Daisy Touglechee!"

Four Corners stuff, the Colorado Plateau . . .

"This is insane," she said. "Practically heirlooms and they're on the floor?" Their own two Navajos hung on the walls, insured for three thousand dollars.

"A lot of expensive stuff," Romero said. "But I wouldn't want to live here."

Particularly alone in the middle of sixteen acres of nothing; and doing what, Sherm wondered. What did the girl do all alone at night in a big, empty house? He traced an X on the dusty oak top of the hallway telephone stand.

"Security fence, dead bolts, alarm system, TV, intercom, every security measure you can think of except a pooch, and none of it did any good." Romero motioned down the hall toward the bedroom area, pointing out the miniature TV camera. "Place is wired like nothing you ever seen. When you drove in, you set off an alarm and I saw your car on the monitor."

"So how did the murderer get through the gate?"

"It's a remote job, like some garage doors, but the motor got gummed and it was left open."

"And the TV and alarm?"

"Sheriff Kline says she missed seeing him because he parked out of camera range." Romero placed a finger in front of his ear and rubbed it through his salt-and-pepper sideburn. "And she probably figured it was her uncle until he started pounding to be let in."

"What do you figure?"

"Well, if he really wanted in, he'd show himself in front of the camera. He was her uncle."

"What if they weren't on good terms?"

"They were. There was a letter from her aunt, Bruner's sister."

"So why does Kline think her uncle would try to break in?"

"Sheriff says he was drunk." Stepping aside for Becky, he said he'd show them where.

The back entrance was through a storage space between the laundry room and an enclosed patio off a double carport. The upper half of the door was dirty glass with iron bars on the outside, chain lock and double dead bolts inside. Romero flipped on the outside light and they stepped out onto a patio filthy with dirt, leaves, stickers, and a jumble of tumbleweeds trapped in the L formed by a storage shed and wrought iron fence. Between the security fence and the low stone wall put up to keep the desert at bay, Sherm could make out the shadowy outline of a satellite dish. Off the patio toward the back was a swimming pool, remarkably clear for its age. Heavily calcified tile framed the waterline, the surrounding cool deck chipped and cracked, diving board missing a key bolt. Both lounge chairs were horizontal.

"Lab took two beach towels off the loungers," Romero said.

Sherm started back and confronted by the empty carport, asked if the lab also took her car.

"No car. Sheriff says somebody drove her."

"Any stray prints?"

"None I heard of."

"Tire marks?"

"Washed away."

Inside the kitchen, Sherm paused in front of the refrigerator, opened the right side, and peered in. Not much: leftover dishes, moldy peaches, a quarter-full liter of Chablis, five beer bottles with an unfamiliar label. He put on his glasses. *Montejo*, a Mexican brand.

In the freezer side there were several frozen dinners, mostly Chinese. Sherm closed the door and was going to ask Romero for the real reason Kline sent him, but the big Mexican was obviously pleased about something. Instead, Sherm asked what he was grinning about.

"Well, it's nice to—" Romero tugged on his gun belt and studied his brown boots. "To see you guys looking so good, you know, after everything."

Sherm took hold of Romero's arm. "I'm sorry. We came barging in like we'd been here yesterday, without so much as a hello."

"Yeah, well, it's nice to have you both back."

"Thank you, Romero," Becky said.

"Come on and I'll show you the big bedroom."

For a room so large that it made the king-size bed appear small, there was scarcely any furniture. A child's bureau and one stool were pushed aside to make room for the plethora of electronic litter. Facing the bed was a new giant TV with two VCRs separating it from an old twenty-five-inch RCA color console. A nineteen-inch model was bracketed to the wall motel-style, along with stereo speakers in the corners. On a metal equipment rack by the bed was a turntable, AM-FM stereo receiver with dual cassette tape deck, a security control box, and a cordless telephone. Wires ran everywhere, some to unconnected ends. Missing equipment, several pieces it appeared. Missing or stolen? What was taken to the crime lab, Romero said, they could find on the inventory.

Sherm asked what the switches on the security box controlled.

"TV cameras out front, in the halls, and out back."

"By the carport?"

"By the sliding door to the pool area."

"So you can't see who's at the back door?"

"Naw, but you can hear." Romero toggled one of the selectors on the control box. "Speakers all over, inside and out."

How would a girl alone react, Sherm wondered, when the electronic eyes and ears warned of a car in the driveway, a man at the back door? He remembered the night Vic and his Indian Guide buddies came up from behind the house when Heather was alone, watching the late movie, and the sound of their footsteps on the deck roused a scream out of her that the boys said scared them shitless.

So Shelly Eagan's cry in the night for help was a 9-1-1 call, then terror diminished perhaps to embarrassment, as it had for Heather, for being so foolishly frightened by imagination.

He asked Romero if he'd seen the body.

"I got here about thirty minutes after the first car. She was naked on the bed like she was resting, but the antenna cable was still around her neck." Romero nodded grimly in recognition of the irony that the murder weapon had been a piece of the equipment that should have protected her.

"No sign of struggle?"

"Like I said, she looked like she just went to sleep."

The big walk-in closet contained few clothes, jeans and slacks mostly, some mannish shirts, T-shirts stacked on the high shelf, and a curious tunic that looked and felt like burlap. Two belts hung from pegs, but no silver cord with a medallion.

Romero poked his head into the closet. "Looking for something special?"

"You haven't seen a silver cord, have you?"

"No, but we can check the inventory."

Sherm came out, picked up the cordless phone, a one-piece electronic push button with MUTE and REDIAL. "Did anyone check this?"

"Yeah, you can use it if you want."

"Not for prints, the redial."

Romero shrugged. "I guess so."

Sherm telescoped the antenna, flicked the side switch to TALK, pressed REDIAL, and held the receiver to his ear.

"Sensa-Vision," a voice answered.

"Sorry." Sherm switched to OFF and handed the phone to Romero. "You'd better tell Kline about this."

"I don't get it."

"The automatic redial retains the last number dialed, and it wasn't nine-one-one."

"She made another call after the nine-one-one?"

"Someone did." Sherm rubbed his chin; why in hell was it *that* number?

The remainder of their visit was taken up with a quick tour of the sewing and dining rooms, library, and another that contained hospital paraphernalia and bed. In this room Shelly Eagan nursed her mother after she was struck in front of her house on Rio Verde. Hit-and-run fatality, Romero said, most likely a DUI.

Could he get someone to let them into Bruner's apartment, Sherm asked. They didn't need anyone, Romero said. The same key worked both lockboxes. He gave them the address, 424 Emerson.

Outside, the scraggly bottomland trees flailed starkly against a sky pulsing with the gray light of electricity.

When they got to the car, Romero held the passenger door for Becky. "Thank you for everything, Romero, but it's my car and I drive." She got in on the driver's side, started the engine, and moved slowly to the mailbox, where she stopped to check both ways that there were no drunks on Rio Verde Road this night.

Safely on their way, she asked who the redial number belonged to.

"Sensa-Vision."

"Sense-ah-who?"

"I think it's a porn shop."

Becky whistled.

"Yeah, just what Bruner needs." Sherm opened the glove compartment to get a tape. "I thought I'd found a loophole, that there was no way someone at the opposite end of the house could identify a person at the back door. Now we have a telephone she could've carried plus an intercom." He picked out a Willie Nelson. "On the other hand, why didn't she identify her uncle over the intercom before dialing nine-one-one?"

"What was that about a silver cord?"

He pushed the tape into the cassette slot and turned up the volume. "Glidden showed me a photo taken from Bruner's wallet of Shelly Eagan in the buff, except for a medal hanging from a silver waist cord. I thought it must have been important to her."

A branching lightning strike cracked the sky over the city.

"Emerson. It's right here somewhere." Becky spotted the street sign and turned off, but they had trouble locating the apartment because the *four* had fallen off the painted cement wall, leaving twenty-four.

Dodging quarter-size drops, they ran for the dark doorway recessed two feet into the otherwise flat front, got the key out of the lockbox into the keyhole, this time without trouble, and ducked inside.

One quick look took in the whole dingy affair. The bathroom, they knew without inspecting, would have a rusty shower stall, mildewed curtains, ring-stained bowls, and earwigs. The brown paint on the kitchen cabinets was flaked, the linoleum watermarked, the Frigidaire chipped, and the living-sleeping area smelled of dogs not properly walked, mingled with latex paint, boiled cabbage, and disinfectant. Decorating the pale green walls were four black velvet nudes, an overexposed photo of a helmeted, bandoliered Bruner, and a framed trade school certificate attesting to his technical ability in dealing with electrical repairs. The hideaway bed was out and made with a GI blanket and starched pillowcase. A lamp with a fringed shade sat atop a blond veneer table jammed between a do-it-yourself chest of drawers and cinder blocks stacked to support two VCRs hooked to a thirteen-inch TV.

Two VCRs, Becky speculated, for copying porno tapes?

Sherm stepped into the kitchen and opened the Frigidaire. It was empty and smelled. "Glidden said there were shoe boxes full of them."

"You expect to find tapes in the refrigerator?" Becky pushed aside the thin closet curtain as though it had fleas. "Here they are."

The boxes were empty, their lids stacked upside down. He turned one of the lids over. On the top was a label, S&M.

She turned another. "They're labeled thematically, see? INCEST."

Another was labeled MISEGNATION. "Very technical but misspelled."

"KIDDIE PORN is neither technical nor legal."

"What are WATER SPORTS?"

"I think it's when people pee on each other."

"Doesn't sound exactly like fun." Becky dropped the lid as if it were someone else's used Kleenex. "Aren't those terribly expensive?"

"Yes, which presents another question; Bruner was unemployed."

"There must have been a fortune's worth here." She pushed the boxes aside with her toe.

A clap of thunder shook the walls as though they were cardboard. "Let's get out of here." Enough was enough; all else was redundancy.

The night sky had opened up, flashing and rumbling, the bleeding downpour soaking them as they raced for the parked Buick.

4

Young Lions and Old Pussycats

Sitting up in bed, book propped against his knees, his right hand buried in Beau's white fluff, he tried *Ulysses* for the umpteenth time, not so much because a long time ago Becky said he should read it, rather to take his mind off the case so he might sleep. No use. He closed the book, dropped it beside the bed, and turned his head on the pillow.

"Honey," Sherm said, "this thing is hopeless."

Becky turned a page of her Stephen King softback, said not to worry, and reminded him that the very essence of the American judicatory system was the assumption of innocence until proven otherwise.

"I meant Joyce."

"Keep trying."

He scratched Beau, cuddled to his mistress, under the chin. "I'm having trouble sorting out the details."

"Joyce was never easy."

"Now I'm talking about the case."

Becky peered over the rim of her reading glasses. "You're getting pretty wrapped up in this. Maybe we should cancel out on the tournament."

"I'll ask Miles to assist. Better yet, I'll assist him."

"Miles reminds me of you."

"A bit less gray and beat-up, I'd say."

"I meant back when you were one of the young lions."

"Now I'm just an old pussycat, right?"

She kissed Beau on his pink nose. "You know what I think of pussycats."

In many ways Miles Purdy reminded Sherm of Vic—so why was he inviting Miles to take a case that would certainly pull him away from wife and kids and in the end probably be lost because of thirty seconds of electronic tape?

Unless . . .

At the pretrial hearing Miles would of course ask—hell, demand—the Frye Rule be invoked, placing the burden of proof on Glidden who would then have to prove the tape scientifically admissible, and he'd already said that voiceprint ID was impossible because they had nothing to compare it with. Yet the judge could accept the aural ID. Ever since Lindbergh said he recognized Hauptmann's voice, the precedent has been to accept aurals. They were not very scientific, though, therefore the Frye Rule. If the tape was declared scientifically inadmissible, it would then boil down to convincing a jury that men who collect dirty movies are not necessarily murderer-rapists. This might be tough, especially with Glidden most certainly capitalizing on data that showed positive correlations between increased availability of pornography and sex crimes, a bit of irrelevance that would place Miles in a position of having to prove the prosecution was leading the jury down a statistical blind alley. However, even if the 9-1-1 tape was admitted, they might break even. It could be used to show that Bruner couldn't possibly do all he was supposed to have done in the time available—although the implication of taking such a line would be that they believed the tape was not authentic, which could really get tacky, for who other than the sheriff's department could've faked it?

No, he wouldn't sic Miles on the law. What he had was a tough enough row, yet there would be that element the recent crop of lions seemed so interested in, the notoriety that stems from defending capital cases. And this was a doozer, the first genuine candidate for electrocution in the state. Even if Miles's loss was a rout, he might still find himself joining the ranks of talk-show attorneys who've become famous defending lost causes. Unfortunately for Miles's ego, he was not of that ilk. Like Sherm, he enjoyed winning.

"I'll handle the investigative chores," Sherm said, "which I like best anyway. Miles can do the rest."

"Shouldn't you call him? The hearing is tomorrow."

"We'd better listen to the answering machine first."

He switched the machine from ANSWER ONLY to PLAYBACK, pushed the speaker button, and settled back to listen.

Two members of the firm volunteered their services in the Bruner case, followed by the inevitable Pauline claiming she'd divined his unlisted number and wanting to know why he'd been so unfaithful. It was hardly worth the effort getting divorced these days, she pouted, when your lawyer ignores you, that if he'd found a more interesting client at least give her a chance or she might just as well stay married to— Pauline had trouble remembering her current husband's name.

Terri was the next caller, to remind him of the hearing at 12:15, Judge Tabor presiding.

The worst.

No forgiveness graced this man's leatherbound book, none. Indeed, the code of retribution cracked like lightning through his early career almost to the hour the Supreme Court cut off his juice. That was in another state and he'd brought his obsession with him, laboring from the wings (if not from the bench), to convince enough of the state's legislators that burning a sinner in this life was the right way to prepare him for an eternity of hellfire in the next. "It's our duty," the *Star* quoted Tabor, "to stoke the furnace of justice."

They called him "Scorchy," not to his face of course; and now this bottled-up avenger was about to be unstopped.

Heat, Fire, Shock, and the Electric Chair.

Terri had an additional piece of news. Glidden wanted to talk to him before the hearing and suggested eleven o'clock at the Saguaro Club. If this wasn't possible, please call; otherwise, he and Sheriff Kline would be there.

Plea-bargain?

Following Terri's call, Aaron Donegan reported in.

"Charlie asked me to work on the electronic aspects of the Raymond Bruner case and, unless you have specific objections, I'll begin with a spectrogram of the deceased's voice on the *original* nine-one-one tape. This will not be an analysis, rather a simple spectrogram proceeding, with a final analysis when an additional recording is located, which there certainly must be, on the presumption of innocence, of course, and that the voice on the nine-one-one tape is an imposter. Charlie has suggested an interesting conceptualization which I'm anxious to explore. I'll be in touch. Good night, Sherm."

He let the tape run. Wrong number; Pauline again, obviously going to babble through whatever remained. He switched her off and punched the autodial button with Charlie's number. The provocative female again, inviting him to leave a message.

"I'm beginning to think we don't exist." Sherm realized he was waiting for a response. "Some additional items bear checking. The timing of the crime as indicated by the nine-one-one tape is highly suspect. How could anyone do all Bruner was supposed to have done in seven minutes?"

Sherm covered their visit to the Eagan house.

"The missing equipment could support a robbery motive. Could've been a computer, maybe experimental and very expensive. Possible attempted corporate theft, something like that; but I'm not sure we could explain rape.

"Also, who drove her to and from work? It's hard to figure someone not driving; then again, her mother was killed by a car. There was an extra beach towel by the pool, which probably indicates a close friend. Locate her friends. Run the tape past them. Also verify the voice IDs with colleagues at AZTECH and Aunt Wilma Bruner to see just how positive they are. Might not hurt to check on Wilma's religious affiliation with Mothers of the Moon. Glidden called it a cult. He's also got a snapshot they found in Bruner's wallet. Shelly Eagan, nude. I'd bet Bruner didn't take the picture. So who did? She had a silver cord around her waist, which seems odd. Likely it meant something special to her, or to whoever took the picture. If so, she probably still had it when she was murdered and it'll be on the Eagan inventory. And yes, we need to take a close look at the inventory to make sure we haven't overlooked a tape that might have her voice on it. Better yet, let's get copies of the inventory for everyone.

"That's it for now—oh, yeah, I read of a fellow who fell in love with a recording, the voice actually. He searched high and low for the woman who taped it. Found her in England." Sherm hung up and selected Miles Purdy's number.

Miles sounded like a pussycat until Sherm asked if he wanted to handle the courtroom end of the Bruner case; then the lion came alive, eager for the meat being tossed his way.

"Were you asleep?"

"Probably; I was going over the Morrison brief—listen, I appreciate this."

"Reserve your appreciation until you've heard Glidden's evidence."

"I've heard."

"Glidden wants a meeting before the hearing, eleven at the Saguaro Club."

"Plea-bargain?"

"Don't know. Look, have Terri clear your schedule and ask her to have Kevin Jorgensen get Pauline off my back."

"Poor Jorgensen."

"Yeah, well, sometimes seniority pays. Let's meet, say thirty minutes before Glidden's ETA."

"Sounds good, and thanks."

"Better save the thanks. See you tomorrow." Sherm reset the answering system.

Becky put down her book. "You didn't tell me MOM was involved."

Sherm stretched out. "Nothing was said about anybody's mom."

"Mothers of the Moon, MOM for short."

"They actually call themselves MOM?"

"It's a perfect acronym. Would you like to know why?"

"I'm always interested in acronyms, expecially when they're perfect."

"They say God is using MOM to reestablish Her ministry here on earth."

"Her?"

"I see by your demeanor that you don't believe God could be a woman."

"I'm probably not alone."

"Well, you'd better mend your ways or Artemis won't let you into Elysian."

"Never heard of her."

"Artemis, Greek Goddess, Apollo's twin sister."

"Now I've heard of Apollo."

"Male chauvinist. Artemis is the Mother Moon, heavenly virgin—"

"Mother and virgin?"

Becky saw that he was kidding and remembered him borrowing from her mythology collection.

His expression became intentionally skeptical. "How come you know all about MOM?"

"It's in all the tabloids."

Now he was skeptical. "Where do you read the tabloids?"

"While I'm having my hair cut. I have to have something to do besides listen to Maurice's anecdotes about his boyfriends. Besides, the headlines are so tantalizing."

"So tell me all about MOM."

"Well, it began with an accident about five years ago during a rehearsal for one of those big production numbers on the Vegas Strip. Sylvia Devereaux, her stage name, and another chorus girl were up on a swing when one of the ropes came loose and dumped them forty feet onto the stage. The other girl was killed and witnesses thought Sylvia was too. The startling point is, that when she came out of her coma, she said she'd died and come back. Of course, she couldn't tell anyone this straight out. All she could do was make noises no one understood. Then her brother said her voice came to him in a vision commanding him to take her off the life-supports. Doctors said she'd surely die, but they were wrong."

Sherm remembered the negligence case that had followed. It had appeared in several journals, and the clincher had been when her lawyer put Devereaux herself on the stand. Her answers were garbled and the casino's lawyers made the mistake of insinuating outright fraud while the jury was being swayed by what they saw: a hopelessly incapacitated yet beautiful young woman. The settlement was a monster eight and a half million.

"With her millions," Becky continued, "her brother built an enormous tentlike structure he named 'Sylvia's Tabernacle' where she teaches that this life is merely a classroom for women to prepare themselves for the eventual resurrection she'd experienced.

"They say MOM puts on a great show, one of Vegas's best, with lasers and hocus-pocus; but it's not your fun kind. Sylvia is a sort of spiritualist who communicates with the dead—I mean missing—I mean—shit." The words had slipped out, words she avoided like bare, hot wires: *dead* and *missing*. Vic wasn't dead, he was missing, and if Sherm had his way, their son would stay *missing* for all eternity. She'd never understood why the families of Vietnam MIAs persisted for so many years, until Vic. Now she knew; missing was worse than dead.

"I'm sorry," Becky whispered, "I'm sorry I didn't tell you I once considered asking this Sylvia to help us locate Vic. The only reason I didn't was I was afraid—afraid she'd tell me . . ." Becky cried briefly. "I shouldn't be doing this, just making it worse, making you feel worse."

She kissed his cheek, and even though he knew their son would forever remain missing and he, Sherm, would never hear a car pulling in late at night, a door slamming, or distant laughter without thinking of Vic, and that he would forever carry the burden of guilt; in that moment, at least, he felt better.

She settled her head on his shoulder, her hair soft and smelling of herbs, and wiped her eyes. "I don't know how I could've considered it, the whole thing's so phony."

"Do me a favor, will you? Tomorrow's your hair appointment, isn't it? So how about some research on this MOM while you're there, from the tabloids and maybe ask around? Someone who works for Maurice has probably read them all."

"How much an hour?"

"Let's see, Ace gets—"

"Never mind, I'll take my pay in trade." She opened her arms. "In advance."

Making love should have made him sleepy. It didn't. His mind was charging all over the place. Becky had climbed over to her side of the bed. For some reason, nature or habit, individuals always have their side of the bed. At least, from a sampling of discussions on the topic, especially with potential divorcees, he assumed all couples conformed to this—which strangely enough, applied to hotels, motels, and perhaps orgies. Does the wife at an orgy with someone who is not her husband have to tell him, "No, you clod, that's my side"? And could it be there are so many unsuccessful marriages because one of the partners demands the other's side of the bed?

Becky stretched from her side to kiss him again. "Night, night, sweetie."

"Good night, honey."

"Night, night, Beau." Her bear had returned to his spot and would be there in the morning. Cats had their sides too.

Sherm wished Pauline Lundquist would find her side soon and leave him alone. With that, he drifted off.

5

The Saguaro Club

An algae-stained fountain had once occupied the center of what had been the Continental Grill during Sherm's apprenticeship. It had been replaced by a minor island of gravel and potted cacti under a skylight cut in the roof to let in a little sunlight. The plastic window, crazed by desert heat, let in more heat than sun, yet the plants survived. Perhaps they could anywhere.

Sherm had to allow his eyes to adjust to the relative darkness before spotting his partner in a booth on the other side of the island, looking cool in his sleeveless terry-cloth shirt and white Levi's in spite of the sizzler this day had already become. Miles glanced up from his papers, breaking out his reassuring grin that—along with a tanned complexion, slightly ruffled sun-bleached hair, and straight taut body— had prompted Becky to say he could be a leading man. He had, however, chosen law, not just to make a decent living or because he enjoyed the courtroom's competitiveness, but also out of a seemingly inborn desire to want to see justice prevail, a trait not uncommon among tyros flushed with the fever of idealism. Vic had met good sense with this same quiet reservation, refuted bad logic with a similar unrelenting harangue. However, Miles was no beginner. He had a wife and two children, and was thirty-five.

His visit to their stubborn client, otherwise unproductive, had yielded the names of Bruner's alibi witnesses, Barry Knight and Edward McCreedy, owner and employee of an adult video shop.

"Sensa-something or other," Miles said.

Sherm let out a moan and explained; then briefly covered the tape and other evidence the prosecution was amassing. In the end, Miles agreed that plea bargaining couldn't be a reason for today's meeting, but he was cool about the avalanche of evidence that threatened to bury their case. Without so much as a headshake, he said that the Frye Rule could probably be invoked, that the tape itself might very well be inadmissible.

Maybe, Sherm granted, but would this be smart? First, any move to block its introduction as evidence would certainly be construed as an attempt to obstruct the smooth flow of justice and likely cause as much harm as good. Even without the tape, the prosecution would be able to draw on the testimony of the officer who took the 9-1-1 call, those who'd identified the voice, and God knows how many others. Second, the tape presented almost as many questions as it provided answers. Briefly, he covered the timing incongruity, but before they could discuss it in detail, they saw Glidden heading for their table, fifteen minutes early.

The prosecutor set his briefcase down next to Miles's and asked if they'd ordered (which they hadn't) before seating himself at the opposite point of the booth's arc, presumedly establishing necessary distance between adversaries. By way of opening things up, he said the county was probably going to buy a light twin and which did Sherm think was the better deal, a used Beech Duchess 76 or a Baron B-55 for about the same price?

Sherm had read that both were good airplanes, but he really didn't know much about twin-engined aircraft.

"Whatever it is, I'll sure enjoy flying it." Glidden went on to explain the obvious to Miles, that he had his private pilot's license, but had not nearly the stature of "the counselor" whose aviation exploits dated "all the way back to when he fought in Korea as a carrier pilot."

"*Fought* isn't quite accurate, nor was I actually in Korea. And I flew Grummans, not a carrier," Sherm pointed out without undue sarcasm. "As a matter of record, I took pictures and ran. Running has always been my sport."

"But you were shot down."

"Actually, I ran out of gas."

"I wish you were as humble in court." Glidden inspected his knife to make sure it was clean. "Have you started flying again?"

"One of these days."

"Better make it soon." Glidden glanced from the knife and caught Sherm's expression. "I mean you'll forget how."

He was about to argue that, like swimming and screwing, unless you didn't know how to in the first place, you never forgot. Luckily, the waitress arrived to take their order: cactusburger, fries, and coffee for Miles, shrimp Louis and lemonade for Sherm, and for Glidden, a pastrami on rye and root beer. When she'd shuffled off, Sherm noticed something he hadn't before; Glidden had the look of a fighter who'd just discovered the other guy could hit. The starch was clearly out of his shorts.

"The Attorney General advises us the tape may be inadmissible."

So that was it. "We're aware of that, Marc."

"We believe the Frye Rule applies," Miles added.

"The prosecutor can work around that." Glidden brushed the sleeve of his powder blue jacket. "The main point is, while the tape itself may very well be inadmissible, there are other ways to get the information contained therein, which would, of course, entail endless hours of perhaps irrelevant testimony with the same end result."

"Look, Marc . . ." Sherm examined his hands. "We don't want to turn a murderer-rapist loose on society." He lowered his voice. "But what if the monster who committed this despicable act is still out there—" His hand shot out, almost taking a passing waitress's tray.

"You're not serious?" A look of sheer disbelief. "You heard the tape."

"Sure I did and I know the voice has been identified. I also know they're still arguing about Lindbergh's identification. Hauptmann fried, yet a lot of people are still convinced, from the other evidence, that he was innocent. And if he was, how many small children we don't know about were kidnapped and murdered by the real perp? But that isn't the point; we've decided not to argue admissibility."

Glidden eyed him suspiciously. "You wouldn't be going to pull something?"

In spite of trying not to, Sherm laughed. "I alluded to this at our last meeting, that the timing appears questionable."

Glidden looked perplexed. "I don't recall your mentioning anything about timing."

"Maybe I didn't." Sherm rubbed his chin, thinking maybe

he should grow a beard. "Hasn't the quickness of all that happened bothered you?" Obviously it hadn't. "It really bothers me, Marc, so much happening in ten minutes."

"It's possible." Glidden removed his hands from the table to make room for the arrival of his root beer mug. "We also have Bruner's prints all over the place, his beer—a not-at-all popular Mexican brand—"

"In addition to everything else that was supposed to have happened, you're claiming he had time to drink a beer?"

"Time to put it into the refrigerator." Glidden sipped from his mug. "Look, we've worked out any number of scenarios, all valid within the given time frame."

"Valid? Marc, any scenario must presuppose he just walked in and raped her. I've seen Bruner." Sherm looked to Miles for verification. "What is he, five-seven, one hundred forty pounds?"

"Smaller, I'd say."

"And judging from her picture, I'd say his niece weighed as much."

"Bruner is wiry and muscular."

"Not that muscular, unless . . ." A strange thought entered Sherm's mind.

"Unless what?"

"Well, to make any scenario work, given the time limitation we're looking at, Bruner would have had to rape her after she was dead."

Something flashed in Glidden's eye. "The pathologist says there's no way to tell when the rape took place." His tone indicated they had considered the possibility. He reached for the handle of his briefcase, slid it next to his leg, opened it, and was reaching in when Sherm's next question about the equipment missing from the bedroom gave him pause. "How did you know about that?"

"From the disconnected cables."

"Camcorder, descrambler device. Lab's checking them

out. Also, some things were apparently removed beforehand, could be equipment from AZTECH Micronetics. She owned a sizable quantity of stock in the company, but also worked in the lab, so she probably had access to whatever she wanted."

"Camcorder, but no voice comparison tapes?"

"No tapes at all. We're working on Defense Department clearance so we can look at AZTECH's files."

The conversation was put on hold for their food to be served; then Glidden handed Sherm the envelope he'd been reaching for. "This is a copy of a letter found in the victim's home. The date establishes its arrival on the day of the crime, which means Bruner visited the home that evening."

Sherm put on his reading glasses and squinted at the lightly scrawled handwriting:

Dear Brother Raymond,

Thanx to you & Shelly the terminel has been approved. Be sure to tell Shelly we appreciate her endever. With out you two we would of been doomed from the start. Now every thing is rolling right along so good we should never hurt again. I still can't believe we got the terminel!

Thanx again. I never would of thought Mother Moon would move in such wonderful ways.

Love,
Wilma

"A lot of misspellings."

Miles wondered aloud why the aunt should be concerned about a computer terminal.

"This letter," Sherm said, "is further evidence of an apparent intimacy."

"Apparent intimacy?" Glidden repeated.

"The girl posed for a nude photograph, didn't she?"

"Who's to say she posed or that it was for Bruner?"

"Or the beer was his or she didn't pick up the letter at his apartment, or—"

"As a matter of fact, our investigation confirms the photo was taken last summer at AZTECH's Hatch Canyon computer camp. We believe another counselor took the picture, maybe on a hike when they stopped to cool off in the stream—you have a daughter, don't you?" Without waiting for an answer, Glidden was off and racing again. "You know how girls are when they're alone. The picture was probably taken as a joke and she kept it as a humorous remembrance, and somehow Bruner came across it and, for whatever perverted reason, put it in his wallet." Glidden took a vicious bite out of his pastrami sandwich before continuing. "After getting drunk he probably looked at the picture and it turned him on, so he grabbed some of his dirty tapes and went to his niece's house. Because she was so committed to her religious group, she probably objected. Her objections led to an argument; the argument to a fight, the fight to—"

"All in ten minutes."

"Stranger things have happened."

"Sure they have." Sherm probed his salad for shrimp. "But none of this is probable."

"We're not dealing with probabilities. We have the victim on tape telling us who murdered her." Glidden sat back in his chair and tugged on the knot in his tie. "And even if the tape is declared inadmissible—I mean Bruner is sick, really sick. We looked at some of the tapes we confiscated from his apartment." Glidden purposely made a face. "They aren't just filthy. That's much too mild a description. I mean, necro—"

"Please!" Sherm held up his hand. "If I find a shrimp in this, I'd like to be able to enjoy it."

Glidden finished off his root beer. "Incidentally, if you'd

used the victim's telephone before checking the automatic redial, the Sensa-Vision number would've been replaced by the number you dialed. Good thing. We had completely overlooked the redial. This is a pretty strong evidence, you know. The last number dialed is the one programmed into the redial system. The last number the victim dialed was nine-one-one; so after he killed her, Bruner called this other number likely to establish an alibi."

A few minutes remained to finish looking for shrimp and still make the hearing on time. There was too much Worcestershire and not enough lemon juice in the sauce Louis, but since there was not enough shrimp it didn't matter. So Sherm abandoned the remaining lettuce, staying to pay the check while the others went on ahead so as not to be late.

Not until he was out on the street did he realize the sheriff hadn't joined them.

6

Precognition

four red lights but no cars.

Sherm jaywalked vacant Eighth Avenue between the new parking garage and the old county courthouse. The street was vacant not because it was hot, rather it was downtown, an area Urban Renewal had transformed into a maze of highrise offices and parking garages and had done little to renew interest either in living or doing business there. On adjacent

B Street, on the block it shared with the county jail, the new courthouse had chinks in its concrete and windows that blew in when a really big chubasco thunderstorm rolled through. Five years and falling apart. The old would surely outlast the new if some misguided demolition crew didn't dynamite it, or a megabomb didn't bring them both down.

Yet the question remained: With all of this concrete and glass, why had the pink sandstone building been left standing? It couldn't have been through oversight, and if by design, hadn't the architects thrown a proper fit? Had nostalgia won out? Was this the Historical Society's one small victory in the midst of so many defeats?

Sherm skipped up the marble steps that led to an arched entrance through the ten-foot-high wall that isolated the courthouse and its plaza from the twentieth century. He ducked to avoid the state flag drooping at half mast in the stagnant midday heat, homage to a circuit judge whose time should've come before Shelly Eagan was born. Framed in the arch, but across the plaza, green streaked and blackened by time, the hollow copper statue of Marshal Estaban appeared to guard the oaken entrance to the court building. Inside the opened oak doors the real guards leaned against the metal detector, waiting.

Sherm's steps carried him through the wall onto the plaza, an area of flagstone walks, wrought iron benches, and zinnia beds enclosed on its other three sides by the domed courtroom building and office wings with tile roofs. Between each wing and the main building, arched passages similar to what he'd just come through led to B Street on the left and C Street on the right. Connecting the two was a covered walkway. A small crowd had gathered along the walkway and behind two television cameras trained on the B Street entrance.

Upon entering the circular tile mosaic laid out around the statue, Sherm stopped to look over the crowd. As usual, two or three ex-counselors and old duffers leaned on their canes and tradition, while others drawn in off the street by the television cameramen jockeyed for advantageous angles—possibly hoping to see themselves on the evening news. Less pushy, the older retired people stood back while some younger ones, probably on their lunch breaks, slouched with their arms over the backs of benches. Two men in blue work shirts, side by side, laughed at a third's joke. A woman alone, perhaps a legal secretary, searched for a familiar face.

In all likelihood, Miles and Glidden were inside.

Sherm glanced at his watch: twelve twenty-two. Seven minutes late and getting sticky.

One of the old duffers moved so close, Sherm stepped back to keep from knocking the man's cane out of his hand and bumped into someone behind him. Turning to apologize, he came face to face with the stern countenance of Marshal Estaban—the perfect icon, Sherm decided, for this court.

Nothing symbolized hard justice better than the uncompromising Creole lawman who (according to the inscription on the plaque) rode out of Mexico to bring law and order with swiftness and certainty. The village was small enough then and the marshal good enough, the inscription read, that he could sit in the shade of the ramada on his cane chair in front of the jail and pick off lawbreakers with his matched pair of turquoise-handled pistols. Estaban was sheriff, judge, jury, and executioner. How Scorchy Tabor must envy him.

Sherm spotted Miles detouring around the metal detector, coming his way. He looked unhappy and a little flustered.

"Did Kline show up?" Sherm asked when Miles arrived.

Miles shook his head and pointed toward the TV cameras. "He's probably putting on fresh makeup—did you know about this? No, you wouldn't have; even Glidden didn't know. I mean, why aren't they bringing Bruner through the back service entrance the way the procedure calls for?"

"Did you ask Tabor?"

"He wouldn't see me."

"I think you hit on it," Sherm said. "All this media exposure is too big for Kline to pass up."

Miles said he'd overhead one security guard tell another that he'd heard on the noon news they'd be broadcasting live from the courthouse at twelve-thirty.

Now Sherm knew why Bruner was late arriving. He checked his watch; it was almost that now.

"A lawyer is supposed to be with his client when he enters the courtroom and here I am like a"—Miles dropped his voice to a whisper—"fucking spectator."

Suddenly, the curious and expectant were being pushed from the walkway onto the plaza by a squad of sheriff's deputies while beyond the metal detector the massive courtroom doors creaked from being pushed open by grunting security guards.

In spite of hard oak benches and poor lighting, the old courtroom aroused considerable nostalgia among the white-haired reprobates who clung to their canes and offered outdated legal advice to their successors. If it hadn't been for them, many believed, the place would have been turned into a landmark long ago. And maybe, in spite of whatever feelings of tradition it evoked, it should have been. The court had the dusky smell of an old library, the odor of obsolescence. White scabs showed in the khaki-colored plaster between faded paintings of dead justices. Near the bench, the figure of blindfolded Madam Justice had taken on the green coat of corrosive time.

Miles asked if Sherm wanted to go inside.

"Let's wait here." He turned to his junior partner. "I'm sorry about what went on in the Saguaro. I seem to be aiding the State's case more than our client's."

"Maybe not," Miles said. "Confusing the enemy is never a bad tactic."

"As long as one doesn't confound oneself in the process—here they come!"

All heads turned toward Bruner emerging from the B

Street entrance, a deputy on either side. Then Bruner seemed to trip; his body appeared to sag as the deputies caught him under the arms. A picture in Sherm's memory caused a shiver: Bruner, the arrogant ex-Army sergeant, bore an uncomfortable resemblance to Oswald exiting the Dallas Police Station.

Becky would've called it "precognition."

What seemed an unnatural movement drew his attention from Bruner, and he found himself staring into the wide and frantic eyes of a young woman whose right hand had dipped under the flap of her knit handbag. Instinctively, Sherm lurched forward, but the old duffer hobbled between them, cane raised, shouting, "Pervert!"

Sherm tried to sidestep the old fool, but the cane came down between his legs tripping him. Sherm landed on his left side and rolled, seeing Charlie not twenty feet away, one knee on a bench, arms raised, .38 revolver locked in both hands.

The plaza reverberated with gunfire at the same moment a stinging ripped the right side of Sherm's face. Then it was as though God himself suspended animation.

From where he lay, the young woman's body was at eye level. A nickel-plated automatic lay just beyond her twitching fingers. Her mouth was agape, a smoldering bullet hole below her eye. A deputy crouched over her, revolver drawn and smoking. Across the mosaic, face contorted, .38 dropped, Charlie Applegate was clutching his bloody leg and looking over his shoulder at the Eighth Avenue entrance.

The floor was littered with people.

Only one person was standing: Bruner. He'd gotten to his feet; his hands were clasped. He was praying—or seemed to be praying.

And in that snip of time, in an atmosphere of silence tainted by the smell of gunpowder, wiping the blood from his eyes, Sherm clearly perceived Bruner's monotonic chant—not words, but a rosary of numbers.

1
Sherman's Law

Sherm had been shot at before, as many as several hundred times during the worst of it against the bridges at Sinanju. Yet they (whoever *they* were) hit him only once that amounted to anything. Not him actually, but his F9F and he was forced to ditch. Yet he hadn't been afraid. Not then. Not now. For, in spite of one lucky hit, the North Koreans or Chinese or Russians or whoever they were, had been lousy marksmen, often inflicting more damage on themselves with shells that fell back to earth than on their attackers. The unfortunate assassin had not been felled by her own shell, but whose had gotten her? Not Carlson's, nor Charlie's. Whose then? And whom was the shot that killed her really meant for?

Charlie had arrived on the scene just as the girl, white, age about twenty-three, pulled her automatic into view. Charlie had acted instinctively, drawing his own weapon, but Tom Carlson, one of the deputies, mistook the action, pushed Bruner out of the way, fired at Charlie, and struck him in the left calf. Charlie never fired, yet the girl was shot and killed, pulling the trigger as she fell so that the bullet struck the tile near where Sherm lay, scattering fragments. Several struck him in the face: on the cheek, the nose, nicking the ear, above the eye. The one above the eye was the worst. It bled profusely, making the wound appear far more serious than it was. Nearly everyone watching would later say they thought he'd received a direct hit.

Maurice was trimming Becky's hair. She'd already loaded the trunk of the Buick with a stack of tabloids Maurice said she could take home to search through for whatever she needed, and was leafing through one looking for a story titled "Miracles of MOM," when Maurice stopped cutting her hair, pointed the scissors at the television screen and asked if that wasn't her husband. Later she would tell Sherm that at first she thought he was kidding; then it was like a nightmare. People were falling everywhere. She saw him and all the blood.

He'd hardly picked himself up and put the handkerchief to his face than sirens were wailing and paramedics pushed through. He had to tell the deputies to get Bruner out before something else happened; then he went to Charlie who was holding his leg and swearing. By then, Glidden was darting about, shouting instructions no one was paying attention to. Miles, indecently calm, corralled and herded them through the courtroom to the judge's chamber where Scorchy Tabor, chin nestled in the folds of his black robe, had been snoozing. Tabor's eyes opened and blinked a quick "How dare you!" before realizing the intrusion was a necessary one, the fire in his eyes subsiding as he looked from Bruner and the deputies to Miles and Glidden, then to Sherm, Tabor crying out, "Good Lord!" and hustling Sherm to the leather couch. Glidden babbled something insane about a tourniquet, Carlson went for a paramedic. Bruner seemed unmoved, back braced, wrists handcuffed behind him, staring off into some private sector where people apparently pray like quarterbacks calling signals.

Tabor came up with a towel, one he might've used for drying his hands after sentencing—an unfair sarcasm Sherm thought to himself, for the old stone face contained nothing but concern. "This is a nasty one." The judge turned to Glidden. "There's a half pint of brandy in the lower left desk drawer." Glidden fetched it and Tabor sprinkled some on the towel, handed Sherm the bottle, then the towel, and told him he'd better have a drink and keep the towel pressed to his eyebrow.

Within seconds though, the corner of the towel was dripping blood onto the carpet, alarming the judge, who turned to the remaining deputy and told him to expedite the paramedic and to turn over his pistol.

Tabor ordered Bruner to the leather chair against the wall under the yellowed print of a battle-clad Joan of Arc. He glowered at Bruner. The pistol in his hand trembled.

Bruner's eyes flickered. "You Tabor?"

"*Judge* Tabor."

Bruner remained sullen for the better part of ten seconds, then, "Why don't you just shoot me, Judge, and get it over with?"

The click of the hammer being drawn to the cocked position startled Sherm. He made a move to get up. Miles raised both hands and said, "Judge—" just as two deputies with a paramedic barged in. Carlson looked as worried as Sherm had ever seen anyone. The paramedic didn't look terrified at all. He applied a clean compress above Sherm's eye. A few stitches were needed, he said, as soon as possible. Carlson unholstered his revolver, held it in ready, and jogged ahead through the courtroom. He checked the ramada area to either side and called out that all was clear before they followed. He stopped them again before the arched outside entrance, checking again before they passed through. He cleared the corner and street, urging them to sprint the final twenty yards to the ambulance—which warbled its way through traffic, arriving fifteen minutes later at the Medical Center Emergency Room where Sherm was joined by Becky who hugged him more times, he was certain, than she had in years. When she kissed him he winced.

"Oh, sweetie . . ." She held him tightly. "And poor Charlie . . ."

"Charlie'll be all right."

"And the poor girl . . ."

He shook his head.

"I wanted to see if you were all right, but the camera was moving all around." This time when she kissed him he kept himself from wincing.

Concerned about her emotional state, Maurice had driven her to the courthouse but the ambulance had already left. She said it was a wild chase across town, that Maurice did splendidly, and she'd paid a cab to return him to his shop. Her arrival in the emergency room coincided with the ninth and final stitch above Sherm's eye.

Nine stitches and a few nicks. Maybe a black eye later. Lucky. Charlie had a bullet in his leg. One person was dead.

When they'd finished the outpatient and insurance paperwork they went to Charlie's room. He was propped up on pillows in the hospital bed. It was hard to associate this oldster in bifocals, whose hair had receded, grayed, and grown ragged about the neck with the fellow who, for twenty years after leaving the Marines, kept the regulation length haircut. But Charlie was doing fine—Percodan, he said. "You look like hell," he told Sherm. "Sit down before you fall down again."

Becky pulled the only chair away from the wall and turned it so Sherm could sit before settling lightly near the foot of Charlie's bed.

"You know," Sherm began slowly, "I couldn't believe it was you on the ramada."

"I was going to give you information my lousy intuition told me you could use—that Donegan thinks the Frye Rule should apply." Charlie closed his eyes and motioned with his forefinger toward an envelope on the medicine stand. "Also the lists you asked for."

"Yeah." Sherm handed the envelope to Becky to stuff in her purse. "You should've sent your tape recorder."

"I talked to yours this morning—the info you asked for."

"I'll get it from the tape."

Charlie opened his eyes on Becky. "How'd you wind up with this?"

"Lucky, I guess."

Charlie frowned. "Can't understand a jabrone giving up the good life of an investigator to run after ambulances."

"Got tired of peeping into other people's bedrooms."

"Nobody gets tired of that." Air rushed faintly through the air-conditioning vents. A wheel that needed oil squeaked. Someone called for a nurse. "I didn't shoot that girl," Charlie said quietly. "Maybe I should've. Everybody was watching Bruner but she had her eye on you and was acting real nervous. Then I saw her piece and she might've got you if the old fart hadn't tripped you; if the other shot from behind hadn't got her."

It hurt when Sherm blinked. "Percodan's gone to your head, Charlie."

"I'm right on this—you got a piece around that dump of yours?"

"Old Harrington and Richardson."

"Not that defective antique. Buy a weapon you can keep handy and outta sight. How about a snappy thirty-eight snub?"

"Too many trigger-happy deputies around."

"How about my suing the county for a couple mil?"

"At least."

"Naw, I should've hit the deck like the rest of you jabrones." The inevitable nurse popped in to tell them that Mr. Applegate should rest now. Charlie promised to be out in a day.

They hadn't left the ward when Sheriff Kline, with four deputies in tow and looking like a man who hoped he wasn't too late, almost bowled them over. He ordered the nearby room checked and when it was declared clear, they were ushered inside.

Kline asked for a statement but Sherm couldn't tell them much because his attention had been diverted at the crucial moment. As for the number of shots, he thought he heard three before seeing the fatally wounded girl.

"We don't know why yet—" Kline removed his hat. "It looks like the girl was after you, Counselor."

With the diffused light of an afternoon turned cloudy slanting through the venetian slats in a room that smelled of dying, the confirmation that he'd been the target wasn't bothering Sherm as much as the crazy questions going off in his head.

They didn't know who she was, but weren't taking any more chances. Kline told Sherm to stay put, protection would be assigned, and they'd see to it his car was delivered. Sherm handed Kline his keys and asked for Romero. Kline grunted what sounded like affirmation as he rotated the rim of his Stetson between his fingers. "Deputy Carlson's here and we're gonna visit Applegate." He put his hat back on. "I hope you realize Carlson did the only thing he could in the situation." Sherm realized and Kline nodded, leaving them with the sound of his Tony Lama's in thumping violation of the hospital's quiet rule as he herded Carlson in the direction of Charlie's room.

Outside, a swirl of dust chased them across the parking lot to the Buick. They got in and Sherm closed his eyes to try to rest them while Becky drove, but the episode kept intruding. It was not as clear-cut as the sight of rotund Jack Ruby stepping into the line of Oswald's advance between camera lens and victim, pistol in hand, the *pop* of a single shot, Oswald clutching his stomach, all of it before millions of witnesses. Half of the population on earth must've seen Ruby shoot Oswald, yet it couldn't have been so clear-cut after all.

Something he hadn't thought of in a long time came to mind, his theory governing the reliability of given witnesses being inversely proportional to the sum of their numbers. This was no more than an extension of what had already been proven—that certain factors reduce the reliability of eyewitnesses accounts. Factors such as weapon focus, and the violence of the event, produce what they used to call, over a navigational radio fix, the cone of confusion. Increases in the degree of stress or violence or the number of people enlarge and intensify the cone of confusion; and those caught in the cone bat eyelashes, blink, look away, close eyes, flinch, duck, bob heads, run, hit the deck.

Even Julius Caesar, it appears, was confused: *"Et tu Brute?"* Neither emphatically nor accusatorily, a question marked by profound disbelief.

Julius Caesar, uncertain witness to his own assassination:

SHERMAN: Tell the jury, Imperial Caesar, what you know of Marcus Brutus's involvement in this plot.

JULIUS CAESAR: Well, he was there with the rest of the conspirators. Of this I am certain. I'm also certain he was concealing a dagger under his toga.

SHERMAN: How can you be sure?

JULIUS CAESAR: Well, all the rest had daggers!

SHERMAN: I see, but you're not really sure, are

you, that Brutus was one of those who hacked you?

JULIUS CAESAR: Ah, well, I guess not.

Et tu, Ruby?
The intensity of this particular cone severely reduced the probability that Charlie's and Kline's perceptions of the assassin's intention were correct; besides, Sherm couldn't think of a reason why anyone would want to knock him off. More important, he'd stopped in the line of fire only to offer a half-assed apology to Miles for aiding the state's case. Except for that he would've passed directly into the courtroom. On the other hand, the girl might have been acting on an unexpected opportunity.

But what about the other shot? Charlie and Kline were surely mistaken; they weren't familiar with Sherman's Law.

Yes, he thought, what we actually see and hear can be as false and misleading as fiction, that the more of us who see and hear, the more ingrained it becomes, the more difficult to dislodge, until it becomes (we believe) the truth.

When Ruby stepped in front of millions to gun down Oswald he could well have been fixing the fiction that Oswald acted alone; yet each assassination, so coldly executed, must have required incredible calculation. Ruby shot Oswald. Clear-cut. No question, no debate, no *why,* and millions of eyewitnesses turn their backs on history to embrace the fiction.

He opened his eyes to see Finger Rock pointing to the cumulonimbus that in a moment would surely dump on them.

As they turned into their driveway Becky suggested he tape the courthouse shooting from the evening news.

Good idea: two channels, two perspectives to view and

analyze as many times as he wished and he would find out what really happened.

Cameras didn't lie.

But when the time came to watch, it seemed as though they did. As the first shot boomed, the cameraman zoomed in on Bruner, no doubt expecting blood. When another shot popped like a firecracker, the cameraman began searching with his lens instead of his eyes. When still another followed, like the thud of a shoe dropping on a hardwood floor at the far end of the house, the erratic panning caught items of such importance as Sherm's sleeve, a deputy's boots, six or seven rear ends, and Marshal Estaban's midsection. The camera finally rested on Charlie's bloody pants leg, accompanied by a stunning narration that went:

> . . . a private investigator, whose name is being withheld, apparently shot and killed an unidentified woman during an assassination attempt on the life of accused slayer Raymond Lee Bruner . . .

Half an hour later, Camera 5 Alive aired a somewhat improved version. Bruner's entrance again evoked the scene of Oswald in Dallas. He tripped and was drawn up by the deputies; then Carlson, who must've had his holster unsnapped, drew his revolver and fired. The *boom* was closer to this camera, therefore louder. The pop of the automatic was hardly discernible. Instinctively, it seemed, the cameraman had followed the sounds of the shots, from Carlson to the blocked view of the girl, a quick pan of the plaza, the marshal again, to the young woman dying on the tile. Channel Five did not speculate on the identity of the assassin. Instead, Lisa Conitti, one of two anchorpersons, reminded her viewers that the complete report from the sheriff's office would be aired at ten o'clock.

During the commercial Becky said she'd seen baby quail by the pond before she left for Maurice's. It was a very late hatch and she hoped the heavy storms wouldn't hurt them. He asked how many, "Maybe eight, but they scurry so, who can count them?" She asked if he'd like to do some steaks outside or did the rain look too close?

He went to the sliding door and saw the storm's edge so close now it was probably raining on the new shopping center. She said she would do the steaks under the broiler. While she went ahead with their preparation, he pulled the footstool up close to the screen and replayed the tape, which proved that Sherman's Law apparently applied to cameras as well.

Even though the two cameras at the courthouse couldn't have been more than ten feet apart, each seemed to have recorded, in several ways, separate events. Could this be a missing link in Sherman's Law, that the number of unique perceptions of a given event is directly proportional to the sum of the subjective viewpoints?

Taking her usual place on the wicker couch by the light, Becky rejoined him, along with Beau, who was in his usual spot next to her. She picked up her knitting basket and asked what were they looking for.

"I'm trying to convince myself I wasn't the target, but all I've determined so far is that the camera shows what the cameraman wants to show, or nothing and everything. In these two, the scene and the persona are the same, yet they appear as separate events."

He got a large sheet of Becky's watercolor paper and drew a diagram of the plaza, entrances, walkway, the marshal. Next to Estaban he placed an M for Miles and an S for himself. At the south entryway an arrow, representing the deputies and Bruner, pointed toward M and S. He marked the probable position of the two cameras, 9 and 5. Finally, between S and Estaban, for Old Duffer he wrote OD. He rewound the tape.

Camera 9 had come on first, picking out Bruner and the deputies even before the spectators saw them coming, but the camera swung to catch the crowd's reaction. "There she is!" He stopped the tape. The assassin's profile stood out, the only one looking away from Bruner. But it was something else that caused Sherm to take a longer look: the remarkable resemblance to the naked girl on the rock.

On his diagram she became an X, the perfect spot for nailing Bruner. In fact, Bruner would've passed so close she could've stabbed him—but even before the crowd began shifting, her movement away from Bruner was evident. Camera 9 returned to Bruner. The rest was chaos.

Less chaotic, camera 5 clearly showed that the girl had come gunning for him. "She probably figured I'd be there," he thought aloud, "because no lawyer in his right mind would miss an opportunity to be on camera. So when this addle-brained lawyer wasn't where Ms. X thought he should be, she looked around until—" *This wasn't right.* "So why didn't she rush right to where he was and let him have it?"

"You're talking like you are someone else."

"I'm wishing I was."

"Is it important why she hesitated?"

It really wasn't. Ms. X could've been uncertain who he was or distracted by OD's move toward Bruner.

Whatever personal sense of outrage had launched the old man on a course between Ms. X and himself, Sherm would be forever thankful for, and now it crossed his mind to present him with some sort of thank-you, if it was possible to pick Old Duffer out of the lineup of old duffers who lined the plaza benches. Unfortunately, his face had not been picked up by either camera.

Becky looked up from her needles. "It seems to me a lot more important to know where the other shot—the one that killed the woman—came from."

"Most likely from somewhere above, roof, top of wall—"

"I'd say it came in much too flat to have been fired from above."

"What do you mean, 'much too flat'?"

"You know, flat, straight, a level trajectory."

"How could you know that?"

"I saw it."

"You saw the bullet?" Sherm knew better than to laugh. "How could you see the bullet?"

"On the TV." She went to the VCR, and ran the tape backward to camera 9 coverage. "Right about—there." She tapped a needle against the screen.

"That's Marshal Estaban."

"Not the statue—the streak across the picture!"

"That's just a streak."

"No, look!"

"A TV camera couldn't possibly pick up the flight of a bullet."

"You aren't looking." Becky rewound the tape and ran it through the scene she'd pointed to. Something streaked across the tube. "See!"

"I see. I just can't believe we're seeing a bullet traveling through the air."

"That's all it can be." Becky placed the point of the needle on his diagram at the Eighth Avenue entrance to the plaza. "The shot came from here."

"I'd just come through there. Besides, it's much too open."

The needle moved out through the entrance. "What's out there?"

"The street, a parking garage."

"That's where the shot came from, the parking garage."

He rested his elbows on his knees and examined the diagram, visualizing the final position of Ms. X. She'd fallen where he had been standing a moment earlier. She'd been hit below the eye. The cameras had begun their search in that direction. Becky was right, the shot had to have come through the entranceway.

He'd almost been caught in the crossfire. It happened in the flap of an eyelid, so to speak. More accurately, in the squeeze of a trigger. If Old Duffer hadn't tripped him, Sherm would have caught the bullet between the shoulder blades.

8
The Evidence

Beau put his front feet on the glass door, tail twitching as he stared out into the mesquite where a curved-bill thrasher alternately sang and clinked its beak against the ceramic feeder. In the outer branches a gaggle of house finches kept their distance. Becky stooped to feed her bear some rare leftover steak.

"This law of yours," she asked, "does it apply only when there are lots of people?"

"Probably not." Sherm remembered another trial, a tragic example of one human and one mechanical misperception, recalling the little girl's testimony: "Daddy had a knife and on purpose . . . he brought it . . . brought it across her . . . Mommy—" The child cried and had to be taken from the courtroom.

"What's wrong, sweetie?" Becky looked concerned.

"I was thinking of an old case where the father was convicted on his daughter's testimony and later he was murdered in prison."

"And Sarah tried to hang herself."

"Sarah?"

"The daughter." Becky stood up. "That's all, Beau."

"When was this?" He hadn't known. "I recall turning the appeal over to someone else because of another change of venue, but I wouldn't forget a little girl's suicide attempt."

"It was a long time ago." Becky moved toward the kitchen. "I'll fix us some old-fashioneds."

The case had achieved notoriety. A national tabloid headlined it THE POLAROID PROOF and ran the picture taken by the girl with the camera, "a present from Santa," of what appeared to be the father about to slash her mother's throat.

The child had planned only to photograph them off guard, a "candid" snapshot. Catching them in the crucial pose had been accidental. The father's story was that the slashing had also been accidental, that he and his wife were arguing in the kitchen and she started waving the carving knife when—yes, it was Sarah who came in. But she was small and couldn't see he was trying to wrest the knife from her mother's hands. Her mother's blood drenched her. A Christmas killing.

His daughter's testimony and a Polaroid picture sentenced him to life in prison where a self-appointed agent of retribution punctured his throat with the sharpened handle of a plastic spoon.

So what happened to the little girl grown up when she realized that the eyes and the mind are not always compatible bedfellows, that there is, in fact, a great deal of infidelity between the two?

Becky handed him his old-fashioned and said she was sorry she had mentioned it, picking at the fluffs of cat hair that had fastened themselves to the sliding door drapery.

A roll of thunder rattled the sliding door. Sherm looked up. The overcast was choppy gray, and a few miles eastward inky black with filaments of incandescence. The tops of the palms a quarter mile away were whipping in the wind as the gray curtain of rain closed in.

Becky balled up the cat hair and dropped it into an unused ashtray. "Listen to the thunder, will you?"

"Gully washer for sure."

"An appropriate finale to a weird day."

"Speaking of weird—" Sherm sipped his drink. "Bruner did something really weird after the shooting."

"Praying is weird?"

"You knew he was praying?"

"Saw it on TV."

"There was everyone flat on his face or back except Bruner; for a moment, everything stopped. It got quiet, like everyone was holding their breath all at once, and I heard him. Not 'Hail Marys' or 'Our Fathers,' but some sort of code."

"That's weird all right." Becky touched the skin below his eye. "You're getting a real shiner."

Lightning so close they could smell it, in concert with thunder that sounded like great windows cracking, sent Beau scurrying to his storm shelter under their bed. Sherm unplugged the TV antenna and switched off the air conditioner just as rain came. The house lights flickered a series of signals before failing altogether, and Becky began setting out candles while Sherm located the flashlight he kept in the VCR cabinet.

"You know what we haven't done in a long time?" Becky said.

"Yeah," Sherm answered with a leer in his voice.

"A *long* time: the old speculation game. How about what happened the night Miss Eagan was murdered?"

"Well, let's see, we were at the Bridge Club being creamed by the twins."

"That's not speculation. You remember how we used to reconstruct the crime."

"With this one I think I can more than speculate."

"Careful, now."

"Okay, how's this? After being aroused by a six-pack, Bruner decides to exhibit his dirty flicks to his niece to get her also aroused, so he pounds on the back door to scare her, which he does—fear being a stimulus to arousal—but when she hears it's only her uncle, she welcomes him with open doors. Uncle staggers in, polishes off another beer, heads straight for the bedroom—he has to because there's no time for amenities—where he promptly inserts a cassette into the VCR, no doubt contemplating another insertion a bit later, which happens to be in less than ten minutes. Of course, the innocent girl is revolted by what her perverted uncle is drooling over and orders him from the premises, posthaste. Loins fired from watching a full five or ten seconds, Uncle makes libidinous, salacious, and unwholesome suggestions as to what he and his virginal niece should do with their genitalia. Being pure of mind and body, she naturally recoils, berating him that he belongs in a zoo with orangutans who bare their red asses before the amazed eyes of little lasses in pink dresses—"

"You're getting carried away."

"And so was Raymond Bruner! Thus inflamed, he grabs the nearest lethal object, which happens to be the antenna cable, wraps it several times around her neck. Because she is faint with disgust, horror, or all of the above, she cannot resist, therefore, no outward signs of struggle. When our Desdemona ceases her feeble resistance, enflamed Uncle strips and rapes her while she's still warm—"

"Sherm!"

"Very quickly too, because she's already informed him she called the sheriff, prior to dying of course. Unlike Desdemona, she fails in her attempt at momentary resurrection. Having satisfied his lust, Bruner calls in his alibi, zips up and zaps out, perhaps tipping his baseball cap as he leaves, with a parting 'Sorry to be a necrophile and run.'"

"Be serious."

"What I've just given is essentially the prosecution's case."

"But they will make it sound different."

"Sure they will."

"So what do you think really happened?"

"Bruner has two witnesses who will testify he was elsewhere. We also have a redial number to this elsewhere made after the nine-one-one call, which tends to darken the shadow of doubt. Shelly Eagan might've been forced to say what she said and whoever forced her was desperate for a fall guy. How it could've been done I don't know, but I really don't think what we hear on the tape occurred within the specified time."

"Why don't we listen to the tape?"

"Good idea." Sherm went for the recorder he kept in his office.

Lightning provided an eerie flickering that illuminated the contents, the mess of unsorted mail and strewn-about books; great-grandfather's Civil War sword; diplomas; an official Department of Defense painting of a pair of Grumman Panthers attacking a North Korean bridge; framed photographs of other airplanes, sailboats, graduations, himself, his wife, and their two kids. It was a room Becky rarely entered. Too many ghosts she said.

He checked the batteries in the old GE recorder by running one of the tapes from the shoe box. "Hi, Mom and Dad—" He snapped it off, one of Vic's taped letters from the summer he worked in Yellowstone. Sherm gathered up the 9-1-1 tape and the letter and returned to the den where Becky, unruffled by the chubasco's frontline cannon, had resumed knitting by candlelight.

They listened to the tape once through before discussing it.

"This is very disturbing, almost as though—I'm not sure how to put it. It's sort of theatrical, and somehow out of kilter. Let's listen to one statement at a time and I'll show you what I mean."

Sherm rewound the tape too far, causing it to run silent half a minute before:

. . . "Nine-one-one, emergency."
"Someone's breaking in!"

Becky stopped the tape. "She says 'someone,' therefore she doesn't know who it is. Also, 'breaking in' suggests a lot of racket, yet there's no other sound on the tape."
"Phones don't always pick up background, especially a ways off, which this probably was."

"Name and address?"
"He's breaking in!"

"Now 'someone' becomes a 'he.' But this has to be an assumption."
Sherm nodded agreement.

"Name and address, please!"
"He's at the back door trying to break in— Twelve-twenty Rio Verde."

"Now the 'he' is located at the back door. To know this, wouldn't she have had to check the intercom switch position and wouldn't she know 'he' was her uncle by his voice?"
"It's also puzzling that three minutes, six seconds should elapse before she speaks again."
"Let's time it; I'll count." Becky pressed the play button and when she reached 1,181 the girl's voice came on:

"I'm sorry . . . it's my uncle . . . that's all . . . he's drunk . . . that's all . . . I'm sorry."

"The line was absolutely dead."

"Glidden assumes she was holding down the mute button the whole while."

"Even though there's a great deal of difference in the way the words are spoken and so repetitive, it's the same voice."

"In the first part she was probably scared to death. When she found out who her visitor really was, it was like a great emotional stopper being pulled."

"Is that what you think?"

"It's what Glidden will attempt to make the jury think. We know that seven minutes later the girl was dead." Sherm rubbed his chin. "Still, beginning with what we have here, I can't see how anyone, drunk or sober, could've raped and murdered and gotten away before the patrol car arrived."

"Which leaves us with three possible conclusions: *a*, Mr. Bruner possesses superhuman capabilities; *b*, the man at the door who was not her uncle possesses superhuman capabilities; or *c*, this tape is some sort of forgery."

Sherm smiled. "You're getting better all the time."

"I certainly hope so. Is the last choice possible?"

"Unless we come up with a voiceprint that can be positively identified as Shelly Eagan's, for comparison, everything is immaterial." He handed her the copy of Bruner's sister's letter.

Becky held it to the candlelight to read and asked if terminal referred to computers.

"Probably."

"From this I'd say Mr. Bruner and his niece were fast friends." She directed his attention to the letter, that it indicated they were working together for MOM. Sherm challenged her analysis, saying it was obviously a computer project they were involved in.

"Not Aunt Wilma," Becky countered. "Not someone who spells e-n-d-e-v-e-r-s, but the important point isn't spelling; it's what kind of endeavors. Surely the 'we' she keeps referring to is MOM, which she writes, 'will never hurt again,' meaning never hurt for money."

"Your angle is probably the right one, but you've got to admit there's an implied interest in computers."

"This proves Mr. Bruner and his niece were working together and he was proud of their success because he took the letter to show her." Becky passed back the letter. "Hardly precursory, won't you agree, to some horrid strangulation." She resumed knitting. "There is, of course, another possibility, that the letter is part of the frame-up."

"Implicating Wilma Bruner?"

"Or whoever wrote the letter, which I'm sure a handwriting expert can ascertain."

The bunched drape was lit as if by neon, followed by a grumbling sort of thunder.

"If it really was you they were after at the courthouse, maybe they think you're so smart you'll figure out how they framed Mr. Bruner and who they are."

"So far, they have nothing to fear." Sherm took a lengthy sip from his neglected drink. "I really doubt anyone would try to kill me so bizarrely on mere supposition."

"Maybe they think you're on the verge of finding out because of someone you've talked to or something you've seen?"

"Maybe we're assuming too much. Maybe the shooting had nothing to do with Bruner." He slid the door all the way open. "Whoever that girl was, they'll say she was acting alone. It's less messy, especially when that one person is dead. No ongoing investigation or expensive court battle, just a funeral plot with a plastic marker." He took a deep breath of the rain-freshened air. "Look, the city has lights."

She put her arm around his waist. "I heard the elf owl last

night," she said, pointing out a black spot on the saguaro in the shallow wash behind the house. "He probably lives in that hole."

He turned to look at Becky and saw the deep sadness on her face. "I'll try to get a picture of the little devil."

The lights came on so suddenly and brightly he half expected the bulbs to blow, but it was apparently an illusion created by their sudden restoration.

The coolness left in the wake of the storm, he said, should be allowed into all of the house, so he went to the kitchen first, then the bedrooms, bathrooms, living room; and when he pulled the drape covering the picture window that looked up at Ridge Road and Finger Rock, he saw the shadowy figure, shielded from the driveway lantern by the intervening mesquite, moving down the driveway toward the house.

9

Five Alive

The frantic surge of heartbeat that sent Sherm's thinking in search of the old and battered and probably defective Harrington & Richardson revolver surprised him; but instead of dashing after it, he waited to one side of the drape as the sound of footsteps transitioned from driveway gravel to porch tile and paused before the door. Sherm might have dialed 9-1-1 had not the gruff muttering prior to the bell been recognized as friendly.

He threw open the door. "Romero, if you don't give me cardiac arrest before this thing is over—"

"Sorry." The deputy shifted his considerable weight to the other boot. "I figured you'd know it was me."

"Who is it, sweetie?"

"Lugosi again."

"We brought your car." Romero handed over the keys. "And this pager. Just push the button and my beeper goes off." He motioned toward the easement side of the house. "I'll park so anybody coming either direction will see the squad car. I'm not here to trap anybody."

"That's good," Becky said. "I'm not here to be bait."

No sooner had Romero returned to the easement than Larry Baron, Channel 5 news director, was on the phone. Lisa Conitti and the Camera 5 Alive crew would appreciate an interview, Baron explained, and they would've contacted him earlier except that their telephone lines were down because of the storm. Baron was explaining as the Camera 5 Alive van arrived.

Beep! Beep! Sherm flinched and picked the pager off the shelf where he'd expected it to remain undisturbed. Romero's hushed voice told him what he could see wheeling down the drive.

"I see it."

"*Madre*, get away from the window!"

"It's only Channel Five."

"Sherm," Romero began with a note of impatience, "please close your drapes and please stay away from windows."

"Roger, over and out!"

How much of this protection crap would there be?

"Mr. Baron," he barked into the telephone, "your crew is already here."

"We'd sure appreciate the interview."

"Okay, okay." Already he could hear Baron's voice on the

van's CB. The phone rang again: Channel Nine. Others began arriving: a platoon of newspaper people, a *Time* reporter, a pair of freelancers, the Channel Nine station wagon. Patrol cars blocked either entrance to the drive, parked on the road, lights flashing. Their home in the desert looked like a goddamned Hollywood set.

Because of deadlines, the TV interrogation was without needless inquiry or pointless cross-examination. The newspeople had better courtroom manners than most lawyers and Sherm liked them, especially the Camera 5 Alive anchorperson, Lisa Conitti, the dark-eyed fox of Channel Five, who bore more than a superficial resemblance to Jaclyn Smith. In tight jeans and T-shirt she looked slimmer and better than she did on the tube. He liked her, but one of her questions threw him. Did he have any idea who fired the shot from the parking garage? He replied no, and asked how she knew it came from the garage. Sheriff Kline told them—them, but not him. Maybe Kline hadn't known earlier, and later the phones were out. Still it bothered Sherm more than a little and when the interview was over he said so.

Off camera, Lisa said she was beginning to have her own doubts about their sheriff.

"A couple of weeks ago he called me about a body they found in the desert. It turned out to be a wild-goose chase, nothing. I was really pissed and when I finally got hold of him he said he didn't make the call, that it was probably a trick, that we should always check back. Which is a bunch of shit. We'd never get a scoop. Besides, I know Tom Kline's voice. Christ, everybody does and I'd just interviewed him!"

Sherm wondered if the sheriff's tenure was beginning to tell.

Becky's interview lasted longer than his, Lisa Conitti probing her feelings during those "terrible moments" she realized what was happening on the TV screen; but when Conitti asked if the crew could stay for live ten o'clock coverage, Becky demurred.

When the mob cleared out almost as quickly as it had arrived, Sherm began to brood. Kline had held out his knowledge of where the shot had come from, so maybe he was withholding the girl's identity as well. Decomposed bodies were identified faster. Police computers gave up data at the speed of light; so what was holding them up? Was Kline trying to mine their case? Was Bruner's thinking so far out of bounds? God knows it wouldn't be the first time the state conspired against an individual.

He picked up the phone and punched out Kline's number. The sheriff wasn't available. There were flooded streets, washes running into trailer courts, lines down. Yet it seemed to Sherm that half the department had shown up for Lisa Conitti. The power of the press. *Priorities.*

They waited for the news, Becky cross-legged on the rug in front of the TV with Beau on her lap, his gentle motor purring to the good life of nestling on so soft a lap.

Channel Five came on with corrections to the earlier version: who was shooting at whom, the number of shots, where they came from. Lisa Conitti wore a disappointing dress. Too much material everywhere shrouded the lovely shape that'd been so evident in jeans and T-shirt.

"About an hour ago," she said, "we talked to Peter Sherman."

He looked ten years older and thirty pounds heavier (and what a shiner!) while Becky—well, she looked like Becky. And when Lisa Conitti asked that one question about her overall reaction to the shooting, she flashed only an instant of concern before her famous smile and the reply, "Oh, so many interesting things happen to my husband."

She was the tough one . . .

"It was not an interesting thing," Sherm objected now.

"Except for a split second's interference you might well be making funeral arrangements instead of basking in the media's spotlight."

"I am not basking."

The scene had switched back to the studio where the camera settled on the trustworthy profile of Lisa Conitti's co-anchorperson, the older Cronkite-like figure who'd picked up on Becky's remark. "Peter Sherman, you may recall, is the man who, in 1983, spent a year and a personal fortune fruitlessly searching for his aviator son."

10 The Morgue

An exhausting day lay behind, yet Sherm couldn't sleep, not because of his injury—it was slight, the pain diminished to discomfort—or because of the thousand questions competing for his thinking—he could lock them out—rather for the same reason he nearly let his life slip away in 1983. Instead of sleeping he prowled the house and it was very late before he joined Becky and her bear. She was asleep, breathing easily, recollections of the Colorado Plateau silent history now. Yet he lay awake a long time and the sleep that came was troubled with fragments of the familiar dreams: machinery that failed, silence in the stark daylight of red canyons and blue sky, yapping bands of coyotes in the middle of stormy nights, sun and snow and the endless search for wood smoke.

The dream awakened him for another long time of staring into darkness, until he remembered he hadn't checked the telephone tape, and so it wouldn't waken Becky, he listened in his office.

Charlie's was the first call. "About the Eagan girl, heir-apparent of controlling interest in AZTECH Micronetics. Consensus has her introverted, intense, intelligent. Graduated from high school at sixteen, college at nineteen, M.S. at twenty-one. Continued work in AZTECH research lab even after inheritance. Described as peasantlike and preoccupied with electronics and religion, which translates to few if any real friends. Only child of Gerald and Dorothy Eagan, Bruner's much older sister. Parents separated but never divorced. Father hit jackpot with new microchip and founded AZTECH. Killed in sports car. Left bundle of stock and big house on sixteen acres of brush and beer cans, also on hundred-year flood plain. A year ago mother was creamed in hit-and-run. Never came out of coma. After she died, Bruner's other sister dragged the girl into a feminist cult who call themselves Mothers of the Moon.

"About Bruner, Raymond Lee, Lee as in Harvey Oswald. Born 1951, Fort Riley, Kansas, middle kid of Tech Sergeant Robert and Frances, both deceased. Two sisters already mentioned. Moved a lot as a kid. Dropped out of high school to enlist. Underage, sixteen, but father signed papers. Vietnam. Exited with Silver Star, DSC, Purple Heart, two clusters, GED HS diploma and some college credits. Wound up at Fort Bliss, Texas in missiles. Married Sharon Bailey. Second tour, Vietnam. Wife died of leukemia. Army says Bruner went bananas and got the boot. Spent next eighteen months in and out of VA psychiatric wards before Vegas to work for sister Wilma. Arrived here this year, supposedly to help niece. No work record but very active draft transactions, all cash deposits. We'll check these Monday. Also, only priors were vagrancy arrests."

"Surviving interests who'd benefit include Bruner and sister Wilma, but all they get is the house and some cash to split. The Mothers are also in for a share, but only enough to complete a cable TV project begun here by the Eagan girl. Major bundle is targeted for AZTECH for carrying on research.

"I'll bring the lists to the hearing. That's it. Don't get run over chasing ambulances."

Deciding he could live without the rest of the calls, Sherm dialed Ace Investigations. Shelly Eagan's stocks and Bruner's cash transactions bothered him, he told the answering machine.

"The money motive is invariably the one first looked at, although it's been my experience that most people realize it's not worth the risk. Becky claims I say this because we have money. She doesn't know yet.

"Nevertheless, there's bound to be litigation over the bundle left to AZTECH, with the major contestant no doubt being Wilma Bruner. With Raymond put away she could wind up with the whole enchilada. Her letter showing up at the scene of the crime is a bit too coincidental for my taste. Have someone check her out, Charlie."

Charlie's papers were still in Becky's purse. Sherm glanced at the inventory, much too complicated to be examining at this hour, checking that there were no items in the alphabetical listing which began with either "tape" or "cassette." At the bottom, in Charlie's scrawl, was the notation, "no record of silver waist cord." He unfolded the AZTECH employee list. The first two names certainly grabbed his attention: Ammar, Majida and Ammar, Najib. Wouldn't it be nice, he thought, to be able to pin the crime on them. Unfortunately, the twins owned the best alibi in the world. On the night in question they were trouncing the Shermans and everybody else in the bridge tournament qualification round.

Unfortunate indeed.

He wandered back to bed and still had trouble getting to sleep; then after hardly any, the telephone and Kline saying it was urgent to meet with him as soon as possible at the county morgue, a deliberately vague enticement having something to do with the identity of the dead assassin.

Barely light out and Kline already calling; was this another of his cliff-hangers?

The sheriff's propensity for keeping his audience in suspense, a hallmark of his incumbency, had earned for him among the courthouse regulars a better reputation for theatrics than for law enforcement. Unfortunately, in a period when the county desert was fairly littered with bodies of drug rip-off victims, Kline was generating headlines over the confiscation of X-rated videos. Somehow he got away with it, probably because the media loved his flair for making the commonplace exciting, and the chiseled image he gave them up front. Tom Kline looking good made the county look good and the electorate feel good about having a sheriff who wore a white Stetson and Tony Lama boots.

Yet there was a Tom Kline voters didn't seem to notice, a sheriff who'd been in office too long and was showing it. Physically, he was developing a gut and a bulbous nose. But it wasn't Kline's looks that bothered Sherm; rather, the way he'd begun running the department with a sort of autocratic paternalism many of his own deputies despised, Romero among them. It may have been this Big Daddyism that prompted the investigation by the state's Attorney General, an investigation which had dried up like the chubasco in mid-August without more than a mention in the newspapers. The state never came right out with what they were after, but it could well have been to find reasons for the department's inordinately large percentage of botched investigations; or it could've been they found out what everyone who lived in the county should've already known, that in spite of the local population explosion, the small town mentality which had dominated for half a century was still very much in force, especially within the circle of hackneyed political relationships surrounding the office of sheriff. Kline had tossed off the Attorney General's investigation with Big Daddy seriousness, telling the public only that it was an in-house affair which was being taken care of. In-house it remained. No one talked. They were like a mountain family, isolated and feuding with the outside, their spokesperson being the tall daddy of the brood, gaunt and handsome Tom Kline stepping out of the woods into the spotlight when the news was good, hiding in the brush when it wasn't.

Sherm looked into the mirror and touched his wounds: ugly little scabs but healing fine. Terrific shiner. He hoped they would turn Kline's stomach. The man deserved it, especially for ordering him from a warm bed to a cold morgue. He hated the cold and he hated morgues. So why was he going? Kline wasn't his CO; she was asleep in the bedroom. He picked up the Remington cordless and began working through the scab field in search of whiskers. He was going, he guessed, because he was like Beau, curious—there was no way now he wouldn't go. He put up the razor, dressed, wrote a note to Becky, fastened it to the refrigerator with a magnetic pickle and departed for the cold morgue.

God how he hated the cold. That day that he ditched to bob like an ice cube in the gray sea until the chopper pulled him from the water, moments from freezing to death, he'd promised himself he would never be really cold again—a promise he'd pretty much stuck with. Of course there were times when the chill seemed to penetrate as deep as it had that day he crashed into the Sea of Japan—winter mornings on the Colorado Plateau when he had to beat the ice out of the coffeepot. But those were times that couldn't be helped.

Kline could've at least given them a clue, but even as he ushered Miles, Glidden, and Sherm into the cold steel glare of the dead room he would say only that he wanted them to see for themselves.

What they saw were the naked, pale bodies of two young women who were remarkably alike, in spite of obvious differences in weight distribution and bone structure—and, of course, the strangulation marks and a bullet hole. As he looked at the girl with the bullet hole, Sherm felt a shiver of recognition that went beyond the glimpse of her he'd had at the plaza. Did he once know her, or was it because she looked so like Shelly Eagan? The two could have been sisters, possibly twins. But never the same person, which was the startling way Kline put it.

"What do you mean they're *both* Shelly Eagan?" Miles asked in such an outraged manner as to suggest Kline had gotten them down there at this awful hour for the sake of what amounted to a practical joke.

Kline removed his Stetson and began rotating it, watching as though he'd just discovered the wheel. "We triple-checked. The computer keeps coming up with the same ID for both women."

Miles shook his head angrily. "Then your computer is fucked up."

"The computer is not fouled up," Glidden said quietly. "Somewhere there was a mix-up and it's going to take time to search out the records: birth certificates, medical data, et cetera. It may take a day, maybe longer, depending on how long ago the mix-up occurred. If it happened when they were born, say by a nurse who somehow switched the records, the process of identification will probably take longer. How long I can't say. It's even possible these two were twins separated at birth. At any rate, we need another postponement."

Under the circumstances, Miles replied, it was not in the best interest of their client to postpone. "We have a witness who places Bruner somewhere other than at the scene of the crime. Now, you say, the identity of the murder victim is in question—"

"There's no question," Kline cut in.

A writ of habeas corpus, Miles said, was clearly in order.

"Think on this . . ." Glidden shoved his hands into his pockets and drew in his shoulders. "To proceed with the hearing now would mean repeating the whole process later." He was, of course, correct.

Sherm gave his partner the go-ahead nod, so Miles conceded the extra time. "But why did you haul us down here?"

Kline put his hat back on. "We wanted you to see for yourselves, that's all." He glanced at Glidden, who had averted his eyes from the bodies and was staring determinedly toward the small window in the metal door to the corridor. Kline signaled the pathologist who'd been working silently at the other end of the room, nodded again without speaking and motioned them toward the door. Miles started to follow but Sherm asked him to wait; he wanted to talk to the pathologist. He had some questions. The pathologist wasn't quite finished—one or two more minutes, he said.

Sherm looked at the dead girls, side-by-side and nearly alike, nearly twins but probably not, no sheet covering their bloodless flesh; and he felt he was violating them with his eyes, seeing in death what was forbidden in life. What gave him the right? Or Kline or Glidden or any of them? Shouldn't they be dressed or covered? He looked away as Glidden had done, depressed, then did what he should have done in the beginning. He covered the girls with the provided sheets. But putting them out of sight did not lessen the depression.

"You have some questions, Mr. Sherman?"

"About the rape evidence."

"What about it?"

"Well, the whole thing had to have happened in seven minutes."

"It doesn't seem probable, but it did. I mean, there's every indication of rape: bruising of the vulva, lacerations of the labia—" The young pathologist's heavy glasses had slipped forward as he looked down and he paused to push them back up the bridge of his nose. "There was a presence of spermatozoa."

"Motile."

"Nonmotile."

"Doesn't it usually take about two hours to die off?"

"That is correct. Unfortunately, I was on vacation and my assistant, though very meticulous, is nevertheless sometimes not hasty enough."

"Nonmotile sperm can be found for weeks, right?"

"A point well-taken, and frankly the amount bothered me. We took vaginal, anal, and oral swabs and came up positive on all three. Now, the average amount of ejaculate is from two point five cc's to five cc's, and each cc contains over one hundred million spermatozoa, so anything is possible."

"But this seems excessive?"

"Well, if she hadn't been murdered, I would say she wasn't raped at all."

Which would be even more difficult to explain happening in seven minutes. "What about the bruises and lacerations?"

"These can occur during intercourse."

Sherm rubbed his chin. "Can the semen be matched?"

"Not with any assurance."

"How about the time of death?"

"Hasn't that been fairly well fixed?"

"Your estimate?"

"I would place it about the same time."

"How close is *about*?"

"Minus up to three hours. Like I said, my assistant—"

"Couldn't he tell by the strangulation marks?"

"Perhaps, if he hadn't been sidetracked into trying to identify the murder weapon."

"Wasn't the cable around her neck when they found her?"

"Yes, but it wasn't what strangled her." The pathologist used his pen to point out the stria along the strangulation mark. "These were caused by something woven and metallic."

"Silver?"

"How did you guess?"

Sherm told him about the photo; then impulsively, almost as though an outside force were guiding his hand, he reached over and uncovered his assailant's face. Like a match flame in his memory: another flicker of recognition. And he had a sensation, like going into a refrigerated theater out of bright sunlight when you know there are people inside but you can't see them and when your eyes adjust you discover you were wrong and you're alone after all; but after you've been sitting awhile you suddenly notice you are not alone, that there is another you should have seen.

The spectral quality of this feeling was unfamiliar, a new dimension, a boundary crossed—

Next, he'd be believing in ghosts. He shook his head to clear these absurd thoughts, but with his last look at the contours of the sheets he knew that neither he, nor Kline, nor Glidden had yet turned the first corner in this maze.

In his funk he'd almost forgotten his partner, who was looking both puzzled and perturbed. With a smile Sherm tried to reassure him, but Miles had seen the passing shadow and was clearly worried.

"I'm all right." Sherm thanked the pathologist who said as they were leaving that he should do something about his eye.

They shuffled down the icy corridor, into the cold elevator, leaving behind the basement smell of embalming fluid, rising out of the dungeon of the anonymous dead, yet unable to rise out of depression or leave behind the chill even as they crossed the sunlit plaza outside in a morning already hot. Sherm said he needed to sit down on one of the concrete benches to warm up.

"God, I hate cold places."

"You used to ski, didn't you?"

"That was different."

Miles leaned over and brought his hands together, clasping them. "Can you believe Kline dragging us down to the morgue like that, so we could see for *ourselves*?"

"That's our sheriff."

"Doesn't he think we'd believe him? You know, like if he used the telephone."

"Maybe he distrusts phones. Some people do, or should. Bruner for one." The sun was beginning to reach his bones. "It's an old prosecution trick. Let the counsel for the defense see the victim. It sort of takes the starch out."

"You don't think there really was an ID foul-up?"

"I'm sure there was, but I hardly concur with the hypothesis that this was the result of twins being separated at birth, especially with Kline's people punching the computer keys. Yet, like the silver cord and everything else connected with this case, it seems to fit a pattern of, shall we say deliberate obfuscation?" Sherm got to his feet. "How about a Saguaro breakfast?"

"I don't know about eating, but I need coffee." Miles brushed off the seat of his pants. "I guess you heard that the shot came from the parking garage."

"Yeah, on television."

"Garage's on the way. Want to take a look?"

As they moved on, Miles said the morning hadn't been the colossal waste it seemed, that he'd arrived ahead of Sherm and learned enough in the five minutes he waited with Kline to make the morbid scene that followed almost worth it. Kline had been in a talkative mood, not about the real reason he'd issued his summons, which had to wait for Sherm's arrival; rather he told how one of his keen-eyed deputies spotted the burn hole in the flag hanging at half-mast over the Eighth Avenue entrance and how, from this single hole, they deduced where the shot came from.

Leading them up the concrete ramp to an elevation above street level, yet not quite high enough to be called a second floor, Miles remarked that high-rise garages always looked like they'd been hit by an earthquake. They crossed a triangle of yellow no-parking stripes along the west side to where a low wall faced the plaza entrance. Whoever fired the shot had parked there.

Sherm reconstructed the rifleman's situation: "It's late morning and getting close to lunchtime so he can't risk setting up a bench rest for the rifle or even have it out in the open long enough to take careful aim because someone might see." Sherm leaned over the wall and looked toward the Saguaro Club. Yesterday he'd crossed diagonally in front of the gunman, out in the open, a clear unobstructed target, his back to the gunman all the way through the arched entrance, and across the plaza. At this range, that would be far enough for even the impressive Estaban to appear small. It was one hell of a long shot from here to the other side of the plaza. So if the shooter was after him, as Kline contended, why wait until he was at the extreme limit of the field of fire?

He expressed his doubt to Miles.

"Kline thinks he pulled in here too late to catch you crossing the street."

"How would he know I would be where I was? No, Miles, there's too much coincidence here. Bruner's the only logical target. This was the backup man."

"There's no way he could've watched Bruner's approach. Look—solid masonry between here and where Bruner entered."

"Ah, but he could've observed him."

"Sure, with Superman eyes."

"On a portable TV."

Miles appeared doubtful. "Why would he wait? Why not get Bruner coming out of the jail?"

Miles was probably too young to remember seeing Ruby gun down Oswald. "Look, there are a dozen ways to deliver Bruner from the jail to the courthouse, but only one way into the old courtroom, through the doors we can see from right here, a clear, straight shot."

"Except for a flag." Miles nodded agreement. "The gunman made a rather interesting choice of weapons, a twenty-two Hornet: military surplus, breaks down, easily hidden."

There were Hornets in their aircraft survival kits during the Korean War, Sherm recalled.

"The bullet was a steel-jacketed tracer."

He wasn't sure he heard right. "Did you say *tracer?*"

Miles had begun moving toward the pedestrian ramp, nodding and repeating that it had been a tracer, which made no sense.

Tracers were used to establish trajectory for follow-on shots; yet the Hornet was a bolt-operated, single shot rifle. And firing a tracer would be like pointing a long smoky finger to where the shot came from. Still, it was either forgotten or no one saw it. Yet someone did: Becky!

"Apparently it was some sort of superload designed for considerable penetration."

"Which makes about as much sense as the rest."

On the sidewalk they were beginning to feel the heat. There were no cars and all the lights were red. On top of the old courthouse the copper outhouse blazed in the sun. They stepped up their pace and nothing more was said until they were inside the Saguaro Club and had been seated by the waitress named Jolene who remarked she wasn't used to seeing members of the legal profession up and around this early. Miles said she'd better take a good look because it would probably be the last time, and ordered coffee and a nut roll with butter. Sherm requested one three-and-a-half-minute soft-boiled egg and toast, with coffee, of course.

Miles said something about Bruner being sure the shots were all meant for him.

"Bruner's talking?"

"I guess the shooting loosened him up."

The coffees and nut roll arrived and Jolene promised the egg would be along in a couple of minutes. Sherm said not to rush. He stirred a spoonful of nondairy creamer into his coffee and watched it break up. Miles buttered the bottom side of his roll, opened his mouth to take a bite, then put the roll down. "Looking at bodies before breakfast always does this to me," he said.

"As long as . . ." Sherm picked up the mug and sipped the coffee. It was cold. He put it down and looked for Jolene.

"As long as what?"

"As long as our client's talking maybe we should go listen."

11

The Client

The way jails cloak their inhabitants with guilt, sometimes even the innocent begin to accept their imprisonment for sins they're never quite sure they didn't commit. Bruner wore such a cloak, his defiance fallen in a pile about him.

Sherm studied the little man who'd lived alone in a bleak

apartment surrounded by shoe boxes filled with pornographic tapes, lost in anonymity, that black whirlpool of despair where the Sirhan Sirhans and John Hinkleys of the world wait for their headline. Was this where Bruner came from? It almost seemed so.

Two deputies had deposited him like a bundle of dirty laundry at the school desk bolted to the floor where he slouched, head down. His hair hadn't been brushed and was greasy looking. He needed a shave and smelled of sweat and bad breath. He was wearing a T-shirt, baggy jeans, white socks, and black shoes. Prison garb. He began rubbing his hands and looked up. His eyes, red rimmed and veined, were nervous and scared.

"You can relax," Miles said with metered patience. "We're here to help you."

"Help?" It came out just above a whisper. "Help," louder still. "Help!" Scrambling to his feet, stumbling, Sherm caught him and tried to seat him but the desktop got in the way. It didn't matter. Bruner had become so virtually comatose Miles had to help get him seated.

Sherm slid into the desk directly facing Bruner, propped his elbows on top, touched his fingers to the sides of his forehead, speaking as he might to a child, necessarily deliberate, explaining the American judicial system, the assumption of innocence, right to trial by jury, basic stuff everyone knew and a few still believed. Bruner was obviously not one of the latter and it didn't matter. What mattered was that he be convinced that his counsel believed. So Sherm took his time, speaking in a way that had once wooed some pretty tough juries into believing, using those same careful strokes of persuasion to cover the canvas of skepticism.

Slowly, completely, with irrefutable generalities; that was how to win. Walk or jog if you have to, but never run. Too many were always running after another case, another client, or (as Charlie put it) another ambulance.

Bruner was coming around. His eyes had slowed down. He looked at his hands. A pathetic grin twitched at the corners of his mouth. "Look, Mr. Sherman . . ." He scratched his hands, his fingers. They were covered with a rash. "I heard from other prisoners—well, they say I'm fucked up, that you was the best around, that you didn't hardly take cases no more, that I was lucky as shit. But I figured, well—they say they got a tape of me breakin' into Shelly's, which never happened, so I figure they got, you know, control, so I didn't trust nobody." Bruner rubbed his hands.

"Yesterday at the courthouse, even before I got there I knew they were settin' me up, and when I saw Shelly—it wasn't Shelly, I just thought it was—I knew they had. And those shots they say was meant for you, I say *bullshit*; those rounds were mine. They thought they had me framed, but I got me a pair of witnesses, so they had to try somethin' permanent." Bruner hesitated, scratched an eyelid, his hands again. "I once shit in my pants in a confessional." He tried to laugh but all that came out was a cough. "This is tough." He rubbed his fingers one at a time. "Fuckin' rash is drivin' me nuts." He brought his hands down hard against the desk. "When I was a kid I'd only confess to the old priest. He was easy on penance."

Sherman waited perhaps a minute, then, "Why not start at the beginning?"

And that is where he began. "I was the middle kid and you know what they say about them, and a only boy, which I guess makes it twice as bad." Bruner told how he was raised by strict Catholic parents, an Army brat, whose father was wounded in Korea and later signed his sixteen-year-old son's enlistment papers. Even Raymond's mother was supportive. She believed, as she'd labored to make her son believe, that the communist infidel was evil, that the Christian soldier, as God's instrument, was the only force strong enough to stop the spread of this evil. So he won medals and was wounded in Vietnam.

Having discovered an inaccuracy in the myth that there are no atheists in foxholes, he returned to his new post in El Paso and searched out a substitute for religion. Across the Rio Grande, prostitution provided a livelihood for thousands of Mexico's disillusioned children. Young Bruner, at first repelled not so much by the act as by the act of paying for it, eventually found himself in concert with these strangely soft children who spoke a language not quite Spanish and wore crucifixes on silver chains around their necks. One of the soft girls, however, gave him gonorrhea, a strain resistant to antibiotics, which very nearly put an end to his sex life and drove him once again to his opposite extreme.

Feeling the guilt bred from a thousand catechism classes, Bruner turned to the succor of his youth, but too much had intervened to allow him to return to where he had been, so he looked for something less mysterious and found it through the girl he married, a West Texas fundamentalist whose religion he'd never heard of.

The former Sharon Bailey provided a stability Bruner had never known. Her stoic acceptance of the meagerness of their uprooted lives and total commitment to serving God's will steered him clear of the usual soldier's pitfalls. She miscarried twice. Though never healthy, she devoted much time to her husband and church, encouraging and praying for Bruner's self-improvement. A measure of her hoped-for success came when the college credits Bruner earned by taking evening classes at UTEP were sufficient for him to enter the Army's specialized missile program. For Bruner those were the happy years of his life, a happiness ended by another tour in Vietnam.

His assignment came as a surprise. His wounds had rendered him unfit for combat, he thought, and his entrenchment in missile maintenance had convinced him he was irreplaceable. He'd contemplated retiring in West Texas without ever having to leave, until the Army decided all of its men should rotate in and out of Vietnam until the war was won. Bruner called it "spreading the guilt." So it was off to war again, this time in charge of Hawk antiaircraft missiles, for six months of protecting the Army in Vietnam against nonexistent enemy aircraft. Near the end, Sharon died of leukemia. Long immobilizing periods of depression followed. He was useless to the Army, useless to himself. He underwent psychiatric care. He tried to kill himself. The Army discharged him.

Over the years, in and out of VA hospitals, his care ranged from outpatient to straight jacket. During one of his extreme periods, his sister Wilma flew to Denver to visit him. She'd come, she announced, with a message from Mother Moon.

Wilma's life, as she related it, had proceeded along a course divergent from his own, a life of dissolution and sin. And when her youth and beauty were spent, she found herself in a pit of degradation performing despicable acts more for carnal satisfaction than for whatever money she could make as a whore.

On the day of Wilma's resurrection, her girlfriend, a middle-aged widow from Ohio addicted to bourbon, slot machines, and being saved, had dragged Wilma into the plastic tent of the Mothers of the Moon in the same spirit as she pumped dollars into the giant jackpot slots, not so much with an expectation of winning, as fascination with spinning wheels. They were so stoked with bourbon, Wilma was not able to later recall exactly how they arrived; but there they were, hands clasped, heads bent, under the beneficent gaze of the mute Sylvia, awed by the incomprehensible moaning being translated into the stream of pulsing words on the giant screen, music and lights, and wild upspiraling of sound and light and heartbeat.

Here Bruner hesitated, glancing from side to side before he spoke again. "When I lost Sharon I lost whatever religion I had, so when Wilma told me this I thought, *bullshit*. But Wilma swore her and this other broad had gone to this Sylvia's strictly on the spur for kicks, that there was no way anybody could've known. Their being there was like a card being drawn from a shuffled deck, yet the words on this screen weren't for just anybody, just for Wilma. Christ, it was a message from Sharon."

Wilma's reaction had been to scoff out loud, from the bourbon probably; however, as the message raced across the screen like print on a teletype sheet, her incredulity sobered into shock. What she was witnessing was beyond belief: a message from her own brother's dead wife begging her to go to him before it was too late, to tell him not to despair, that she was safely in the arms of Mother Moon.

Wilma Bruner had reeled out into the neon night struck as dumb as Sylvia, trying to answer her friend's gibes, but all she could do was moan, and the sound of her own moaning was like an electric shock to her brain. She clamped her hands over her ears, screamed out her friend's damnation, and caught a cab to her motel where she forced herself to throw up, then sit on the shower stall floor with cold water beating against her head until the muddle cleared and she could speak again. Afterward, she put on the only dress she owned, packed, and flew to Denver.

"She couldn't know where I was," Bruner went on. "Nobody could. I wound up in Denver in the VA hospital. I didn't plan. I didn't tell nobody. I got there accidentally. So when Wilma showed up I couldn't believe her. She said it was a miracle and offered to pay my way to Vegas. I wasn't in shape to argue. Shit, I wasn't in shape for anything. So there I was in a fuckin' tent with my name being spelled out on a big TV screen and a message from Sharon telling me to take hold of my life and I believed it."

Bruner became mesmerized not so much by the word as by the woman. Sylvia was queenly, saintly, virginal even; that virginal quality of latent sexuality. So he found a way to serve. Not personally. Electronically. He'd worked with army missiles and knew about black boxes; so he stayed on, watching and wanting, serving the speechless woman whose god was Mother Moon.

Here, Bruner went on hold, waiting for an invitation to continue, and Sherm sensed reluctance. The story had been a long one but not much of a confession, at least not yet. What remained was important, so he had to keep the pace, maintain the calm, let the confessor tell it his way or it might not be told at all.

Patience, old priest, Sherm told himself.

Miles's chair squawked against the floor.

"Go on, Raymond," Sherm said, keeping the anticipation low.

"I dunno—" First the eyes, then the hands, rubbing the fingers. It was coming back, the ghost or whatever. "You got questions you want to ask?"

"I'd rather hear you tell it your way."

"Ask me what you want to know." Bruner was not about to carry the ball on his own.

"Well, okay. Let's see, you said you stayed on with Wilma and—they call it MOM, don't they?"

Bruner nodded.

"And you repaired this electronic message board?"

"Repaired, worked on it, did what I could."

"Did they pay you?"

"They helped me, gave me three squares a day, a roof. Wilma was the one involved, then Shelly after Dorothy died."

"Shelly's mother?"

"Yeah."

"The letter from Wilma indicated you and your niece were working on a project for MOM. Is that why you were here?"

"What letter you talking about?"

"The one Glidden found at Shelly's. It was addressed to you."

"That was one reason . . ." When no additional reasons were forthcoming, Sherm asked if Wilma had introduced Shelly to the Mothers. The answer was "Yes, sir."

"Raymond, the postmark on the letter presents a problem in that it indicates you visited your niece after your mail delivery on the day she was murdered."

Bruner nodded again and haltingly told of going to the house because Shelly called and said she had to talk about something she couldn't discuss over the phone. She would meet him at the front door. When he got to the house the gate was ajar as usual and the front door locked. He rang the bell several times and when there was no answer, went around back thinking she might be by the pool. He knocked loudly and called out her name. When there was no answer he left, dropping the letter in the mailbox. It was about six o'clock. Four hours and thirteen minutes later Shelly Eagan called 9-1-1.

"Do you have any idea what it was she wouldn't tell you over the phone?"

With this question Bruner's agitation became again apparent, his "No, sir" perceptibly shakier, the nervousness in his eyes returning, and a general perturbation as though he were not quite telling the truth and whatever he was hiding was causing this agitation.

"Where did you go after you left Shelly's house?"

"Jack-in-the-Box, then to the apartment to watch the tube. Knight called a little after nine wanting a favor so I went over to his place."

They'd been mistaken about Bruner's addiction. He was not the world's most insatiable voyeur. Instead, he stored the tapes for Knight, the owner of Sensa-Vision, because the new antiporn law specified stiff criminal penalties for "presenting obscene exhibitions." Private residences were excluded from the search and seizure provision, a dodge, Sherm knew, that could backfire on the middleman because a residence so used became, in fact, a warehouse. The law contained the usual abstraction about community standards and no clarification whatsoever of the word *obscene*. This recent product of the reactionary *Star*'s crusading was a terrible piece of legislation certain to result in plenty of litigation.

"How long were you with Knight?"

"Let's see, I got to the Sensa-Vision about nine-forty. Knight wanted a tape I didn't have so I brought a different one and he raised hell. I was there till about ten-thirty."

"Where did you go after you left Knight?"

"I had to have the right tape at this guy's house by eleven."

"Was this Edward McCreedy?" McCreedy was the other half of Bruner's alibi.

"McCreedy was at Knight's."

"Can you think of anyone else who saw you there?"

"There's Earl, the kid who works the paraphernalia counter; but shit, he might not want to say so. He doesn't want his mom to know he works there."

"Knight's testimony will have to be corroborated."

"You ain't callin' me a liar, are you?"

"I'm calling on you to remember names."

"It ain't exactly a social club down there. People don't look at each other much." Bruner spread his hands in a gesture of surrender. "We got a deal, Knight and me, which is gettin' around the new law. I don't think that'll do me much good; you know, gettin' a bunch of perverts to testify they seen me in a porn shop."

"They don't electrocute people for violating antipornography laws."

"I ain't so sure." Bruner meant it. "Look, ask Knight; he'll remember."

"I'll contact him on my way home." Sherm glanced at his watch. Could it be so late? "One more question, Raymond."

It might be a bombshell but it had to be asked. "What about the numbers?"

Bruner snapped back much too quickly.

"Right after the shots you were reciting numbers."

"I hardly remember anything." He glanced over his shoulder toward the door, going at his fingers again. "I was scared shitless."

"You don't remember saying the numbers?"

His eyes were on the move again. "You think I'm guilty, don't you?"

"I think you'd better level with us."

"I think you'd better level with me."

"Fair enough," Sherm replied. "The prosecution has a tape of your niece's voice saying you are trying to break in. Minutes later she's found murdered. The number in the auto-redial of her telephone is the Sensa-Vision, which makes it the last number dialed from that phone, Barry Knight's number, also your alibi. Then someone tries to shoot you—two people try, and you start mumbling numbers. I was there; I heard you, Raymond."

"You're wrong about this, Mr. Sherman. And Shelly didn't make any emergency call. They're connin' you—you and me and tryin' to make you think I'm guilty."

"It doesn't matter what we think, Raymond. Our job is to defend you. But it matters what the jury thinks and we have to know the truth, all of it."

Bruner got up and went to the door. He grabbed the bars and called for the guard. Just before the door was opened he turned and said as calmly as he could that it would be best for everyone if they'd forget about the numbers.

Outside on the mall between the jail and the new courthouse, Sherm and Miles settled on the first bench they came to. Miles let out an exasperated sigh and said he knew one thing for sure.

"What's that?"

"It's hotter than hell out here."

"True."

"Another thing, we've got to do something about the way he looks."

"Also true."

"Was he really chanting numbers?"

"Yeah."

"What do you make of it?"

"I don't." He turned to his younger partner. "Do you think he killed her?"

"Like you said, what I think doesn't matter."

"It matters—" Sherm stretched; he needed to run. "I've been dragging my heels because I couldn't believe Bruner couldn't be guilty. Now I'm not so sure. That tape isn't right. I mean something besides the timing; yet for obvious reasons I've been half afraid to have it analyzed. Now, well, it might be wise to have Donegan run a spectrogram. And have Charlie clarify the triangle of Bruner's relationship with his niece and this MOM bunch. Also run background on everyone involved. There'll be a lot of information, so have Terri hire whoever she needs to set up a twenty-four-hour command post. We'll call in a minimum of twice a day and anytime we come up with something we think important. Whoever mans it should relay the information to you, Ace, and me right away, which should help cut down on unnecessary duplication and the number of surprises.

"One more item. The old duffer at the courthouse who saved my ass. See if we can find a chore for him. I have a hunch he'd enjoy working again. Right now, I'd better have a chat with Mr. Knight."

12

Sensa-Vision

While the bank flashed a mere 103 degrees, down next to the blacktop it was closer to 125 degrees. Sherm swore. Whoever blacktopped these streets deserved whatever fires awaited in the end.

The 103 gave way to HAVE A NICE DAY! and when the light changed, he tried his best to improve his day by beating the next light. No such luck; red caught him. He glanced again at the top of the bank, still asking him to ignore the temperature and have a nice day. If it got much hotter would the message read, THE END IS NEAR?

It got hotter: 104. Out of the shadows of buildings now, mired in traffic that was backing up, intense heat rising from tar so hot it had turned to liquid.

He located the adult shop in what was principally a residential area, remembering it from a year earlier when it came under fire from local antipornography crusaders. They claimed Sensa-Vision's presence destroyed real estate values; but anyone could see that the run-down condition of the neighborhood had little to do with the porn shop's intrusion. Broken fences plastered with yellowed paper separated the commercial from the residential, where rusted swing sets were missing seats, battered garbage cans lay on their sides, and a 1971 Maverick squatted on its axles with sun-browned peels of vinyl hanging over jagged window openings. The lawns were overgrown with buzzard's nests of Bermuda grass.

On Sherm's side of the fence an off-keel Dumpster blocked the fire lane, where stagnant puddles from the night's storm were caked like slow-healing sores. The air smelled of dog shit.

Sherm put the XI/9 between a Continental Mark something and a '49 Studebaker pickup.

Sensibly, construction of the shop had been as unobtrusive as possible, sharing a Spanish-tiled, adobe brick building with a beauty salon, an unusual alliance, Sherm thought. Even its name had to be looked for to be seen—somewhat less an assault on the senses than one got from the shopping center sign a block away.

Inside was a different matter. It smelled of Lysol and something that reminded Sherm of their one brief visit to the cat breeder. From a rusty vent near the ceiling squeaked a swamp cooler doing its best and failing. Sherm commenced to sweat and wonder if this womblike dankness was intentional. Patches of raw cement showed on the floor where the linoleum had been scuffed away. The flaked walls were stained. This was certainly not fancy. It didn't have to be. Porn shops were frequented mostly by burned-out, older men. There had to be others, of course, the simply curious as he was about the glossy array of magazines with ejaculatory titles, sealed in polyethylene and costing sixteen dollars each, two for thirty. And what sort of man would surround himself with such trappings? Inflatable Big Dick and Cherry Pops, vibrators, enlargers, plastic vulvae, rubber penises, grotesque plungers, and other appendages of the pubic region; plus all sorts of erotic salves, sprays, powders, and pills.

Because the hairy youth on the stool behind the counter fit a preconceived image, Sherm assumed he was Knight. He was watching a twelve-inch TV mounted on a bracket near the ceiling. A sign by the TV advertised cassettes for sale, rent, or trade. The TV show was "Sesame Street." Without taking his eyes off Big Bird, the youth asked if he wanted tokens.

"Tokens?"

The youth blinked his watery eyes. "For the booths." He hitched his thumb toward the darkened vestibules.

"Are you Mr. Knight?"

The youth squinted at him as though he were crazy. Sherm introduced himself and stated his business.

"He's in back." The thumb again, this time toward an opening that appeared to lead to a storeroom. "Barry," the boy called out, "Bruner's lawyer's here."

Knight obviously spent a great deal of time on himself. His hair, flecked with gray and something like twinkle dust, might've been done in the beauty salon next door. His jaw was lightly powdered to cover a stubborn shadow that couldn't be shaved away. A gold chain converged through a grove of gray and black hair to its hidden juncture beneath a blue satin T-shirt. He was tanned and muscular about the arms and shoulders, but flab pushed out at the midsection above the wide leather belt.

"Peter Sherman!" Barry Knight grabbed hold of his hand and turned to the youth. "Earl, this is Peter Sherman!"

"Yeah, I know."

"No, you don't know!"

"For Christ's sake, it was me told you he was here."

"*The* Peter Sherman, the one on TV yesterday!" Knight was jabbing a forefinger at Sherm's wounds. "Look!"

"Damn!" Earl exclaimed.

"You gave us one nasty fright, Mr. S. I hope you don't mind my calling you Mr. S. We were watching TV when it happened. Good grief, your wife must have been frightened nearly to death." Knight's eyes went over him with the cold quickness of a shopper at the packaged meat counter. "You need something for that eye, but I don't have any liver."

Sherm pulled free of Knight's feeble grip. "Could we talk?"

93

"Certainly." Knight turned, gesturing limply. "My office?"

The paneled room was small with several leafy houseplants and a filled bookcase that extended from the beige carpet to the ceiling. There was a maplewood table and three matching chairs. On the table was an assortment of paraphernalia and a volume of *Grey's Anatomy*. Knight said for Sherm to seat himself, please excuse the phalluses, and how much he admired people in the legal profession, that he himself should never have turned down the opportunity to enter law school. "Or medicine, which was more in my line of interest. I am fascinated by the human body." His fingers came down on *Grey's*. "I think I should have been a splendid surgeon. No, not surgeon, I simply cannot stand the sight of blood. Perhaps something in gyniatrics. No, that neither. Is there such a specialization as, ah, genitourology?"

"I think you just made up a word."

"Well, there should be." Knight touched one of the plastic penises. "Aren't these awful? I swear I've seen better-looking at the delicatessen."

"Mr. Knight, I have some questions—"

"Call me Barry, please."

"Barry, the night Bruner's niece was murdered, was he here in the Sensa-Vision between nine forty-five and ten twenty-three?"

"I've already informed the sheriff that Raymond was sitting in the same chair you now occupy during the period in question."

"Will you sign a sworn statement to this effect?"

"As much as I occasionally become frustrated with Raymond, I wouldn't wish anyone the unfortunate circumstance of being sizzled in the electric chair."

"You're certain of the time?"

"Actually, I had promised one of our—what do you attorneys call them, clients? Yes, well, Raymond was holding a fine cassette which I had promised to one of our clients that evening at precisely eleven, but Raymond showed up here at quarter to ten and said he couldn't find it. I was furious. One of our best clients was going to pay one hundred dollars just for the privilege of taping this particular cassette. Raymond dredged up a substitute but it was so awful you wouldn't believe. We watched it on the television there in the corner." The TV was behind a rubber plant and Sherm had overlooked it. "We had just a terrible argument, so you see why the time is etched in my memory."

"I'm not certain I understand why Bruner was delivering the tape."

"Actually, for reasons of circumvention and security, circumvention of an unconstitutional statute and security for the protection of an exceptional line of video cassettes, one of which Raymond was supposed to deliver—are you familiar with the Mythos line, Mr. S.?"

"Not with it or any other line."

"Highly original, exciting, and especially controversial; however, much of the subject matter is considered taboo by certain narrow-minded elements; so we hand deliver to reduce the risk to our client and especially to make certain the tape does not fall into enemy hands. You may recall the so-called kiddie porn scandal. Good grief, to listen to the uproar one would have thought those children were *not* having the times of their lives."

Knight lowered his voice. "Mythos depicts holy perversions you might say, mishmashes of mysticism spanning aberrations from totemic to animistic." Knight paused, with an expression that asked if Sherm understood. He tried to look as though he did. Knight saw that he didn't. "Well, *totemic* implies a belief that an animal or natural object is related by blood, and *animistic* is a belief in—"

"Spirits."

"Precisely, Mr. S.!" Knight smiled broadly. "I apologize for my patronage. In this business I'm not used to dealing

95

with educated people. You see, ethnography was one of my many college majors. A total waste of time then, yet here it is, a rebirth—you own a VCR, of course?"

"Of course."

"Then you really must view at least one Mythos, Mr. S., before certain narrow-minded elements eradicate them from the marketplace. Earl, would you find a Mythos for Mr. S., please."

The boy appeared in the door opening, glared at Knight, and shuffled toward the back of the shop.

"Hopelessly addicted," Knight whispered, but he didn't say to what. "Earl," he called out, "make that *Nymphs!*" He dropped his voice to just above a whisper. "Along with many other depictions, the tape reveals incestuous defloration. One scene is an absolute gem. After circumcision of the labia minora, a virgin nymph assumes the anthropomorphic role of—no, no, I mustn't spoil it for you, Mr. S."

Earl loomed in the doorway. "It ain't here."

"It's in the safe, Earl."

"The safe's locked."

"We certainly have trouble keeping track of that tape. Excuse me." Knight scurried through the doorway.

"Don't bother," Sherm called after him, but Knight was gone.

Earl shrugged, turning to Sherm. "He forgets where he puts things."

Sherm asked Earl if he knew Bruner.

"Ray? Yeah, I know 'um."

"Do you remember if he was here Friday night?"

"The night his niece was murdered? Yeah, I remember he was here, but I ain't sure what time." He squinted at Sherm with his rheumy eyes. "I don't think I'd make a good witness."

No, Sherm thought, you probably wouldn't—but Knight most certainly would. He had a manner about him, like every mother's sonny boy, a sure hit with juries. Great when you're ten; disaster at forty. Knight pushed past Earl into the office, panting. "Mr. S., I'm sorry." He wagged his head. "*Nymphs* is nowhere to be found." He turned to the rheumy-eyed youth. "Earl, I'm very upset, please leave us and see if you can find another Mythos tape for Mr. S."

"Ah, Barry," Sherm said, "you needn't bother. What I'm really here for is to find out if there are corroborating witnesses."

"Corroborating? You don't believe me?"

"No, no, we need—"

"Of course, I understand. Earl so upset me by misplacing the tape I wasn't thinking of the jury. Well, let me think." Knight put a finger to his lips. "There was Earl, of course, but he probably wasn't aware of the day much less the time. Oh yes, yes. I'm certain Edward will remember. How could I have forgotten? Edward was in on the transaction." With a flair, Knight took a pen and jotted down the name and address of Edward McCreedy on a business card and handed it to Sherm. "I don't think there were others who would remember. Men seldom look at each other in here."

Sherm thanked the pornographer and got up to go just as Earl returned with the tape, threw it on the desk, and headed back to "Sesame Street."

"All of these are quite good, Mr. S." Knight dropped the cassette into a plain brown paper sack, rolled it closed, and gave it to Sherm. "Tell me where you live and I shall see to it, when Earl remembers what he did with *Nymphs*, that it's delivered to your house."

"That won't be necessary."

"Please, I don't like to go back on a promise."

"My home is quite out of the way, Calle Vista in the foothills north of—"

"We're neighbors, Mr. S.! I live just above you on Ridge Road. Do you know the house with the gazebo?"

The house with the gazebo was Becky's favorite.

Outside, the first big drops of the storm that had loomed out of nowhere were making popping sounds on the surface of the parking lot. Sherm scrambled to get the hood open and the top out and onto the X1/9. A hot wind kicked up a swirl of dust. He fastened the top on and settled behind the wheel, taking a last look at the Sensa-Vision.

Why were men vulnerable to such trash? Could it go back to when they lived in trees and had to keep whole harems happy or to those more recent neolithic times when man was a rare creature in a forest dominated by Amazons? Whatever the source, this powerful itch seemed always ready to jump in and bugger men. Just men. Women seemed relatively immune. They were not the voyeurs who crowded the cloaked closets of Sensa-Visions to plink tokens into the slots of machines and steam in their own hot breath for the privilege of masturbating.

He started up and moved out. By the time he reached the main street, the rain had become a steady downpour.

13

The Great Escape

It was as though the moisture evaporated from both gulfs had suddenly been released, turning the street into a river his little car floated on, the pair of taillights ahead the only other color in an atmosphere suddenly drenched in the eerie yellow half-light of the storm. A crack of lightning, concentrated on a transformer fastened near the top of a pole, flashed and exploded with such intensity that even the impenetrable curtain of rain, in that moment, evaporated.

He swerved across the double yellow line to miss a piece of pole that fell in his path, and when he glanced into his outside rearview to see the damage, he saw instead a white Mercedes pressing in. He slowed to let it pass. The Mercedes slowed. He could barely see the woman driver. The man beside her was aiming something black. Sherm rolled down the window, wiped the rearview with a Kleenex. The something black had a barrel.

He pressed the gas pedal; the Mercedes caught up easily. He took the next right, then left onto a circle all the way around; his pursuer followed. On a good day his top speed would be seventy. He mashed down on the accelerator and hoped for a good day.

This was like some made-for-TV nonsense; nevertheless, here he was in the great chase scene in a 1.8 liter bug being pursued by a God-knows-how-many-liter Mercedes that could run him over and probably not feel much of a bump. "Ridiculous!" If someone really wanted to get him, why not wait till he was out of the car in the open. This made no sense. Normal people did not chase other people in cars.

Midway in the block, with the Mercedes's bumper aligned with his rear deck, Sherm wheeled into an abrupt U-turn, shooting past the German car, cornering sharply through the stop sign, darting in front of a 7-Up truck which braked hard and blasted its horn. He moved to the far left of the right hand lane to keep the truck in his pursuer's line of vision until he reached the road fork, one branch parallel to the Rio Verde, the other crossing it.

He stayed on the parallel branch until the last possible moment, cranked the wheel right, shot back through the changeover lane, across the double stripe, against the flashing red light; but the Mercedes was far enough behind to negotiate the fork without losing control. Shifting at maximum RPMs, Sherm accelerated to seventy into the twenty-five MPH section leading to the Rio Verde crossing. Ahead, a sheriff's car was parked, lights rotating, by a yellow warning sign: DO NOT ENTER WHEN FLOODED. Two deputies were moving a ROAD CLOSED barrier into position. Here was help at hand. Sherm slowed and suddenly the white Mercedes filled his rearview.

Courthouse—shot—dead girl.

Better to explain later than wind up tagged in the morgue. He floored it, roared around the deputies and the barrier, hoping he could get through, hoping they might come after him and the white Mercedes.

The first dip in the road was dry. Downshifting, braking slightly, skidding up onto the middle hump that separated the two normally dry river channels, he saw more than a mere trickle, but it was still upstream. At that moment, water in the second crossing was only inches deep. Just for that moment. Upstream a three-foot wall was only yards away. It caught the Mercedes as it bottomed in the dip. Sherm saw it in his rearview, floundering.

He let the X1/9 unwind. At forty he felt he was coasting, coasting home.

Four deputies crouched beside two patrol cars in the driveway. Had the gunman come for a second try? Heart pounding, he skidded to a stop and jumped out. One deputy pulled his weapon and when Sherm stopped to look back, another grabbed his arm and locked him rigid against the side of a patrol car. He heard and felt handcuffs snapping into place.

"Sir, you're under arrest."

Someone was reading him his rights. The fourth deputy began searching the X1/9.

"What the hell—where's my wife?"

"Take it easy, fellow."

The driveway gravel crunched and Sherm could see it was the Mercedes, muddy and not so white. The woman and the man got out. They were in uniform. The male deputy was holding a radar gun.

Another patrol car, this one marked, pulled up. Putting on his big hat and unhappy face, the sheriff crawled out.

"Counselor," Kline asked with quiet resonance, "what the fuck were you doing?"

Sherm had been correct in his assumption that normal people do not chase other people in cars, with one exception: law enforcement officers do chase traffic violators. The beginning, he explained, had been innocent enough. He'd crossed the double yellow during a rain squall to avoid a piece of telephone pole. Understandable, Kline conceded, and the patrol car, seeing the lightning strike, had closed in to make sure he was all right. But Sherm sped away, and what followed was neither understandable nor rational—and included nearly every traffic violation in the book and a few they would have to look into. He would, he said, just as soon forget about the matter, but he had no choice this time; every patrol car in the county heard the call. Sherm would have to plead his case. They unshackled him and checked his driver's license.

"Mr. Sherman, your license has expired."

Kline shook his head. "Which about completes it."

The deputy who had been searching the Fiat emerged with a triumphant smirk and Knight's brown paper bag. Kline removed the video. "Contraband, Counselor?"

The illustration on the box depicted fellatio and neither participant was female. "Ah, I was checking on a potential witness and, ah—"

"We'll have to check on this." Kline turned to the deputy. "Go tell Mrs. Sherman what's happened and she can follow us if she wants." He motioned Sherm toward his patrol car. "I'll take you in, Counselor."

He got in the back, Kline beside him. Having run the gamut from numbing stupidity to burning embarrassment, Sherm began to feel a rising sense of outrage. "Where in hell did you get money for a Mercedes, for God's sake?"

Kline had the nerve to laugh. "The dealer loaned us three, betting they'll be cheaper to maintain and hold up longer so the county will start buying them."

Sherm raged at the indecency of not flashing a light or blowing a siren!

"They were. Might there have been a little panic, Counselor?"

"Damn it," Sherm blurted, "you saw what happened at the courthouse!"

"I understand; I hope the judge will," Kline said. "I also recall telling you to stay put."

"Yes, sir!"

"Until we get whoever's behind this, I want you to stay where we can protect you—home."

Hell or high water, Sherm thought.

Becky pulled her Buick in behind and followed them onto the street. Sherm slid down in the seat. God, how many times had he raved at the tube for just such nonsense and how many times had Becky urged him to calm down. What would she think of this escapade? What could she think?

"My husband," she might tell the judge, "detests movies which feature automobile chase scenes. He rants and throws soft things at the TV screen whenever he sees what he calls 'perfectly serviceable machinery' being demolished. He insists that such depictions, in addition to being monumental wastes, are also dangerous illusions to be planting in immature minds, which anyone watching such shows surely must have—"

They were clear of the foothills now, on a long, straight

backroad to the freeway, and Sherm said the judge might not understand and could Kline possibly lend a little support?

For a moment Kline chose silence, then: "Sure, Counselor, I'm always willing to lend a friend a favor."

Lend. What would the interest be on this loan?

They transitioned into the freeway traffic flow and the truck they fell in behind quickly adjusted to fifty-five. Kline leaned forward as though about to instruct the driver; instead, he spoke to Sherm. "Mind if I ask why you took Bruner's case? What I mean is, you've been out of the criminal courts for several years, so why pick this one?"

"You said it, 'several years'; it's now or never and I'm not quite ready for never."

"Bruner doesn't deserve you."

Before he could thank the sheriff for his left-handed compliment, Kline said the identification had been partially straightened out. There was no doubt now that the girl Bruner raped and strangled was his niece, Shelly Eagan. The other girl was still being checked out.

Up ahead the bridge spanning the freeway loomed like a cenotaph, a concrete platform for the bodies of two dead girls, an image he couldn't shake even as they were entering the County Jail and Becky, who'd caught up, scolded Kline's driver for having exceeded the speed limit. She then turned on Kline, but his beeper saved him. A jeep was overturned in a flooded arroyo with a woman hanging onto one of its wheels. The chopper was on its way. So was Lisa Conitti's Camera 5 Alive crew. Kline snapped back that he was also on his way, and with a tip of his well-known hat was off before anyone could say good-bye.

They were finishing the paperwork when Romero lumbered up, surprised to see them just as he was about to go on duty at their place. Recounting his escapade as succinctly as he could, Sherm concluded by admitting he'd let his imagination trample his better judgment.

"*Trample* is a good word," Becky agreed. "Traffic court tomorrow."

Romero tugged at his worn leather belt and said he'd walk them to their car. When they were well into the parking lot, he glanced around, making certain they couldn't be overheard, and in a voice even more subdued than usual, said he really wasn't sure of anything except that certain people seemed to know more than they were letting on.

"This morning when I checked in, one of the guys in the department told me the sheriff had him open up the Eagan house for some FBI guys. He said they hooked some electronic gear to those loose cables in the bedroom and messed around for a couple of hours. He said they cussed out Kline about every two minutes for moving that stuff that was there. Finally, they called someone on the phone and while they were tinkering, asked the person at the other end if they got the signals. From the way it sounded they got one of two."

"Did they say what kinds of signals?"

"Not exactly, but they talked about scrambling one of them."

"Not unscrambling?"

Romero shook his head.

Sherm forced an appreciative thanks, but he had the kind of feeling he got after too much of a bottle of cheap wine.

Once Becky and he were on their way, he muttered about Kline's stonewalling for several blocks before covering the day's events as best he could. A trio of conspirators, lack of sleep, exercise, and food, made him forgetful and she had to ask for clarification on several points. He needed a meal and some sleep. He hadn't jogged in two days. Physically and mentally he was worn-out.

"Heather called. She saw the shooting on German TV and she's glad you're all right," Becky said. "I told her we made the bridge finals and she wishes us luck. Also some good news—Charlie's out of the hospital and back on the job and, although somewhat hampered by a cane, he says it's almost worth it to be able to park in 'handicapped' spots. He called shortly before your posse arrived. Before that, your favorite client, Pauline, called to say she was upset about your injuries. She saw us on TV and wanted to know if it wasn't time we enacted some sort of handgun legislation. Moffet next door was also upset about our dog."

"We don't have a dog."

"I told him but he went right on being upset." Becky continued, "Two newspeople called wanting to know your feelings about electrocution. I told them you've never tried it. And Miles wanted a time to get together before the hearing."

"Oh, hell," Sherm groaned, "I'll be in traffic court."

It was cooler now, windows down and driving so the air streamed in, pungent from the storm which had become a thin, irregular edge of captured sunlight. Becky caught each synchronized light as it changed to green so that the total sensation was one of fluid motion. She had never had an accident. His last one was six months ago. Had she been in his bucket seat this afternoon instead of him, they would probably be sitting home eating dinner. She would have slowed to let the tailgater pass; that failing, she would have pressed on to open road. Most certainly she wouldn't have risked life, limb, and driver's license to elude a figment of her imagination.

Was it entirely imagination? The Mercedes could easily have been following him all day. Whatever, he was too hungry right now to think of much else. "How about Milano's?" The red checkered tablecloth spread out in his mind began filling with food. "Antipasto, spaghetti with mushrooms and meatballs, Chianti—"

"You talked me into it!" Without changing pace, she ducked onto a side street, swung into another, and slowed for Milano's. It was dark. There was a sign on the door: CLOSED

105

TUESDAYS. "Whoever heard of being closed Tuesdays?" She pulled away, accelerating smoothly.

"Why did I have to mention antipasto, spaghetti with—" Not so smoothly and for no apparent reason they'd begun slowing. "What's wrong?"

"I'm not sure." A reflected band of light from the inside rearview shone across her eyes. Although it was still daylight, the car that followed a half block behind had turned on its headlights. "When I slowed for Milano's, it slowed."

"I see the lights."

"I'll take us home, directly, deliberately. No chase scene, okay?"

"Okay." But the juices were flowing.

The lights stayed with them up the main street, into the foothills, onto the meandering blacktop roads where big houses squatted like giant Colorado River toads among the saguaros. Becky swerved into the driveway, activating the garage door which opened before them and closed behind them like a dark mouth. Nevertheless, Sherm had turned in his seat and through the brief opening saw the same muddy white Mercedes.

14

Speculation and Assuagement

Along with Sherm's reading glasses, Becky found the beeper between the cushions and the wicker. He put on the glasses and checked the beeper, intending to ask Romero to inform Kline that they really didn't appreciate being followed. No answer. He carried the beeper to the refrigerator, plunked it on top, and dialed Glidden on the kitchen phone. The County Attorney, a taped voice informed callers, was attending a movie premier benefit for indigent orphans, sponsored by the Marshal Estaban Brigade.

Sherm slammed down the phone. "Everywhere I turn it's goddamned Estaban!"

"Easy, sweetie, easy." Becky pushed him out of the way to get the meals she'd prepared and frozen for such emergencies, from the freezer to the microwave. In no time at all he was putting away the last of what turned out to be one of his favorites, sliced pork roast with stuffing and gravy and fresh peas and carrots. As she rinsed the trays to stack them in the dishwasher, Sherm kissed her on the cheek.

"That's for assuaging my hunger."

"Everyone should be assuaged once in a while."

"I'll fix the old-fashioneds."

Becky got the dishwasher going and settled on the couch with Beau, assuring him that Mr. Sherman's bad humor had been a temporary state brought on by something Beau could relate to, hunger. When the drinks arrived, she eyed them suspiciously, remarking they were "darkish." The end of a long day, Sherm said, from morgue to being pursued over half the county, required strong drink.

"If we were being followed strictly for our protection," she asked, "wouldn't Sheriff Kline inform us, especially after what happened?"

"Kline has an unfortunate flair for mystery and intrigue, and I wouldn't be surprised if he believes we're somehow better off not knowing."

"I don't think you give him enough credit—how's about a little speculation?"

Too tired, he said, settling beside Beau, but at least there was no more to speculate about her seeing the bullet; and, catching her triumphant smile, he confessed, "I should've learned long ago never to doubt my wife. This tracer, however, complicates rather than helps. Tracers were made to leave smoke trails so gunners could adjust their aim, which surely isn't the case here. It's unquestionably absurd that an assassin should use a bullet that leaves a trail back to where he's supposedly hiding."

"You're speculating reasons for *not* using a tracer bullet."

"Why the shot in the first place? Why the courthouse plaza? Who was shooting? Who was being shot at? The setup makes no sense. Only one person, Bruner, was certain to be there; everyone else just happened along."

"You and Miles didn't just happen to be there." She got busy gathering up the tabloids she'd left scattered about.

"Sure we did. If Glidden hadn't asked us to meet him at the Saguaro—" Becky stopped to study his reaction. "I think I'm running out of speculations."

"You haven't made any."

"Okay, okay, so our gunner has this twenty-two Hornet he bought from Bob's Military Surplus which he wants to try out. He's one of those characters who likes to shoot holes in stop signs and has to go to the courthouse to get a permit to shoot something. When he parks in the garage and looks across the street, he sees the arched entranceway with good old Marshal Estaban like a silhouette target at the far end of a shooting tunnel. Our gun nut, unable to contain himself, grabs his rifle and a box of stolen shells, unaware they're war surplus tracers—which I'm sure were never manufactured for the Hornet—and potshots the marshal. Unfortunately, the flag, which had been hanging motionless all morning, decides to flap and he misses the marshal, with tragic results."

"How's that for speculation?"

"Not bad."

"Not bad? That was the most ridiculous scenario I could think of."

"Your speculation could contain elemental truths."

"Elemental, eh?"

"Elemental," she repeated, concentrating on sorting the tabloids. "I found some interesting stuff in these while you were chasing around the county."

"Being chased," he corrected. "Such as?"

She held the top one so he could read the headline.

MOM OR MOB?

"Listen to this:

Has Sylvia swapped her Elysian Fields for mob money? People on the strip aren't the only ones asking. After discovering that huge deposits into MOM's piggy bank kept bankruptcy at bay, Nevada's gambling commissioners are looking into the possible coupling of MOM with MOB. Sources say MOM's riches were squandered on a TV miniseries that smelled to heaven—oops, Elysium. Sorry, Sylvia.

Do you think organized crime could be involved in Miss Eagan's murder?"

Sherm thought a minute about the potential overkill at the courthouse. Historically, the mob avoided wasting innocent people. No, this seemed more like the work of a terrorist, which made even less sense. He asked what other tidbits she found in the tabloids.

"Well, there's lots about who's firkytoodling whom—"

"They use *firkytoodling?*"

"No, 'doing it' is about as far as they dare go, but we all know what 'it' is, don't we?"

"Innuendo with never a witness."

"Like back when they picked on poor Jackie, only now it's poor Sylvia. First was the honeymoon, when they all loved and referred to her as 'the sainted mute.' They virtually canonized the poor girl. Look at this early headline."

HAS GOD SENT HIS ONLY DAUGHTER?

"Definitely excessive."

"Then Sylvia, rather her brother acting on her behalf, decreed that all future interviews were to be exclusive, meaning sold to the highest bidder. With that announcement the honeymoon was over. See."

MUST MOM MAKE MORE MONEY?

"They seem to enjoy alliteration."

"They've had plenty of fun with the acronym too." She flashed a headline, printed in red:

WAS MOM A HOOKER?

"This one makes the *National Enquirer* read like the *Wall Street Journal*."

> Show biz pop cult, Vegas's own MOM, admittedly has been hooker haven since word go. When pressed about its pandering to ex-members of world's oldest profession, Sylvia's oversize Ouija board tells critics to take a gander at the Big Book and check out pals of a chick named Mary Magdalene.
> But Sylvia, honey, the big word board doesn't tell us if the One and Only Herself turned tricks while plying her trade on the strip.
> Come clean, Sylvia. After all, could you be in better company?

"Sounds like poor MOM really pissed off the press."
"You're beginning to alliterate, sweetie."

"Been listening to too many tabloids." Sherm rubbed his temples with the tips of his fingers. "This is all very intriguing, but is it worthwhile? Sometimes too much information can bog you down, and I'm really beginning to feel bogged."

"Before you bog out completely, did you notice all the decks on the Eagan inventory?"

"Yeah, stereo, VCR. You'd think she would've recorded her voice sometime."

"I meant cards, decks of cards." She dug out the alphabetized list and pointed out the items.

The item he saw was *bicycle*. "That's her bike."

"No, after bicycle it says deck. Look at the quantity. A single person wouldn't have six bicycles."

He hadn't noticed the number. "Who do you suppose the idiot was who listed this stuff by brand name?"

"Probably a computer—and here, KEM—KEM decks, four, and KEMs come in pairs."

He didn't see the significance. "I'll bet we have more than fourteen decks scattered around."

"And we play tournament bridge. What did this single girl living alone play, solitaire?"

"They were probably her mother's. You know how those things accumulate."

"I think it's worth checking on."

"Could be." But his tired eyes had fallen on an item above KEM, JEZEBELS, and he remembered the brand name from the annual, unsolicited Victoria's Secret catalog he never failed to scan for its femme fatales. The quantity, twenty-one, made it an item definitely worth checking.

He picked up the phone to call the command post before going to bed. Terri answered and he scolded her for putting in too many hours.

On such short notice, she explained, it was hard to find someone, but another girl was coming in at midnight and two more tomorrow. The big news was, of course, what Sherm had been put through, then there was the sound of papers being rearranged and he gave her a list of items for Charlie to check out, concluding with the card decks and underwear.

"Underwear?"

"Underwear can tell a lot about a person."

"Charlie says Donegan's real bent out of shape about our sheriff's mix-up on the IDs of the dead girls. He, Donegan, says these days everybody is in the computer, so somebody must be hacking it, whatever that means."

Nobody escaped the computer, the daily mail proved. "Congratulations, P. Sherman, your name is on the list of possible ten million dollar winners," ad nauseum. Apply for credit, donate to charity, put money in the bank, or subscribe to anything and you wind up in the computer. After mailing a guarantee for a video game cartridge, Sherm was deluged with ads for rock music tapes and acne cures; and they still received computer-generated junk for Becky's mother who spent her last nine years in nursing homes. So how was it possible anyone could escape the electric tentacles of the computer?

15

Whitewings

Shortly before six, Sherm rolled out of bed, brushed his teeth, put a clean adhesive strip over the cut above his eye, brushed his hair almost into place (checking the bristles for additional loss); donned his sweatshirt, white trunks, tube socks with the blue 34s Becky had embossed, and the blue and white Nikes; downed two glasses of cold water from the Amana tap; checked the temperature and humidity (77 degrees, 51 percent), and was out of the house by ten after.

He scanned the area from the rise at the top of the drive. The patrol car in the easement was the only vehicle in sight. He hoped no one lurked behind the dark green screen of jojoba along the road.

Becky called the plants "whale savers" because oil from jojoba nuts was being substituted for whale oil. When all the nuts ripened she would be out gathering them, not for the buck or two a pound but to save the whales. How many years had it been since they last saw whales on one of their sailing trips out of San Carlos? How long since their last sailing trip? Weren't the kids along and weren't they still kids?

He set out on a slow, even pace because of the miles to make up and more humidity than he was used to. A cap of middle clouds spread like a washboard across the sky, keeping the sun under wraps until it angled high enough to burn away the overcast and begin recycling moisture up into cumulous turrets that in late afternoon would grow into the hulking front line of the chubasco.

From the top of a rise he could see the city laid out in grids of low flat houses separated by streets wide enough to turn a hearse around, where most of the people in the county lived and where he would be just as happy they stayed. City below, mountains above. And what mountains, the westernmost ridges with precipitous canyons as beautiful as anything along the Colorado. And sticking out near the top of it all, Finger Rock.

Until they began installing expensive homes on the ridge between him and his "finger," he'd always thought of Finger Rock as part of his front yard. Since then, these past several years, it had been carrying more than its share of symbolism, seeming more than an accidental geological landmark, perhaps Mother Nature's gesture of last resort.

He moved to the middle where it was smoother going. The road, severely potholed and strewn with stones and weeds, paralleled a wash that flowed during the chubasco and kept the heavily shrubbed cactus forest alive with rock squirrels, scorpions, quail, cottontails, diamondbacks, and larger animals that hadn't been so occasional when they first built the house back when the javelina ran in herds and bobcats left tracks in Becky's garden—

A picture snapped in his mind: Vic running into the den breathless with excitement, jabbering about the mountain lion at the pond, and sure enough there was one.

So long ago . . .

Shrugging away the prickle of remorse, he stepped up his pace. "One-uh-two-uh-three-uh-four." Lift the legs; pound the macadam. Get body and brain alive again. "One-uh-two-uh-three-uh-four."

He turned onto a jogging path for a couple of laps through a natural park of uncleared desert. Measuring his pace to keep from slipping on the gravel, he passed a saguaro with arms enough for an octopus, scanning the trail ahead for rattlesnakes; but it was already too hot for snakes. He started down a steep embankment toward a pond containing water beetles and pollywogs, through the cluster of mesquite along the high-water mark, then back along the rim past an army of battered saguaros whose arms were tipped with the splitting red fruit that a month ago had been white flowers and now swarmed with gnats.

A white-winged dove landed on one of the arms and began pecking. They were always around when the fruit ripened. Atop the saguaro, a bit unsteady because of the spines, the head-bobbing whitewing was an unstable, silly creature, but in flight nothing would catch Sherm's attention quicker than this same silly bird hurtling through a forest of giant cacti, wings fixed, head raised to clear the erratic flight path ahead as it weaved, dipped, and swerved, using wind and air currents, losing altitude but never terrain clearance, a reckless low-level flyer flirting with the danger of impalement on the thorny spikes of miscalculation.

Other birds, less bold, flapped safely from tree to tree or soared upward on rising air currents. Not whitewing. He courted disaster just for the fun of it.

A pair hurdled the pond, disappeared behind the mesquite, and reappeared atop their separate saguaros to resume their silly bobbing.

How much longer would his memories keep him grounded?

The cap of clouds was thinner now, like a gauze bandage with the sun coming through. It was even beginning to smell hot. He stopped to remove his sweatshirt, tie it around his waist, and dump a tiny bit of gravel from one Nike. He put it back on and reversed course. It'd been a good morning, five miles more or less without encountering another human being when suddenly he came upon the last man in the county he would've expected to see on the road at approximately five till seven on a hot July morning, dressed as though he'd just been through a sporting goods style show, in loose and silky red shirt and shorts with white seam stripes; matching headband, socks and shoes; and red leather wristbands. But the man was definitely no jogger, and not jogging. He was stooped over, hands on hips, chest heaving, looking as though he were about to throw up, have a stroke, or both.

Sherm stopped a few feet away. "You all right, Mr. Knight?"

His color was washed out, almost gray. His eyes bulged. He tried to talk but there wasn't enough left in him to get out more than something sounding like "Airey."

"Pardon?"

A coughing attack, interspersed with tubercular wheezing followed, together with, "Barry."

"You'd better sit down, Barry." Sherm pointed out a mesquite-shaded slab of rock.

"Yea-ss . . . bettah sit." Knight lowered himself slowly.

"Sure you're all right?"

"Yea-ss."

"Do much jogging, Barry?"

"First time." He gulped for another breath. "Maybe last."

"You should take it easy first time out."

"Yea-ss . . ." Knight pulled up his shirt and grabbed a hairy handful of flab. "Gotta lose this."

"There are less risky ways." Sherm looked toward Ridge Road. "That's quite a jog from your place to here."

"Heavens, I haven't run *that* far." Knight placed his ring finger on his lower lip and glanced about as though he'd just discovered himself in the ladies' room and was trying to think of a good reason for being there. "I drove down looking for a park that's supposed to be around here and when I couldn't find it, I decided to jog anyway. I've barely covered a quarter mile I'd guess, though most of it uphill."

Sherm told him about having the tape confiscated.

"Good grief, the fickle finger of law is everywhere." He threw up his hands. "C'est la vie—thank heaven it wasn't *Nymphs*."

"I'll pay for its loss."

"Heavens, no, I practically forced it on you." Knight looked at him evenly, grabbing onto a gold chain that had been hidden by the shirt. "Besides, after the drubbing we took when they confiscated Raymond's tapes, this is hardly worth fretting."

"Those were your tapes?"

"Well, let's just say I had an interest in them." One branch of Knight's chain angled oddly toward his armpit as though caught on something there. The red, silky shirt was too loose to make out the outline of whatever it was. Knight let go of the chain and managed a smile, however insipid. "By the bye, I located *Nymphs* and you really should take a look at it—or have you already?"

"No, I haven't."

"Well, you're in for a treat." There was a reflective cast about the pupils caused by minute movements, something in the way Knight looked at him that sparked the feeling of having been maneuvered into a space he would as soon have left vacated; then Knight seemed to relax. "Let me bring it around, say lunchtime?"

Something of so much interest, Sherm decided, should be looked at. "Fine, but take it easy, okay?"

"I suspect my jogging career has terminated."

Sherm did a couple of steps in place. "Don't give up so easily."

"I never give up, Mr. S."

"Good . . ." Sherm moved off at a steady, pounding pace. "See you later." Glancing up, he could see the gazebo but not the house, and someone in a white gown, it appeared, but there was no way to be certain at such a distance; then he caught it, a glint of glass, and realized they were being watched, that Knight could've watched him leave the house. He glanced over his shoulder—Knight was gone—then back to the gazebo. The white gown was also gone. A lizard skated across the road; a car was coming up. Sherm turned abruptly onto a side road. The car followed. He glanced back: a Mark something. The Mark slowed. The driver's window zipped down as it pulled alongside.

"Mr. S.!"

Sherm did a quick take on possible escape routes, then back to Knight in his loose red shirt, hand dipping for something—but when it came up there was only a harmless sheet of paper.

"It's our sworn statement, Mr. S., Edward's and mine. I've been carrying it around since yesterday."

They both stopped.

Sherm took the paper from an obviously pleased Knight. "I'm sorry I didn't make it clear, Barry. We prepare the statements; all you have to do is sign them."

He of course understood it had to be in the correct jargon and all, but Sherm might as well keep it. Knight waved into the rearview as he drove away.

When Sherm got back to the house, Becky was at the kitchen table sipping coffee, still in her robe, reading a tabloid propped against the spherical vase used to contain mail more often than flowers. When she looked up, her eyes sparkled with a glint of discovery. The answer to Bruner's enigmatic chant had been in the tabloids all along. It was, Becky explained, a form of numerology.

"People can pray in numerology?"

"In this country one may pray as one wishes. It's more or less tied to astrology and based on a belief in the magical power of numbers, in MOM's case four and its multiples."

"Absurd."

Becky waved her hand over the vase, assuming the role of fortune-teller to plumb its crystal depths in her worst Zsa Zsa imitation. "Duz not meester belief in zee teachinks of Galileo who sez zat zee book of nature is written in mazematical characters?"

"Meester Sherman duz not belief zat numbers pozzess magical powers."

"Does meester belief in zee computer?"

"Touché."

Becky folded the tabloid. "The ability to divine numbers was one of the lost secrets given to Sylvia in Elysium, a gift from Artemis herself in the form of a mandala, a religious design based on numerology, sort of a square within a circle divided into quarters, worn at all times, usually as a pendant, by devout MOMs. And get this, Sylvia wears hers on a silver cord around her waist!"

"Ah, I know of someone else who wore a silver cord around her waist."

"Right, and when you hold it and recite the secret numerical sequence, the mandala protects you against all sorts of things."

"So Bruner prayed for a lucky roll—and got it."

Becky nodded and asked how he felt about breakfast by the pool.

Sherm kissed her on the top of the head. "I'll get into my swimsuit."

While slipping into his blue trunks, Sherm mulled over Charlie's advice about keeping a weapon handy, deciding it wouldn't hurt even if it was an antique. He went to the office closet where they hid their poverty period cedar chest, and rooted through long johns, ski sweaters, stocking caps, Becky's wedding dress, a silk Japanese kimono, Heather's graduation robe, and a tatter of Vic's baby blanket, until he uncovered the only handgun he had ever owned, the slightly defective Harrington & Richardson .22 purchased in a pawnshop on his way overseas.

To survive after his plane was shot down, he had thought he might have to shoot a rabbit or something; and because it was considerably lighter and more accurate than the GI issue .45, he packed the revolver on all his missions. It was with him in the sea. Afterward, it was impossible to clean out the rust and the gun often wouldn't fire. Yet having a weapon, no matter how old or battered, would probably make him feel better, as it had over Korea, even though logic had presented a half dozen more probable outcomes: being hit by flak or cannon shell, explosion, fire, freezing, bleeding, drowning—in a word, *death*. To carry the .22 on the slender possibility that he would bail out and have to shoot some hapless bunny to stave off starvation made packing a gun of no more probable value to him than carrying an extra rabbit's foot would have been for the bunny. And when the flak finally came to him, in one of those moments of incredible clarity which seem to pop up only in the middle of nights or during periods of intense stress, and knowing he couldn't make it back to the carrier, he'd thought of it this way: The key to survival was to get down in one piece as near as possible to the rescue ship and get picked up by the chopper before the ten minutes it would take to freeze to death were up. In actuality, Harrington & Richardson served only to weigh him down that much more and offer itself as another possible snag where many already existed. If he could have, he would have tossed it before he ditched.

Sherm weighed the pistol in his hand. It could never do more than weigh him down. Its cylinder had been knocked out of alignment, causing misfires. Its prominence alone could panic a potential assailant into pulling his trigger first. Like everything else in the chest, the revolver was a piece of sentimental junk. He put it back under the blanket tatter where whatever security it might offer would be served, just as Becky came in to announce breakfast. She asked what he was doing in the cedar chest. He closed the lid. "I was looking at Harrington and Richardson."

"That nasty old man?" She was wearing large reflective sunglasses and a bikini. She kissed him lightly on his wounds. Inwardly he smiled, conscious of his pride. Sometimes she acted like a little old lady, but there was no doubt looking at her now that here was one foxy woman.

"I buried him in the chest."

"Good." She kissed him again. "I'll be out to the pool with breakfast pronto."

He left by the office sliding door, across the deck, down the walk to the pool which had been sited away from the house in the open, surrounded by a low, slump block wall, with a clear shot at the mountains above, the basin below, screened from the road by citrus and sage, from the neighbors on two sides by jojoba and hackberry, with only the short side open to the Moffets. Supporting his weight with his hands flat on the cap block still cool from the night, he looked at the peaks in the distance, already losing definition in the glare of the summer sun, and patted his right hand against the capping. Solid job, a fine time. He and Vic had put up most of the wall after the contractor left them with a poured footing.

He shucked his thongs, dove in, swam ten laps, climbed the steps at the shallow end, and glanced up at the sound of a "*Hooo-hooo-hoo-hooo*," a whitewing, staring as a small child might, more questioning than curious.

"I wish I knew *who*," Sherm answered; and hearing Becky sliding the door, went to help her with the trays, which they put on the white wrought iron table.

Over the scrambled eggs, toast, and coffee, he told her about running into Knight.

"Don't you think jogging is risky?"

She was right. His exercise could've cost him his life. "Well," he said after chewing awhile on his error. "Mr. Smut's coming over around noon with an X-rated video cassette."

"We're going to watch a dirty movie in the middle of the day?"

"We're not going to watch it; I'm going to tape it for later study."

"Study?"

Sherm finished his coffee. "Exactly."

"You don't wish me to watch it?"

"It's not your kind of movie."

"What's my kind of movie?"

"Oh . . . *Gone With the Wind*."

"Phooey, I like raunchy stuff as well as the next guy."

"Come on, what've you ever seen?"

"Well, there was that time in Juarez."

"Twenty years ago and you made us leave before the show even got underway."

"Seeing the donkey was quite enough."

"Knight indicated this is pretty raunchy stuff."

"Raunchier than a donkey making love to a girl?"

"Making love isn't quite accurate, and all we saw was the donkey."

"Haven't you any imagination?"

"Not that much," he answered.

"What can be so raunchy about a movie titled *Nymphs*?"

"I told you I haven't much imagination."

"What if you get horny and I'm not there to assuage you? I mean, isn't that what they're all about, to make dirty ole men horny?" She tiptoed across the hot stone to the edge of the pool, dove in with hardly a *kersplash*, went for the bottom, and swam underwater the length of the pool once, twice. Watching her swim underwater, quite suddenly he sensed the passage of an inexplicable fear of some half-expected, indefinable catastrophe, as though she would never come up, and he got to his feet ready to go after her, but she was swimming, not drowning, and came up after two and a half laps, hardly gasping, smiling now and the smile brought back a more pleasant remembrance of a time they both got more than a little bombed and Vic and Heather were in California visiting Grandpa. Becky left her bikini in the pool and when she got out, as though competing for a Mrs. Nude America, Sherm asked if she'd forgotten the Moffets and all the small boys with binoculars. She'd responded by hopping onto the diving board, where old Moffet or the boys couldn't miss her, and told the world to eat its heart out. Shortly afterward, Sherm remembered, Moffet had his first stroke.

Becky settled onto the lounger and began spreading tanning butter on her forearm. He knelt on one knee and kissed her shoulder. She stuck a finger in her ear and gave it an ineffective shake. "Got some water in my ear all right. Remember the time I kept hearing whistles? I thought it was Vic and all the time it was water in my ear." When she finished buttering her legs, she removed the bikini and asked him to butter the rest of her.

"My pleasure." He took the jar and began with her bottom. "What would you do without a bottom butterer?"

"I could probably make arrangements."

The present arrangement was one they had been enjoying since no one was around who could pop in on them, although—for reasons she never explained—Becky had never worried about Heather, as though she would have known not to barge in. Rather it had been Vic who sometimes took the wall in one vault to land in the pool and stay under just long enough to make his parents squirm before coming up, pushing the hair out of his eyes, and grinning devilishly. Even as a twenty-one-year-old law student such actions had been part of his repertoire, impulsive and impetuous—characteristics which perhaps should've tempered Sherm's decision that Sunday morning he handed over the keys to the Cessna and told Vic to have a nice flight home. These thoughts always started out good and always wound up on the Colorado Plateau. He tried—God how he tried not to let them.

"You've stopped buttering."

"Sorry . . ." He went to work with the tanning butter, smearing it where it had no business.

"Hey, watch it, guy!" Becky propped her chin on her hand to keep an eye on him. "Just keep to the areas exposed to the sun."

"Did you know," he asked, "that during the eruption of Vesuvius the Pompeians made love on the streets?"

"You've mentioned that before—so what if they did?"

He shrugged. "It sounded appropriate."

"It sounded like a nonsequitur—you lawyers are all alike."

"You've tried us all?"

"Nearly all." She punched him on the shoulder. "Why should I submit to your crass advances just because the Pompeians tried to get a quickie before they were buried under a ton of ash?"

"Back in those days—" He rubbed the bruised spot. "At least they got their fair share of ash."

"Ho, ho."

"We'd better get all the ash we can while we can. Besides, you know what they say about older being better." And that's all it was, a saying—certainly true at twenty, perhaps at thirty when the heat of desire is combined with the fruit of experience in such as way as to produce masterpieces. But that, they both knew, had long since passed, which was no reason not to try. "Think of it this way. Though it may not be as good, I certainly guarantee it will be longer—referring to the duration."

"Well, I guess that's all right, given the correct time and place, which this is neither. You know me, good-old-lights-out-in-the-locked-bedroom-with-no-exceptions."

There'd been more exceptions than rules, he recalled with pleasure as he began tugging at the string on his trunks.

"What are you doing? You'll sunburn your thing."

"Not if it's not in the sun."

"Oh no—what if someone comes?"

"Yeah, me."

"Someone might drop in—Romero—"

"Romero's not here."

"Heather?"

"Heather's in Germany."

"She might've gotten a furlough!"

"She would've written."

"Oh—" Becky laughed provocatively. "I must think of something else then."

"Don't bother."

"All right . . ."

The whitewing was setting out on a wild flight through the thicket of conventionality, and she was playing along, but her skin showed apprehension in the form of barely perceptible goose bumps. Her eyes too reflected this apprehension, the playful spark heightened perhaps by being out in the open under the eye of Him—or Her. And as they embraced she struggled in the most cooperative ways, closing her eyes not in surrender, for the rest of her had become an equal aggressor: mouth, limbs, body . . .

Her eyes opened wide, and in a resolute though suppressed voice, at the worst possible moment she said, "Someone's coming!"

He held back the temptation to wisecrack because she was right. "Hi-ho, Mr. S!" the voice rang out like one of the Dwarfs', but not a dwarf, and the voice of the pornographer was near.

16

The Pornographer

As though he sensed what had been going on behind the wall that separated them, Knight kept a discreet distance. For this Sherm was grateful. His initial attempt at dressing had resulted in the suit going on inside out. On the other hand, Becky had slipped effortlessly back into hers, wrapped a towel around herself, and had gone through the gate to greet their unexpected guest. He heard the pornographer apologize for being early, that he got home and was getting ready to go open the shop when he realized the tape was in his game room and dropping it off on his way would be much more convenient. They were by the pool having coffee, Becky said, and wouldn't he care to join them? Knight said he would, but first he'd better get the tape out of the car so he wouldn't forget it. Good, Sherm thought, with that guy around he certainly didn't want to be caught with his pants down; so he started toward the bedroom via the back way when Becky ran him down and grabbed his arm.

"Where do you think you're going?"

"To get my pants on."

"And leave me with that, that peddler of penises?"

Sherm knew better than to laugh. "I'm not exactly going to leave you."

"You better come right back," she said, pouting, "before that pervert has a chance to rape me."

"He won't rape you."

"He will, I can tell. You should see the way he leered."

"Who could help himself?" He placed his hands on the small of her back, slid them down and pulled her to him.

She slapped his hands away. "Not now, you idiot."

"He won't care. Fact is he might want to shoot a video."

"What I've always wanted: porn queen." She beat her fists lightly against his chest. "Please hurry; I don't know what I'll do if the conversation drifts to genitalia."

"Act like you know what he's talking about."

This time the punching was heavier. "Hurry!"

"I won't be a minute."

Sherm bounded onto the deck, through the door to the bedroom, kicked off his suit, grabbed a pair of denim slacks along with a blue knit with some sort of reptile on the breast, which he slipped over his head on the way back out. No need to have rushed. They were inside the pool area by the wall, Knight with his arms folded across the breast of his brown corduroy jacket, overdressed and in the wrong color for the climate, in vivid contrast (like Manet's *Luncheon on the Grass*) to the nearly naked lady at his side who'd let her towel slip and was staring agape toward the mountain. When she heard his approach she turned, surprise unchanged, and with a flap of her hand pointed in the general direction of the cliff mansions nested on precarious aeries along the last road north where impossible lots had been sold for twenty times what the Shermans had paid for their acre.

"Mr. Knight lives up there."

He knew she had mixed feelings about those homes, in awe of them who could build where a slight tremor might send them, their homes, and their swimming pools crashing down the cliffside; yet she'd never quite forgiven the developer for having sold off those few acres between them and the National Forest, especially for not having advised them of his intention first. They hadn't lost the opportunity of having a magnificent view of the basin, for there was no way to improve the one they already had; and, as Knight was quick to point out, Ridge Road's mountain view in no way compared to their own. Only a few of the cliff dwellings, in fact, caught even a piece of Finger Rock, most looking onto the rocky southern slope of one of the lesser mountains. It was the ranging mountains beyond, especially the Finger itself, they'd been denied access to when the lots along Ridge Road were sold.

"Mr. Knight lives up there." Her voice almost squeaked and even though Knight was pointing to his house ("Not the biggest, the one with the gazebo—"), Becky seemed to be struggling with the notion that such a person could own a home on Ridge Road, not immediately comprehending that this person not only lived up there, he also owned the house she most admired. "The big white one?" she finally asked.

"That's the one."

"I've always wanted a gazebo," she whispered.

"I built it myself, with help of course." Knight was obviously pleased someone had noticed his gazebo. "As you can see, it hangs out," he went on. "Everything hangs out: house, pool, gazebo; so if there's ever an earthquake, we'll really become bosom neighbors. Are there ever quakes here?"

"Hasn't been one in over a hundred years," Becky said. "We're quite overdue, you know."

Bewildered by this sudden hostility, Knight tried a show of wry appreciation for her rude humor. His lower teeth were crooked, perhaps a reason for not smiling much. "I should hate for that to happen." He gestured limply in the general direction of Ridge Road. "I love my house." Another gesture, limper still. "I should love it; I paid twice what it's worth." The closed-mouth smile again. "I love the desert even more. The forests of my home state, Michigan, are green and beautiful indeed, but represent an ordered quality I resent. Everywhere one looks, the trees are lined up like telephone poles. I love the desert's chaotic abandon, its uninhibitedness, the jumble and flurry. The desert—this desert is still celebrating its orgiastic rite of birth and renewal."

Becky asked if he cared for a cup of coffee.

"Well, thank you, no; but a glass of water would be most appreciated."

She suggested they go inside for the water and the air-conditioning, and as they proceeded toward the house, Knight declared that his brief experiment with jogging had just about finished him. "I compounded my error by going home and plunging directly into my hot tub."

"You have to cool down, not heat up."

"So I discovered when my head began swimming and my body wasn't."

Sherm slid open the den door and motioned Knight toward the chair opposite the TV, but Becky said no, don't sit until she'd brushed off the cat hair. She slipped into the old muumuu she'd bought in Hawaii, did a quick once-over with the "Magic Brush," poured the ice water, and asked if this was his first summer on the desert.

"Thank you, yes, my first summer on this desert." He gulped the water. "But, please, both of you please call me Barry; it's my name after all." He reached into his waist pocket, removed the cassette and, with a certain anticipation of expression and voice, said *Nymphs*, as though contemplating the damage the contents of this plastic missile would inflict on the moral fiber of its viewers.

"I'll see this gets back to you," Sherm said.

Anticipation became consternation. Knight drank the last of the water and set the glass daintily on a clay coaster. "I'm really sorry, but you've got to understand that if the *moron* majority is allowed to continue their disgusting travesty on the First Amendment, *Nymphs* could well become the single most valuable piece of tape in existence. In other words, Mr. S., because of what happened to you yesterday, I simply cannot risk leaving it."

Knight's substitution of *moron* for *moral* sparked Becky out of her funk, bristling for battle: "Are you implying that people who do not share your perversions are morons?"

"Certainly not, Mrs. S., but I do resent moronic encroachment on my personal and financial freedoms by a group so intellectually inferior they apparently do not understand a word of their own Bible."

"I don't see what the Bible—"

"If that particular book were filmed literally and in its entirety and sold across the counter on video cassette, they would be pounding the pavement in protest, toting placards demanding the abolishment of such a perverse anthology of gratuitous sex and violence. Certainly you must agree, Ms. S., that this literature is nothing more than a series of sexual encounters and wholesale slaughters."

"I've read the Bible, Mr. Knight, and I think you're missing the point."

"Barry majored in ethnography," Sherm said.

"*Porn*ography!" Becky cried out, turning on Knight. "You're a smut merchant, an exploiter of women and children—"

"How old do you think Eve was, Ms. S.?" Knight, to Sherm's surprise, appeared unruffled.

"Genesis, which happens to be the first book of the Bible, tells us only that Eve was a woman."

"A woman in that time. Yet in these times a thirteen-year-old is considered a child, and whoever admires a thirteen-year-old who is, in actuality the quintessential *woman*, is considered by these morons to be guilty of the most heinous of crimes: kiddie porn, they call it. And should I also mention that I have studied biblical literature as part of my *eth*nographic training?"

"Then you should know Genesis contains no mention of Eve's age."

"Her age must be inferred from the description of her shameless innocence. Besides, chronological age is immaterial. Eve was innocent of the knowledge of good and evil, which makes her, I believe, a de facto child. And you cannot deny that Eve, or Adam for that matter, was naked and felt no shame; or, to quote Genesis, 'the two became one flesh,' unquote, which certainly cannot be misconstrued. Further, Eve engaged not just in what is defined by the morons as *wholesome* sex, but also rather flagitiously in bestiality; therefore, an accurate opening of any such film on 'the greatest story ever told' would, of necessity, depict numerous heterosexual encounters followed by a thirteen-year-old girl experiencing coitus with a snake!"

In spite of himself, Sherm let slip an appreciative laugh. Becky, though not quite as angry as before, was not laughing. "Eve's chronological age," she reiterated, "is not immaterial." She turned to her husband for support but he was enjoying the argument too much to risk shutting it off.

Knight bit his lower lip and wagged his head. "I fear I have just engaged in what I most abhor, an attempt to force my values on someone else. I apologize, Ms. S. Will you accept my apology?"

Becky let out a slow, exasperated sigh.

Knight turned to Sherm. "I have obviously bruised your lady's sensibilities." He turned his appeal back to her. "In my circle of affairs I seldom encounter refinement; yet I must hasten to explain that this group who would force their particular values on all of society do not just threaten to eradicate my particular perversion, rather my entire existence, my business—" He waved limply in the general direction of his gazebo. "Everything I possess: my home, my pool—"

"Your hot tub."

"Yes, dear lady, even my hot tub."

"I'm sure they'd let you keep your hot tub."

"I am not proud of what I do nor am I necessarily ashamed." At this point Knight was looking at Becky strangely. "I was raised, I think, rather well, and my mom, God rest her soul, was a refined woman who might—no, would certainly not approve of the business I fell into really by accident. Neither would she infringe on my freedom so long as my freedom did not infringe on another's freedom. My mom was a fine woman, a good woman, respected and admired and never less than a lady. She dressed elegantly. Do you know that in all my life I never saw her in slacks. Always dresses. Very often she would wear gowns in the evening even when she wasn't going out. She would put on a gown and come to my bedroom just to sit by my bed and talk to me. I suppose Dr. Freud would make something of that—and she wanted me to become a doctor, not, as you put it, Ms. S., a 'smut merchant.'" Here Knight paused, his feelings surely bruised. "And I would have been a good doctor because I am interested in people. I'm not like those lobster-shelled Puritans who brandish their morality like armor while electrocuting human beings. I love people. I learned that from my mom. She was the kindest, most beautiful . . ." Knight lowered his eyes. His outburst had not only softened Becky. Much more. Her hand moved as though she were about to reach out, but she held back, and there was a look in her eyes Sherm recognized. Had the merchant of penises joined those like Mr. Bruner who were nice no matter their transgressions?

"Barry," Sherm said, "since yours is an only copy, why don't we record the tape so I can see it later, then when I'm through you'll have two copies?"

"Or twenty." Knight looked to heaven. "I'm sorry, Mr. S., but each copy diminishes the value of the original."

"You have my professional word there'll be no additional recordings."

Knight seemed not to be paying attention. His eyes settled on Becky who'd moved to the window to look outside. "Barry," she said gently, "my husband has a professional interest in your tape. He believes it may contain information relating to Mr. Bruner's case. He would very much like to view and analyze it. As you know, analysis takes time."

"Well, I didn't know." Knight seemed genuinely surprised. "You should have said. Of course, of course, go right ahead."

In the minute or so it took to set up the recorder, Knight talked about his own equipment.

"The VCR is Sherm's toy," Becky said. "I claim technological innocence."

"Toy it usually is," Sherm added, "although of late it's had some practical workouts."

"It *is*, as Ms. S. prefers, but a wonderful toy. Don't you find it quite thrilling to see yourself on TV?"

"Not when I'm being shot at."

"Of course I've never seen myself being shot at, but I have been able to observe myself in less life-threatening positions and it has been fun."

"I'll bet," Becky said.

"What kind of positions?" Sherm feigned naïveté.

"Well, one can tape his or her golf swing, you know, to analyze and improve his game."

"You play much golf, Barry?"

"In this clime? Heaven's no! But just this morning I used my camcorder and VCR to improve my jog."

Becky and Sherm looked at each other.

"I jogged in front of my camcorder, then watched myself. I didn't want my first time out looking like some waddly old fag bouncing down the park path." Knight was pleased with his candor. "Of course there are drawbacks to becoming enamored with one's own image. For instance, my first wife claimed I spent more time watching myself than I did her, which was true."

"Are you married now, Barry?"

"Once was quite enough! I don't know why I call her my first wife; I suppose because she was. Do you film at all, Mr. S.?"

"No."

"Well, you should take time out from your jogging and try video. With a camcorder a man can be an artist in his own home. You shoot a scene, preview it, erase what you wish to shoot over, all in a matter of minutes. The major advantage is, of course, privacy. You can do whatever you wish with whomever you want and you don't have to worry about others seeing it when it's being developed; or, if you wish, you may share your videotapes with others sympathetic to your needs. A most lucrative service at the shop is the tape exchange. Singles, couples, even families are involved. If you think you would be interested, I can drop off a couple of tapes for preview."

Becky groaned.

"You're quite right, of course. Home recordings are garbage. At least what you're recording—well, you're in for quite a treat."

"He certainly is," Becky said without so much as a batted eyelash.

"You have viewed the Mythos line and Mr. S. has not?" Knight asked incredulously.

"My bridge circle. We watch them all the time."

Knight seemed relieved she was kidding. "You have a nice sense of humor, which would blend well with the club I belong to."

"Don't tell me, it's a video games club."

"Everyone is *really* nice."

"You have such a nice gazebo and nice hot tub and nice camcorder, I'm sure your friends must be nice."

Unruffled, Knight stumbled on. "They really are and we have so many laughs together. We just laugh all the time . . ." His words trailed under Becky's iron glare. Knight cast an imploring glance in Sherm's direction.

No, Mr. Knight, he thought, you got yourself into this and you're going to have to get yourself out. He watched Knight pick up the empty glass and twirl what remained of the ice with his middle finger. "Why am I always playing games? I mean, here I am with two intelligent people and I'm trying to drum up interest in another of my childish games. I just can't seem to grow up. Why?" He clearly wanted an answer.

"It's a fairly common male malady," Becky said.

"My first wife didn't think so, always wanting to know when I would grow up like other men."

"She either didn't know men or didn't recognize their games when she encountered them."

Knight shook his head. "Mr. S. doesn't play games."

It was Becky's turn to laugh.

Sherm made a noise of disapproval. "My wife's deprecatory amusement notwithstanding, I must confess to playing and having played the gamiest games devised, war being the absolute, the courtroom trial another. I love games, especially winning. Everyone does. My wife is especially addicted to contract bridge."

"You really play bridge!" Knight fairly exploded out of his

doldrum. "Mom was a brilliant player. She taught me to play before I was in high school. I also take my games seriously and almost always won when my partner was good."

"You should find a steady partner," Becky said.

"I don't have one, you see."

"Play at the Bridge Club. They'll get you a partner, and who knows, maybe you and she will click." Becky's eyes went up slowly, indicating she realized too late what this might lead to, and Sherm suppressed his delight in imagining one of the club's matrons being lured into one of Knight's games.

"Barry may prefer to find his own partner," he said in defense of matronly honor.

"Would one of you be my partner?"

"We are partners." Becky pointed to Sherm, then to herself.

"I've heard so many couples fight over bridge hands."

"We have arguments," Becky said. "Never fights."

"Once I defended a man who shot his wife for unnecessarily trumping his good trick in tournament play. We pleaded justifiable homicide and got the fellow off."

"That's almost true," Becky affirmed.

"We're aware of our individual shortcomings."

"At least one individual is," Becky added.

"Maybe we could find *me* a partner so we could play some night?" Something in Knight's look had nothing to do with bridge.

No way, Sherm thought.

"Well . . ." Becky began, but Knight jumped to his feet, startling them.

"What a gorgeous pussycat!"

Beau was slinking along the edge of everything, having decided to come out from under the bed, his hideout from all potential threats, thunderstorms to strangers, his curiosity able to stand so much.

Knight beamed at Beau safely stowing himself behind the

lamp table in an inaccessible corner where he could still keep an eye on the goings-on. "I have three Siamese. They don't shed like Persians but they certainly do their best to tear a place apart. I've simply given up on cloth and gone to nearly total plastic."

A *clunk* in the VCR told them the tape had transferred and automatically rewound. Sherm gave the original to Knight, who thanked Becky for the ice water, imploring them to call as soon as they found a partner, and if he located one first, he would call. When he was out of the house, Sherm said she'd better dig out the old chastity belt.

"I wouldn't think Mr. K. would be much of a threat to members of his opposite sex, except the way he looked at me certainly wasn't gay."

"I suspect you remind him of his mom."

"That's not very flattering."

"I think he means it to be, but you may be right. This morning while jogging, I looked up and saw a woman by his gazebo."

17

Marrying Sam

Knight's visit ran them late. They rushed through their bathroom and dressing chores and Becky asked if she looked all together.

"Just right." Sherm kissed her and, unthinking, grabbed the keys to the X1/9 out of the dresser drawer. The drive to town gave him time to elaborate on Bruner's narrative and he'd reached the point where sister Wilma had taken Bruner to Las Vegas when they came to the Rio Verde bridge and ahead, a pea green and cream patrol car waiting on the intersection light suddenly reminded him. He tried not to brake too abruptly as he swerved into the Dunkin Donuts parking lot and told Becky he'd forgotten to mention that his driver's license had expired.

"How could you forget that?"

They'd switched sides and he was fastening his seat belt when the patrol car crept up on the right side. The deputy, a young woman, asked to see his driver's license.

"I'm not driving," he said.

"You were, sir. May I see your license?" Sherm fished it from his wallet and handed it over. "Sir, this license has expired." She asked the deputy in the patrol car to run a check on the mobile digital terminal; and as his number was being pecked out on the keyboard, Sherm could visualize all the tiny semiconductors in the police computer switching from one silicon chip to another, taking him apart a layer at a time until all that was left was either a good circuit or a bad circuit. Which would it be? Had they already punched Peter Sherman, traffic menace, into the police computer?

"Sir," he heard the youngster say, "would you please step out of your vehicle." Bad circuit. "We have to take you in."

"Officer, I'm already being taken in." He tried to smile. "We're headed for traffic court."

The deputy, apparently satisfied with Becky's appearance, nevertheless checked her license. "All right." She said she would meet them in traffic court to file this additional charge.

When Becky broke the silence she did so with a vengeance, rebuking him not so much for having gotten the ticket as for his total lack of concern. She'd never gotten a ticket in her entire life, which he'd never realized, and how could he be so dumb?

"Dumb?"

"Dumb!"

It turned out to be very dumb. Kline had been called out on a homicide. Worse, the judge was Fordyce, who was not really a judge but a justice of the peace, the incumbent in his particular district for as far back as Sherm could remember, who always ran unopposed and always won because as the "marrying judge" he'd tied the knot of nearly every couple in his district who hadn't married in the church. Judge Fordyce appeared disinterested as the deputy related the saga of this latest misdemeanor; but when Sherm tried to set the record straight, the judge raised his eyes like pop-up headlights.

"Sir, you had better hire yourself a lawyer."

"I am a lawyer."

Fordyce tapped his mallet against the bench. "Have you been in a fight, sir?"

"Your Honor did not see the attempt on my life on television?"

"This court does not waste its time watching the boob tube."

"This was on the news, Your Honor."

"I just told you, sir, that this court never watches television and any additional reference along that line and I shall hold you in contempt."

His last appearance before Fordyce had gone about the same. Vic had been cited for failure to signal. He was sixteen, and when he said he did signal, the justice informed him that he couldn't have or the officer wouldn't have cited him. That particular line of logic had rendered Sherm as speechless as he was now.

"Your Honor, I plead not guilty to all charges."

The gavel came down suddenly and so loudly that Sherm could not help but flinch. "Date of trial to be determined by the superior court; bond set at one thousand dollars; see the bailiff over there." Fordyce pointed in the wrong direction. "Next case."

"One thousand dollars for a traffic violation?"

"Next case, I said!"

"One thousand is an unreasonable—"

"Sir, the way you drive is unreasonable, and this is the first and last warning you shall receive. Next case!"

Becky's hand closed around Sherm's. "Come on, sweetie." She whisked him through the proceedings and away from the stuffy court into the heat of the day; and when he set out walking, she said the car was the other way. He was sick of cars, he said, all cars. He never wanted to ride in another car. It was five blocks to the office. Becky fell in behind and told him they weren't jogging.

Abruptly, he stopped. "How come you never jog with me anymore?"

"I do," she said, "just a second ago, but it's too hot to keep up."

He took her arm and proceeded at a more reasonable pace to the office building where they entered the lobby through the electronically operated door and crossed the marble rotunda into the open elevator. Becky pressed the sixth floor button. A Mexican lady with a little boy wearing a Budweiser T-shirt got in, went up a floor, and got out. Sixth floor. Sherm inserted himself into the opening while Becky got out. It was twelve steps to the firm's office.

Terri looked up from her computer to give them her best smile. She was pretty but not disturbingly so, with black hair, brown eyes, and a figure that tucked nicely into tight jeans. Her nose though was flat, her mouth too wide, minor flaws that kept her from being a doll.

"Hi," she said, "when's the bridge tournament?"

"First round, Saturday," Becky answered.

"I'll be rooting for you."

Sherm said they'd need it and asked how the hearing went.
"No hearing." Terri nodded toward Miles's office. "Pauline Lundquist—I think Lundquist is her present name."

The divorcée was seated with her sheathed legs crossed, the slit in her long skirt positioned so all of both legs showed below midthigh, legs Charlie once described as the best this side of the Hassayampa, not a bad compliment for a lady who wouldn't see sixty again. Unfortunately for everyone, the woman possessed vocal chords.

"Peter *and* Becky, how nice. I was just telling dear Miles what a bad man you are for never returning my calls. You just don't know how much I need the sexy sound of your voice to cheer me up. You don't mind my talking this way, do you, Becky darling?"

"Not as long as you remember he's married."

"Well, I'm married too and that's the problem. Why did you go back to that horrid old criminal law when nice people like me need you so?"

Sherm ignored her question and asked Miles what happened at the hearing.

"Canceled." Miles flicked a look Pauline's way.

Sherm turned to Pauline. "Kevin Jorgensen is a fine young attorney."

"That's the major problem; he's too young. How on earth did Kevin ever obtain a law degree at *his* age?"

"He's twenty-seven and married."

"Twenty-seven, oh my, that *is* a good age; but I do hope he isn't *happily* married. That would be such a drag. You know, don't you Peter, that you and Becky are the only happily married couple in town, but even with you two I keep my hopes alive. Nothing is forever." She looked from Sherm to Becky. "Are you two fighting about something?"

Becky shook her head. "We just came from traffic court."

"You're taking traffic cases but you won't handle another of my little old divorces?"

"It was my case, me who received the citation."

"Citations," Becky corrected.

"You are fighting! Listen, Peter, if it goes badly you have my unlisted number."

So does every other man in town, Sherm thought to himself.

Pauline uncrossed her legs and popped to her feet. "Must be rushing. Do you still go to Maurice, Becky? Isn't he a darling? As gay as a pink petunia, but I *really* don't care. You know, I think I like gays better than men; they're always so nice."

"Maurice is nice," Becky agreed.

"Didn't I say so?" She looked from Sherm to Miles. "You men would do well to take lessons from a gay. None of them would ever ignore a lady's phone calls. Well, ta-ta." Pauline swished out of Miles's office, voice trailing after her. "It's off to Maurice's. Bye, Terri."

"Bye-bye, Pauline."

"Christ," Miles muttered, "first the hearing, then this."

"What went wrong?"

"Bomb scare. We were all set up when Kline's men stormed the court and ran us out: Tabor, Glidden, Bruner, everybody. I left my briefcase behind but they wouldn't let me back in. How did your morning go?"

"Would you believe a thousand dollars bail?"

"A thou— Who was it?"

"Marryin' Sam."

"Figures—Terri," he shouted, "can you come here?"

"We have a guest. Mr. Wanamaker."

"Bring him along." He turned to Sherm. "Wanamaker's your old duffer."

Before Sherm could express his gratitude, the grizzled retired counselor began raving about being forced to evacuate the plaza. "I told 'em I was investigatin' a case, but they went and kicked me out anyway. Punks!" Wanamaker's head jerked about as he checked each of them, presumably to make sure no punks were present. "They pushed me around and I'll sue their britches off. Damn! What say, Purdy, wanna crack at 'em?"

"It was a bomb scare, Eustace."

"Damn sight more'n a scare. It was old Marshal Estaban. They wanted to kick him out just like they kicked me and all the rest out. Damn, I've been going to the courthouse nearly sixty years, even when it was hot as chili peppers in hell. So who do they think they are, those punks who kicked us out? Hell, I told 'em, don't you know who I am? I'm the one saved that Sherman fellow, but the punks—"

"Whoa, Eustace, whoa!" Miles held up his hand. "I don't understand why they wanted to move the statue."

"He's fulla TNT."

Miles feigned interest in his pen, and Terri covered her mouth with her hand, but Sherm could see the old duffer was absolutely serious. And TNT explained a lot.

"Good work," Sherm held out his hand. "I'm that Sherman fellow and you just solved something none of us were able to."

"The tracer!" Becky exclaimed.

Miles smacked his pen against his forehead. "To set off the TNT!"

"I don't get it," Terri said.

"Me either," admitted Eustace Wanamaker.

"A tracer would've acted like a fuse to ignite the explosive stashed inside the hollow copper statue, which, judging by his size, would be about the size of the bombs we dropped in Korea, quite capable of taking down a bridge." Sherm's voice began sinking with his feeling. "Or a courthouse."

All except Wanamaker, basking in the glow of discovery, took on Sherm's mood. Even Miles's customary self-assurance had temporarily abandoned ship. "Now we know," he said, "why the rifleman stationed himself in the parking garage and attempted what appeared to be an impossible shot."

"Why, why would anyone want, want to kill. . . ?" Terri didn't need to finish her sentence for Sherm to answer.

"In situations like this, people aren't the actual targets. An idea or ideal, or knowledge itself is what the assassin is out to destroy, as we see in acts of terrorism."

By now most of Wanamaker's euphoria had drained away. The old man nodded grimly, about to add something when the telephone cut him off. Terri answered. The court had rescheduled the hearing for 10:30 tomorrow. Sherm said he could make this one if they didn't get shot, arrested, or blown up in the interim. The phone had barely been put down when Charlie called, asking if they'd heard about the explosives.

"Just did," Sherm said.

"There's more to this mess. You know about McCreedy?"

"Our potential witness?"

"Less than two hours ago in his bachelor apartment, McCreedy was blown into very small bits, which is why I'm here instead of there and why Kline didn't show up to fix your traffic ticket. He gave me this personally, only we know something he doesn't. We put a tail on Knight and my boy says he followed him from your place straight to McCreedy's. But Knight never got inside. The bomb went off—"

"We need to talk, Charlie. Can you meet us at the Saguaro?"

"Be there in fifteen."

18

Sixes and Tens

Arriving at the same time as the cheese crisp and pitcher of margaritas, Charlie hobbled into the dark interior of the Saguaro Club on the shakiest cane Sherm had ever seen. He wore a coat and cursed the heat. The waitress, an older woman named Lorraine whom everyone called Flo, brought him a chair and started to go for another menu and margarita glass, but Charlie called her back saying he didn't much enjoy Kool-Aid, what a man with one shot leg on a day in hell really needed was a Coors from the bottom of the cooler. No menu either; all Mexican menus were the same and he'd have the number six.

"That's soup, enchilada—"

"Chili relleno and frijoles," Charlie continued. "I know my number sixes, Flo, and eights and tens. But at my age in my condition there ain't many tens hanging around." He grinned at Becky. "They're all taken by shysters and such."

Terri asked Miles if he didn't think Pauline and Charlie might make a pair.

"A pair to draw to," Charlie interrupted. "Pauline gets married so she can get divorced. She's a lawyer groupie."

That, Sherm observed, was patently absurd.

"Not so," Charlie said. "Some women get sick just so they can get with their doctor."

"Ah, but doctors touch, handle, do things even husbands aren't permitted. Lawyers talk."

Becky reminded him that sex is primarily a function of the intellect.

"Fact is I almost married Pauline the time your spouse hired me to investigate her fifth, or was it sixth divorce? Anyway, she's nowhere near the six-to-ten range except for her legs, which don't make up for the minus-one mouth. But how about you, Becky, how would you like a jabrone who doesn't think he's so smart, isn't quite so ugly, and's a whole lot more mature?"

"Senior citizen," Sherm added.

"Hear him, veteran of World War None." Charlie reached into his coat pocket and brought out a red lollipop. "Want one?"

Becky said she would stick to margaritas.

Terri laughed. "Lollipops?"

"Charlie started carrying them after experiencing his Kojak identity crisis."

"Ha, ha." Charlie pounced on his beer before Flo could pour it, took the bottle halfway down, sounded an "ahhh," and said, "If you gotta know, I carry them because my doc told me to quit drinking." Terri stared at the half-empty bottle. "This ain't drinking; it's beer. I gotta fool myself, especially at chow time. Doc says no martinis, and lollipops handle the trick." He turned to Sherm. "You still running in this heat?"

"Five a day."

"Miles or minutes?"

"Meters."

"You must be crazy; it's hotter'n hell just walking."

"Take off the jacket."

"You want me wandering around with my piece flapping in the breeze?" Charlie patted the bulge under his left arm. "Cops would shoot me on sight."

"They do anyway."

Charlie shuffled his silverware. "How come they never give you a knife in this dump?"

"They're afraid you older folk might cut yourselves." Sherm held up a knife which Flo, who was setting out the plates of food, promptly snatched, saying he wasn't supposed to have that.

Charlie's laugh was crisp and quickly over. "Let's see, why am I here? They say the first thing to go is your memory." He scratched his nose. "Wish I could remember the second."

"McCreedy."

"Oh yeah, after Knight left your house he drove to McCreedy's and parked across the street a couple of houses away. It was hot as hell but he sat there about eight minutes, like he was making sure the job got done. After the bomb went off he drove to his shop. In the shambles they found a twenty-two Hornet Kline believes was McCreedy's, which fits, maybe too good."

Charlie continued with what the investigation had turned up. His source, an agency in Vegas, identified McCreedy as Edward Creedmore, former employee of Bart Robin, aka Bartholomew Rabinowitz, aka Barry Knight. All three called themselves entrepreneurs.

"His first enterprise in glitter town was an escort service with Bart himself as an escort, primarily for other men. But Knight made his big money as Rabinowitz, real estate promoter. His last enterprise of consequence was a cable TV scheme which the Vegas city fathers torpedoed due to Knight's alleged dealings with suspected gunrunners. Creedmore fits into all this as Bart Robin's personnel manager. *Procurer* is probably accurate. When the Robin Escort Service was sold, they both migrated to our fair city, apparently to open a similar operation.

"The Vegas agency may've also given us a handle on the girl killed at the courthouse. I say 'may' because we're having all kinds of pains with the computer."

"Terri said Donegan was upset."

"When he looked for info on Knight he came up dead. Same with McCreedy. And you know about Kline's problem. Donegan's pretty sure someone hacked the data; but he says there's gotta be a backup somewhere."

"What about the girl?"

"From what we got from Vegas, she might've worked for Robin Escort and come here with Knight and McCreedy. She might've even lived awhile at Twelve twenty Rio Verde; but the real kicker is that Wilma Bruner arranged for the girl to meet Shelly. Also, you asked us to check out Wilma's whereabouts on the big night, which is something no one seems for sure to know. She left Vegas the night prior, scheduled to visit a number of cable outfits in hopes of getting the Mothers on TV in different cities. One of her scheduled stops was here, but Wilma says she only got as far as Phoenix when she saw the news about the murder and was so upset she returned to Vegas.

"Something else, about Wilma's sister's *accidental* death Shelly's mother, that is. Blood-alcohol level was double what it takes. According to the Eagan girl's testimony, her mother was so drunk she went to the mailbox for a check she was expecting, this at twelve-forty A.M., and was apparently sitting in the road when she was hit. Blow to the head. No tire marks, paint, et cetera. The woman never regained consciousness anybody knows of. She was put on a life-support system and transferred to the residence where Shelly took off from work to care for her until she died. Listed cause of death is some mishmash about complications arising from injuries suffered in a previous accident. And get this, no autopsy."

"A multimillion dollar estate and no autopsy?"

"More like hundreds of millions."

"And no autopsy."

"I think you've got it," Charlie said. "Reasons given were close relative present at time of death and they don't perform autopsies on organ donors unless there's reasonable doubt, which my suspicion thinks there should've been. Dorothy and daughter definitely didn't get along because of mother's boozing. Also, Shelly adored her father and blamed her mother for the split."

Motive enough and worth thinking about, Sherm agreed, but wrong case.

"The girl thought so much of her dad, she hired a tutor to teach her the finer points of what had been his favorite game when he was alive—which also happens to be yours and accounts for the card decks you were curious about."

"Who was the tutor?" Becky asked.

"A woman who works at AZTECH by the name of Armor or something like that."

"Ammar, Majida Ammar?"

"Sounds right. One of the boys got a phone interview. Says she was hired to give bridge lessons but the couple of times she went to the house, the mother got in such fights with the Eagan girl she finally just gave up." Charlie put on his bifocals to scan the list he'd taken from his jacket pocket. "Oh yeah." He peered at Sherm. "Ah, you have some special interest in underwear?"

"Just adding to my collection."

"This should make you happy. Our little girl seems to be addicted to some pretty sexy stuff."

"Knight's been nosing around like a puppy, like maybe he wants to talk—maybe about underwear; who knows?" Sherm checked under the shredded lettuce to see what was hidden. "I think I'd better ask him."

"Don't press it, Sherm." Charlie picked up his cane and poked it toward the entrance. "Whoever's behind this crap is still out there. It could be Knight and all we got to do to put him away is tell Kline about him being at McCreedy's."

"We can't afford to hand over our only surviving witness."

148

Withholding Knight's involvement, Miles reminded him, could have serious repercussions.

"We won't withhold, we just won't rush over with the news, just like they haven't hurried to tell us where the courthouse shot came from or that the antenna cable wasn't the murder weapon. Besides, we don't know Knight was actually involved."

"And if they ask?"

"Put them on hold and leave them there. Look, it's a risk worth taking."

Miles warned against excessive delay. Charlie expressed reservations, saying Knight was tied to everything. Knight, Sherm argued, had volunteered to be their witness. Becky reminded them that volunteering was a meaningless gesture for someone planning their termination. Sherm didn't like the direction the conversation was taking and asked if Donegan had come up with anything on the 9-1-1 tape.

"He says he's having equipment trouble."

"Not exactly speedy, is he?"

"Methodical as hell and one hundred percent reliable, which is why I hired him."

"Plug." Sherm remembered Donegan's remark. "What's this, ah, conceptualization of yours he mentioned?"

"I said the nine-one-one call could've been a tape."

"Which would account for a lot, for example, the Sensa-Vision number in the redial."

"The one you discovered." Charlie turned to Becky. "How about joining Ace? We need a brainy investigator to offset damage done by the senior counsel."

19

Unnatural Objects

On the way home they'd stopped at the Gourmet Emporium for a special tuna the supermarkets didn't stock, which Sherm said Beau liked because it was expensive. Her bear, Becky disagreed, was only being considerate in preferring what was convenient. As though aware of the treat in store, Beau was at the door to greet them, all twelve pounds of fluff emitting hungry meows and rubbing Sherm's leg all the while he was opening and dishing out the expensive tuna onto a saucer from their best china, "A special plate for a special bear," Becky said.

When Beau was served, Sherm settled to the carpet in front of the VCR.

"Can't wait, eh?"

"My curiosity hurts."

"I'll bet." She said she had to get some more green yarn from the storeroom and would be right back.

Knight's tape ran blank a full two minutes and was through in less than ten. Sherm wondered if Knight had all his marbles. He rewound and started over.

"You're gonna watch that again?" Becky passed through, headed in the opposite direction. "I know there's a skein of Kelly around here somewhere."

The tape began without a title. Good thing: *Nymphs* had little to do with nymphs. Appropriately pigtailed and pantaletted at the beginning, the nymph (there was one)

150

promptly revealed herself to be a hirsute whore in a cheap hotel room.

Although he'd seen plenty of smut during the obscenity trials of the late Sixties, Sherm never considered himself an aficionado. Knight did and it was his business; yet this thing could not be termed, in any sense of the word, *classic*. Rather it smacked of the you-show-me-yours variety of child's play. The bearded fellow appeared embarrassed throughout, which in addition to his advancing years may have been why he never quite rose to the occasion.

Definitely not classic.

Her quarry bagged, Becky returned to her knitting station on the couch.

Sherm switched off the set, disappointed that *Nymphs* apparently contained no clues. The click of needles drew his attention to his wife's slender legs showing along the slit below her denim skirt, legs that even at forty-eight were more nymphish than the whore's.

"I can't imagine why Knight went to the trouble of getting me to watch this thing."

"Maybe he likes you."

"Maybe he got the wrong tape."

"You don't think you missed something?"

"What's to miss about an ugly whore and an old man?"

"Don't give away the plot."

"There is no plot; it's laughable."

"I need a good laugh."

"It's so bad even the guy in the movie can't get a hard-on."

"That's laughable." Becky put aside her needles. "Besides, I don't wish to view it for its erotic effect; I want to see if I can spot its significance."

He was about to tell his darling wife that even the donkey show they never saw probably had some sort of redeeming virtue, perhaps imagination coupled with certain athletic and artistic talents, whereas this piece of smut had none. Watching it could ruin their whole evening. He was about to open his mouth to say all this when the phone cut him off. She asked him to answer it elsewhere and, annoyed that she should want to watch it alone, he trooped off to his office.

Glidden, Miles said, had called him wanting to know what he and Sherm knew about Knight. "When I went into my surprise routine, the sonofabitch hung up."

"So much for Glidden."

"My head was still buzzing when Charlie called with the info that the explosion that ripped McCreedy was a time bomb set for eleven A.M. He also says the official version is that McCreedy was the courthouse perp and accidentally blew himself up."

"That would be convenient—where's Charlie getting this stuff?"

Miles paused, then, "I'd rather not say on the phone, except his source is the best. Don't you think we'd better let them in on Knight?"

"First thing in the morning."

"Yeah. Oh, they finally got an ID on the girl. Kline thinks somebody fed in the wrong data, read off the same card twice or something like that."

"Which is an easy way out. What happens if the police computer has been tampered with? The entire data bank would be compromised, sending a considerable amount of evidence, fingerprint, voice and other data, past and present, down the tubes. Courts could be tied up for years just on appeals."

"Christ—which reminds me, tomorrow's hearing will be in the new courthouse. Glidden will let us know the room number at ten. All very secure this time."

"No more shoot-'em or blow-'em ups?"

"I hope not."

Sherm was about to bid good night when he realized Miles hadn't given him her name. "Who was she?"

"Let's see, I wrote the name down. Here it is, an easy one—Sarah Jones."

"Thanks and good night." Sherm got up from his desk and headed down the hall. Becky was standing under the arched entrance to the den, arms limp at her sides, with an expression Sherm had not seen before.

"I warned you about that video," he said. "Did it make you sick?"

"No."

"Then why are you looking that way?"

"The stupid thing made me horny."

Anyone who got horny watching *that*, he argued pleasantly, had to be a little perverted. Becky snuggled closer, taking care not to disturb her bear curled up at their toes, acknowledging the truth of his observation, except that it was more than a little. He assured her he was not objecting to having perhaps more than a little, only that her reaction to the tape surprised him.

"What do you expect for the first one I ever saw?"

When had he seen his first, Sherm wondered, in college at one of the monthly Franklin smokers even the Unitarian minister turned out for? Before the movie, there was always the stripper, straight from the big time in Kansas City. They picked on bald-headed men, who loved it. All quite depraved, yet not even the wives of the bald-headed men seemed to mind so long as their men didn't come home too drunk or lose too much money at poker.

One particular movie stuck in Sherm's mind. He couldn't recall the title, if it had one. "It starred Candy Something-or-other," he said, "a B-film actress who never really got known until she made this old blue movie. After that, every lad with lead in his pencil knew when you mentioned Candy you weren't talking about the confectionery variety. When I saw

Candy, they'd flown the film in from Texas and charged an extra dollar. It was black-and-white, a little out of focus, and scratchy. It was also shot in a motel and there were two ladies and a gentleman; but one of those ladies was Candy, so the scratches and focus didn't matter. It was what I'd call 'classic.'"

"Did you say, Unitarian minister?"

"Yeah, why?"

"Sounds kinda smutty to me."

"Not really, they just did it. No kiddie porn or buggering."

Her hands moved over him, exploring the territory. "Do you suppose Mr. Knight could get us a copy of this Candy Something-or-other?"

"They say she made only one dirty movie."

"Tried it once and didn't like it, huh?"

"Got busted and spent five years in the Texas State Prison for Women."

"Wasn't that back when they were electrocuting people for being communists?"

"The funny part is when she got out she took up with some evangelical bunch. I remember seeing it in the paper. Could've been Baptists."

"They like repentant sinners, not ones who've actually sinned; but isn't it odd how thin a line separates religious and sexual experience? Sometimes I wonder if the good fathers are aware of where they came from. Doesn't it strike you as a paradox?"

"There's a whole arena of human behavior I'll never fathom."

"Could be we're all voyeurs at heart, loving movies and TV, and sometimes just people watching. It has to be curiosity. Still, I picture myself when I was a kid. Sex was so disgusting I refused to believe it was the way people were made because I couldn't believe my mother and father would do such a thing. In the early school years a girl is caught midway between a time when curiosity really is a factor and an age when slip-ups mean disaster, an age of innocence when one yearns for perpetual maidenhood, not motherhood. Baby dolls have been left behind, menstrual cramps are still in the future. It's a perfect time, the only time a girl can be a girl without being threatened—which is what makes kiddie porn so despicable." She reached to scratch her bear under the chin. "Whatcha think of all this firkytoodlin', ole bear? You want to see what you're missin', huh? Or is ole Beau just curious too?"

"Better brief him about cats and curiosity."

"Naw, Beau ain't never gonna die, are you?" She squeezed him and kissed his pink nose. "You heard all the goin's-on and came runnin' to protect your mom, right? And when you saw it was just firkytoodlin', you jumped up so you could watch." She pressed the great white fluff to her bosom, and when Sherm remarked that watching was about all a neutered cat could do, she made a face at him. "Don't make fun of my bear just because he's not a ladies' man." She put her feet on the floor, still hugging the cat. "Even bears have to take a look now and then, right, Beau?" She kissed him again. "Now we're going straight to the kitchen and get what you're really interested in, the rest of that good tuna the mean ole Sherm didn't feed you when you were half starving after being home by yourself all day, poor baby. And if the mean ole man promises not to make fun of my bear no more, I might bring him a glass of chilled Chablis."

He promised and watched her go; without his glasses she looked like a naked little girl with a cat in her arms, the irregularities of age washed away; and he could imagine Becky as fleeting innocence being spirited from his bedroom, and in that moment and to a small degree he sensed the attraction innocence itself transmitted to the core of perversity. It bothered him, this flaw. He closed his eyes, aware only of the whir of the air-conditioning fan. Sleep, he thought, was what he needed. He didn't want to think about anything, especially not about little girls. Sarah . . . ah, Sarah Smith? No, not Smith . . . not Smith and Wesson . . . Jones.

"Here's your wine, sweetie."

Sherm opened his eyes. She was there, his own little girl arranging their pillows against the headboard so they could drink without dribbling. He sipped once from his glass before asking where he'd heard the name Sarah Jones.

Becky nodded, biting her lip. "You know, we just talked about her—the Polaroid."

Sherm said her age would be about right, but this was just too much coincidence; the girl killed at the courthouse couldn't be the same Sarah Jones.

"Jones is quite common," Becky said almost apologetically.

Common or something unaccountably irrational at work? He shook his head. Relationships were causal; reason ruled.

"Look, sweetie, she was probably a street person."

The phone jangled him out of his funk. He punched the speaker button. "Hello?"

"This is Miles. Looks like we're back on Baltic."

"Baltic?"

"Square one on the Monopoly board—Bruner's confessed."

Utter disbelief. "You say confessed?"

"In writing. Kline says when he told him about McCreedy, Bruner came unglued and started yelling that he killed his niece."

Would this go on forever? "Did you talk to Bruner?"

"He refuses to talk to anyone, but we have it that Kline told Bruner he wouldn't get the death penalty if he gave them a signed confession."

Sherm mulled it over a moment. "I don't think this confession will hold up, so let's let it rest for now and give our client time to think over what he's done."

When he'd hung up, Sherm turned to Becky. "You know," he said, "I half don't blame Bruner. Good God, tracers and statues filled with TNT—the work of fanatics, madmen, or what?"

"Miles was wrong."

"About Bruner?"

"About Monopoly. The first space is Mediterranean. He shouldn't miss his metaphors."

"You mean mix."

"Miss, a complete miss. There's a community chest between Mediterranean and Baltic. And it's a rectangle, not a square."

"You certainly know your Monopoly."

"We played a lot when you weren't around."

"Maybe there's some good news on this." He switched the recorder to PLAYBACK CALLS and pressed the speaker button.

The first voice was Pauline's: "Peter, darling, I'm calling to inform you that I am seriously contemplating a crime, any crime. Not that I'm a criminal, mind you, a person more sinned against than sins. It's a necessary risk I must take in order to secure your attention since, all of a sudden, you have taken to criminals. So I shall become, to wit, a criminal so you will take my case. On my list of contemplations are robbery and murder, no rape though. What a horrid crime that is! My third husband, Carl, used to say—or was it Monty? *Whomever* said rape was a state of mind. No, it had to have been Fred. He was the professional rapist. To Fred, making love meant crushing fragile females with the sheer bulk of his corpulent self—"

Although Pauline's intimate revelations should prove interesting, they would also prove endless. He moved the selector to FAST FORWARD, eye on the counter, then to PLAYBACK.

"Of course, Gerald possessed any number of idiosyncrasies—his definition, not mine. Actually his idiosyncrasies were absolute perversions—"

Gerald's perversions would have to wait, but Pauline was still on Gerald the second time he stopped. The third time the tape was almost to the end and still *her* voice. She would've run the tape right off the reel, if that was possible, if it hadn't been for "Laverne and Shirley." "I love their reruns," she gushed. "They remind me so much of growing up in the Fifties." She'd been well-grown, Sherm was certain, by the time the Fifties rolled around.

Pauline promised to call again after the show. Sherm checked the counter. Almost out. He waited through the spot where the answerer told the caller to leave his or her message after the *beep*. This was followed by a protracted period, the space in which breathing at the other end begins to raise hackles. Only there was no breathing, no sound at all, like being put on hold without being told.

It was a good thing he wasn't holding the phone or he might have suggested something anatomically impossible and the call would turn out to be long distance, a stuck relay somewhere along the line, Heather from Germany. But this wasn't Heather. A girl, but not Heather. And he knew who it was. He knew this voice better than Heather's. This voice he'd analyzed, studied, and listened to several times. This was the voice on the 9-1-1 tape.

The voice said, "Peter Sherman, you know who I am, but do you know, Peter Sherman, the fires of hell burn hot. The fires of hell burn hot for Peter Sherman. The fires—" Out of tape.

"Damn, damn, damn you, Pauline!"

"Sweetie, calm down!" Becky held onto his arm.

"That damned Pauline is goddamned going to give me a damned coronary!"

"You're going to give yourself a coronary."

"She just wrecked a piece of prime evidence."

"Pauline didn't wreck anything—calm down and think what we've got, a tape Mr. Donegan can compare the other one with, and analyze. Don't you see?"

Sherm calmed. He did not believe in ghosts. Becky was right. What they had, proved something; though he wasn't sure what. Or why? Why would anyone be so stupid? If this was the same voice, as he was sure it was, it virtually proved either that Shelly Eagan was still alive or that the 9-1-1 tape was phony.

Too many questions, too few answers. He went for a glass of milk, poured most of it down the drain, and returned to bed. His mind was a thicket of activity. He couldn't sleep.

The light came on. Becky went to the medicine cabinet and came back twisting the people-proof cap of an amber prescription bottle. She tipped it into her hand and held it out. "Take this."

He took it and studied it. Round, yellow, with print too small for ordinary eyes, and too small to be of much use to a grown-up, the pill nestled in the palm of his hand somewhere near the end of his lifeline, and for that reason a case he'd studied way back in law school came to mind: Nutrand vs. Auto Air Inc.

A professional palmist named Madame Nutrand had gotten her hand caught between the belt and compressor pulley of a newly installed auto air conditioner. Her hand was mangled and it was argued she had been deprived of her livelihood, therefore should collect substantial damages. The equipment, her lawyer maintained, had been so positioned by Auto Air Inc. that it was extremely hazardous to lift the hood and check the oil with the engine running, in fact almost impossible to do so without incurring injury. Auto Air Inc. argued it was the only place in Mme. Nutrand's French-built automobile they could put the damn thing and that they'd warned her of the hazard before installing it. She called them damn liars and they said only damn fools checked the oil with the engine and air-conditioning running. The sides might have gone on damning each other forever had the attorney for the defense not gotten the plaintiff to boast that one of the powers of a palmist was foretelling future events. The next question broke the case: If Mme. Nutrand was able to predict the future, could she not foresee the consequences of placing her hand where it would most certainly be mangled? As Sherm remembered it, there was a small settlement, not enough to buy a new hand.

"I don't need this much valium," he said, turning the tiny pill over. A line down the center divided it precisely into two half moons. "I'll take half."

"It's only five milligrams and it'll make you sleep."

"I'll sleep, all right."

"No, you won't. You've got a million thoughts on your mind."

"You know how aspirin affects me."

"This is valium, not aspirin. Now take it."

"On top of all that alcohol is dangerous."

"You had one glass of wine."

"And a pitcher of margaritas."

"That was hours ago—and *four* of us had a pitcher of margaritas. Now swallow it."

He stared at the pill, insignificant, a speck really, yet it seemed unnatural to swallow anything, no matter the size, without chewing it.

"Take it."

He hated pills—needles—even thermometers. His tolerance to what he termed *unnatural objects*, which included anything not immediately recognizable as food or drink, entering the body by any means via any normal cavity was nil. He'd never smoked a cigarette or eaten a Twinkie and he wasn't about to take a dangerous drug.

Becky slid her hand under his and tipped it toward his mouth. "Come on, sweetie, live dangerously."

"Better set nine-one-one in the autoredial, just in case."

"I can manage three numbers."

"I sure hate pills."

"I guessed that."

He hardly felt it go down. "It isn't making me sleepy."

"Give it a few seconds."

"Pauline could piss off a pope."

"Pauline just likes to talk."

"The call might've been a warning, but because of her we'll never know."

He began to experience a sort of rising-sinking sensation during which it came to him how he would use this latest call. He smiled. Like Glidden's evidence it was almost too good to be true. When Becky snapped off the light he was sinking into darkness.

20

Percentages

Under the double impact of heat and humidity, Sherm canceled his run, surely a mistake in light of the couple of tough days and a bridge tournament that lay ahead. But the cancellation gave him time to get angry at the *Desert Star* for having a field day with the prospect of Bruner being fried in the state's brand-new, never-used "electronic" chair. There was even an article on the computerized hot seat that pointed out its more humane attributes, such as no executioner, and the chair's ability to make the end painless and ultimately final. No half-baked jobs; semiconductors would see to that.

"They're killing people with computers now," Sherm complained over coffee.

"Wasn't that the original intent with missiles?"

What really galled him were the stories disclosing the "irrefutable proof" as "an actual tape recording of the defendant breaking into his niece's home," and the rodent-brained editorial restating the view that punishment should always fit the crime, that admission of guilt was an irrelevant factor and should remain so. No crime or name was mentioned.

Sherm teetered on the edge of an outburst as irrational as the editor's argument; the storm was becalmed, temporarily at least, by the digital time display on the microwave, which said he'd better move.

While dressing, he decided on an evening jog if the rains cooled things down. The *Star* predicted a 20 percent chance, whatever that meant, 20 percent of the readership would be rained on, or 100 percent would be rained on 20 percent of the time? All he'd come to rely on was that 20 percent usually meant that by four in the afternoon there was a 90 percent chance it would be raining.

He folded the newspaper's editorial page and put it in his briefcase along with the cassette of last evening's calls. Becky drove while he tried to think out these latest developments. Unfortunately for the case, there wasn't a whole lot that needed thinking about. Bruner's confession had pretty well sealed it—

Except for one small item.

As it turned out, the small item became the only point of controversy in an otherwise speedy hearing railroaded by an unusually jolly Judge Tabor who dispensed with everything he could, explaining his haste by pointing out that the hearing had already taken up three times as much time as it should have and since the defendant had already confessed there was really no reason to continue. It would have been over in fifteen minutes had not Sherm asked for a ruling on the admissibility of the 9-1-1 tape to prevent it becoming an unnecessary bone of contention during the actual trial. Tabor saw no reason to argue the applicability of the Frye Rule when the tape in question was no longer a necessary exhibit in the question of innocence or guilt. Sherm said he had no intention of asking that the Frye Rule be invoked. Glidden, immediately suspicious, wanted to know why Sherm should be concerned when the prosecution had already announced they would not be introducing the tape as long as the defendant pleaded guilty.

"Clients do change their pleas, as ours has once, making it to our advantage to prepare a defense against this most incriminating piece of evidence."

Delighted, Tabor admitted the 9-1-1 tape as State's exhibit number one in the event it became necessary, he said, in the further prosecution of the case against Raymond Lee Bruner, and was about to close the proceedings when Sherm cleared his throat and spoke so quietly even Miles had to ask, "What?"

"What did you say?" Tabor's eyes dared Sherm to delay the adjournment.

"Your Honor, I said I have one more small item."

"Small item?"

"Yes. Since Your Honor has admitted State's exhibit, I ask that this—" Sherm reached into his pocket and fished out the cassette. "This tape also be admitted."

"What tape is that?"

"Sir, this contains a voice identical to that which the State purports to be Shelly Eagan's voice, the same allegedly slain by Raymond Lee Bruner." He rubbed the scab over his eye. "If you so desire you may have my wife's and my sworn statements along with irrefutable technical proof that this voice was recorded live last night on my home telephone answering machine." Sherm swallowed hard. *Watch it, old priest.*

"Also, Your Honor, we believe that a spectrograph analysis of this tape will reveal that the voice recorded last night and the one now labeled as state's exhibit one to be one and the same voice."

Glidden was on his feet. "Proving what?"

"Well, ah . . . that the deceased is not dead?"

Becky couldn't help herself; she applauded.

Marc Glidden was not applauding. He fumed at what he called "an unconscionable tactic no doubt in anticipation of a change of plea." He argued that there could be no spectrographic analysis of either tape because there was no authenticated voice of the murder victim on record. Only after going on in this vein for several minutes did he seem to realize that he was arguing the defense's case, if there should be one.

Tabor would have none of it. "Mr. Glidden," he finally interrupted, "your argument presents an academic objection which is irrelevant at this stage of the proceedings. Since the court has entered state's exhibit it must do likewise for the defense, especially when their exhibit is in essence purported to be—ah, so distressingly similar."

Throughout the proceedings Bruner had remained a bit nervous but under control, a man clearly resigned to the kind of fate that had taken his wife and older sister. He was under heavy guard, four deputies, one in advance, one on either side, one behind. Kline wasn't taking any more chances. Even the location within the new courthouse had been kept secret until ten minutes before they convened in the cramped room in the small claims section.

Glidden nearly collided with Becky as he stormed down the narrow aisle ahead of Sherm and Miles, leaving his young assistant behind. At the door he apparently remembered something forgotten and turned, a move that confronted him with the decision either to recognize or ignore the defense counselors.

Sherm spared him. "Marc, I hope you realize there wasn't time to notify your office."

"You had time to run a spectrogram."

"I said we *will*, not that we have."

"And what about your key witness, Knight, and the McCreedy killing? You better not be withholding evidence, Counselor!" Without waiting for Sherm's response, Glidden motioned his assistant through. "Come on, Margot."

"He must think I'm up to something," Sherm said to Miles.

Miles simply raised his eyebrows.

Sherm reached into his briefcase for the editorial. "Have Terri Xerox a copy for Raymond. We'll wait until morning to meet and hope the prisoners down there talk some sense into him. They seem to be the only ones on our side."

Miles said he'd have Donegan run a comparison analysis of the two tapes; then, "This new one, have you thought about what it's saying, 'the fires of hell'?"

"I think someone is trying to scare me but I haven't the slightest idea why."

"Well, anyway, I was thinking about what Charlie said yesterday at lunch—Jesus, he called me at home to get me to talk you into staying put until this is straightened out."

Sherm wanted to hug Miles. "If someone really wanted me, they've had plenty of opportunity." The nod became a no. "It was Bruner they were after and I guess they got him." Sherm thought of asking Miles if he and his family would like to join the Shermans on a late autumn trip to San Carlos, but for some reason he couldn't quite get to it.

Becky drove them to Milano's for their somewhat belated antipasto, spaghetti, and Chianti. Milano's had always been a favorite in spite of the tacky wall painting, an obligatory addendum for small Italian restaurants on side streets, depicting plazas and olive groves, gondoliers and leaning towers, spread in rigid acrylic over the walls. Carriages appeared cemented to the cobblestones; horses' legs were out of synch. Human figures were sticks of uncooked spaghetti. Worst of all, this atrocity appeared to be organic, growing with the passage of time. Sherm could remember when there was only one lovely tree on a knoll overlooking the Tyrrhenian Sea. Even the ceiling had taken on inflexible clouds and stationary birds. Would the floor be next, followed by tables and mirrors?

Who was this mad painter? Could it be Milano himself? Was there in fact a Milano? Or was the restaurant named for the city of Milano? After so many visits over so many years, this was something Sherm felt he should know, yet he didn't and probably would never ask.

After they'd ordered, Becky said she'd been thinking about the case so much she wasn't sure she could concentrate on their bridge game.

"I mean, it's all so mixed up and confusing. There's no connecting thread—who was the professor in law school you said was always harping on finding the theme by seeking out its correct analogy?"

"Jeremiah Bedford." How did he phrase it? *Analogy: the inference that certain admitted resemblances imply probable further similarity.* No, Sherm would never forget Jeremiah-Two-Note's "Analogy and Theme in Crime Detection," a hypothesis no doubt borrowed from his colleagues in graduate literature. But Sherm's problem had always been that he mistrusted inferences no matter how soundly based. It was too easy to make a case out of the color of a man's underwear. Of course, an attorney's job was to provide enough "admitted resemblances" so the judge and jury would make their inferences in his client's favor. Bedford wasn't right but he was essentially correct. Without inference there could be no trial.

"We called him our 'professor of fictional crime.'"

"I'll ignore the obvious slur on my background in literature."

Somehow the Chianti had been delivered and poured. "But you know, I think the guy brainwashed me. While mulling over Sherman's Law after the courthouse fiasco, I thought of a perfect analogy to Oswald and Ruby: Caesar and Brutus."

"Good, and what was the theme?"

Sherm sniffed the sharp fragrance of the wine before taking a sip. "Assassination?"

"Assassination is a subject. Theme is the recurring unifying idea, the motif. Such as alienation, liberation, the vulnerability of idealism, or the irrepressible conflict of opposite personalities—"

Sherm raised his hand. "It's *c*!"

"What do you mean, *c*?"

"The third one, *c*'s the answer."

"To what?"

"Oswald, Ruby, and Kennedy: vulnerability *whatever*."

"So I was lecturing."

"You're right though, assassination is not a valid theme."

"We must look for the larger implication."

"Less explicit than implicit."

"Right!"

"Jeremiah used to say that."

"Your memory isn't so bad after all."

"Wish I could remember what it meant."

"What is implicit in the slayings of Caesar and Kennedy?"

"The murder of a national leader?"

"Subject."

"Ah, conspiracy?"

"You're getting close."

"The perpetual struggle for power?"

"Bull's-eye!" Becky blew her star pupil an appreciative kiss. "It began with God and Satan, not so much a struggle between good and evil as pure and simple conflict over who was in charge. Whether one is good or bad is subject to interpretation. Not subject to interpretation is that any successful assassination invariably results in a transfer of power."

"There are people who'd be upset by this analogy."

"So be it. But let's look at Mr. Bruner's situation. For example, take Kafka—"

"You take Kafka. I find him only slightly less tedious than Joyce."

"In *The Trial*, K is arrested, tried, and executed and never told why."

"I remember the case; are we ever told?"

"Not really."

"A good author always tells us why."

"Franz Kafka was one of the great writers of the twentieth century."

He picked up a bread stick and broke it in half. "You're implying certain similarities between K and Bruner, both at the mercy of an outside uncontrollable force for which there is no apparent explanation; yet there are possibilities which, when they graze my thoughts, I would just as soon ignore."

They had to be thought about, she said, and she was right.

"Okay, let's begin with the bizarre numbers prayer, which seems to indicate Bruner's slightly more than casual relationship with Mothers of the Moon. And the connecting thread, the theme if you will, is a plentitude of electronic devices."

"Subjects again. Try 'blind adherence to faith' and 'man's misuse of technology,' Jonestown and Frankenstein being analogous. But you're right; everywhere we look we see the stuff. Could be a sign of the times, though. Did the letter say they'd approved a computer terminal or was it just 'terminal'?"

"Just terminal."

"Ms. Bruner seemed barely literate so maybe terminal was the wrong word. Maybe the letter referred to the cable TV hookup that's been mentioned."

"Could be; and Bruner's porn connection makes for some pretty interesting inferences."

"I see a picture." Becky put her fingers to her temples and closed her eyes.

"Not the fortune-teller bit again."

"This isn't soothsaying; this is straight from Dr. Bedford's lectures, nasty details like a nude picture of a good little MOM taken at a computer camp, and semen, all of it non something."

"Motile, *nonmotile*'s the word."

"Not moving, dead; therefore, she probably hadn't bathed or gone swimming between the time she had sex and when she was murdered."

"Does this MOM embrace some sort of excessive sexual ritual?"

"MOM supplicants take a vow of celibacy, like nuns."

"Yet, according to the pathologist, she might've engaged in a regular gang bang."

"He used the term *regular*?"

"He said he wouldn't have been surprised to learn she wasn't raped."

"Ah, a potential theme: uncontrollable lust; but there were beach towels by the pool, which means someone probably came to swim, maybe the same someone who drove her to work and was with her at the computer camp. Now you tell me, she worked even though she didn't have to?"

"She practically owned AZTECH."

"Therefore, she had other reasons for working: interest in job, friends, whatever."

"She left a bundle for research so you're probably right."

"Maybe she was researching something that was hooked up to those wires in the bedroom. But how do *we* hook up lust, technology, and faith?"

Sherm thought a moment before commenting on the switched IDs, people not being where they belonged in the computer, the questionable 9-1-1 tape and of course the strange call from the same voice as the one on the 9-1-1 tape.

Becky recalled an analogy in their own family—Vic's interviews. He'd taped and rearranged a Reagan press conference, then injected his own questions, some of them pointedly obscene. So couldn't someone have put the words on the 9-1-1 tape together from other recordings, like a ransom note pieced from newspaper clippings?

Anything was possible—even that the waitress was about to serve the antipasto.

Milano's antipasto was a meal in itself. They nevertheless dug into the complicated Italian salad trying to catch up for the missed lunch, thinking without talking while they ate.

Because Shelly Eagan seemed so sexually undesirable, both in life-style and physical appearance, Sherm had dismissed any evidence of promiscuity, assuming as Glidden had, that she had in fact been raped—beauty not being a prerequisite for becoming a rape victim. Unfortunately for the case, the opposite might be more statistically correct, especially since rape is recognized as a crime of violence rather than one of lust. Thinking subjectively, though, with all of her wealth and influence, couldn't she be someone to lust after?

This was not the first time Becky's thoughts were nearly identical to his. "Considering the semen, the erotic underwear, and all the incongruities, isn't it possible we've got the crime turned around?" she said almost the moment it entered his mind. "Suppose instead of an unattractive bachelor girl devoted to religion and work, we have a lady with the wherewithal to do whatever with whomever she can buy? Suppose she's the voyeur, only she wants to carry it further and become a piece of the wonderful world of pornography?"

"And the Sensa-Vision call was hers, not his?"

"Exactly."

"So the nine-one-one call originated somewhere else by someone who could've taped it in advance." Sherm plucked a black olive from the lettuce. "Someone who has tapes of Shelly Eagan's voice, possibly recorded from this new MOM terminal."

"Someone who found out about Ms. Eagan's sideline and didn't approve one bit."

"Someone who wrote the letter that framed Bruner."

"And couldn't prove where she was the night of the murder."

"And may have used the silver cord symbolically to ritualize the murder."

Becky said it, "Aunt Wilma," then shook her head. "I'm not sure. So much just doesn't fit."

"If we could only get our hands on one of those MOM tapes."

The spaghetti arrived too soon but it didn't matter. The wine and their mutually arrived-at solution had brought on a glow, if not of elation, close to it.

Outside, the twenty percent chance of rain had become a one hundred percent reality.

21

Another Call

Thunder and lightning were no longer a duet, the interval between flash and bang a bit longer with each display, until the storm rolled away like a growling celestial indigestion.

Without bothering to change, Becky had gotten out a deck

of cards and was sitting cross-legged on the rug, a north-south bridge hand in front of her. Beau purred, looking like a champ.

"Appears your bear is winning."

"My bear always wins—this hand from Sunday's paper offers anyone with psychic ability a definite advantage. South is declarer with a singleton club in his hand and three on the board; and west, the preemptive hand to south's left, has at least seven clubs; therefore, south knows east can have no more than a doubleton, okay?"

"Got it." Sherm knelt to smooth Beau's fluff.

"Declarer is faced with the natural finesse to dummy's king, jack, ten of clubs. A problem though, south needs a club entry to get to the good hearts. Am I being followed?"

"You are, and I'd play my club to the king on the board to cover the queen on the right, in east's hand."

"Why would you do that? Your left hand opponent preempted—"

"With the ace and six little ones."

"He should have ace-queen."

"He bids a weak preempt."

"If the ace-queen is on your left, he gets in with a spade and runs the clubs. You're down a bundle."

"Ah, but if the queen is on the right I can stop the run with the jack, switch to the spades, and make the contract for a top board."

"Your gamble is too risky." Becky clasped her hands between her ankles.

"Maybe it's not a gamble."

"Maybe?" Becky sighed. "But you got it right, which is pretty lucky."

"Not luck, ESP."

"Maybe."

"Or maybe I read the newspaper."

"You, you—" She glared at him, though a smile was about to break through. "You cheat!"

"Precisely my attitude toward the twins; however, reading the newspaper is not cheating."

The smile broke through and she put out her hands, a gesture of willingness to play the game even though this was not the hour the game was usually played. Sherm's eyes flicked to the blank TV screen then back to the famous smile.

"Why don't we make ourselves less uncomfortable?" she whispered, pulling him to her.

Knight's second interruption was only slightly less disruptive than his first.

"Ignore the call," Becky said, "let the recorder take care of it," little realizing she was probably the only person this side of the Hassayampa capable of not answering a ringing telephone—a habit, she once explained, acquired during Sherm's young lion period when he invariably took on more clients than was humanly possible to handle.

The pornographer had found a bridge partner: "We would very much enjoy your company," Knight said. "And your expertise. When we talked earlier I had no idea of your extreme talent, that you and Ms. S. actually are going to play in the Southwest Club Tournament! What a marvel you are, Mr. S.: pilot, detective, famous criminal attorney, championship bridge player. I thought you only jogged. My partner's name is Gloria Woodward, no relation to Joanne. We really look forward to picking up a few pointers on the fine art of contract bridge from a pair of experts. I do hope you will—"

"Well, ah . . ." It was probably a proposition, but a lot of questions could be answered in an atmosphere of games and fun. "You heard about McCreedy?"

"Wasn't that awful?"

"You know you're our only witness now."

"Good grief—but aren't we being rather academic? I mean, poor Raymond has admitted his guilt."

"But we know he's not guilty, don't we?"

"Well, we know where he was when the murder was supposed to have occurred. Now I know how busy you must be, Mr. S., but you must eat and we're planning the dinner, say sevenish, with cocktails of course, and an evening of bridge. Please say yes," he pleaded.

"We're really busy."

"Then you *really* must relax. Gloria's such a bridge whiz and my cook is simply the best in town."

"I don't think so."

"*Please.*"

"Well . . ."

"Good! It's a date, then. Bye!"

No sooner had he hung up than Sherm began to regret having been pulled into the dubious pleasure of an evening with Knight. He rolled over on the bed, taking Becky in his arms. "Now, let's see. Where did we leave off?"

"Hold on, what have you got us into?"

"We're going to play a little bridge."

"With that—that penis peddler?"

"I thought you got to like him."

"I never said *that*."

"This could be our opportunity to ask a few questions, you know, in a more relaxed atmosphere."

"I'm sure the atmosphere will be relaxed."

"This conversation isn't doing us any good."

"Neither will Mr. Knight's *bridge* party."

"You'll get to see his gazebo."

"Maybe I don't want to see his gazebo."

"You want to see my gazebo?"

"I've seen your gazebo." Becky's smile faded. "And for all we know, Mr. Smut is behind all this."

"I say he's a real pussycat." Beau stirred at the foot of the bed and jumped off.

"I don't think my bear appreciates the comparison. Are you prejudiced against gays?"

"I'm not prejudiced; I just wouldn't want my daughter marrying one."

She hit him lightly on the chest. "Fat chance. Heather's just like you."

"I hope not."

"I meant, sweetie, that she doesn't like weird people either."

"I like you."

"I'm not weird—well, maybe a little."

Whatever weirdness was about to transpire never took place. That rude interloper, the telephone, sounded another of its alarms and Sherm, in a flash of anger, snatched it from its cradle, prepared to blast whatever insensitive bastard had the gall to call at such an hour, but there was no one to blast.

He recognized the sound, rather lack of it. The same as the night before, on hold. He pressed MUTE and said, "Here we go again."

"Is the recorder on?"

He nodded. There was a sound like the faint hissing whisper of an unused AM frequency early in the morning in the middle of nowhere, on the Colorado Plateau—

How many mornings did I sit shivering in the Blazer twisting the dial for something?

Then the voice, distant, hollow, and suddenly very clear: "Hello, hello, is anyone there?"

"Who is this?"

"Heather."

"Goddamit, Heather's in Germany!"

"I am—are you okay, Daddy?"

Pleasantly surprised that it was Heather, he was at the same time mildly distressed by how grown-up she sounded. God, what had the Army done to his little girl?

"Let me talk to Mom."

This seemingly unwarranted rebuff put Sherm to sulking while Becky, relieved that this call in the night was not the result of accident, ill health, or bad luck, made the standard inquiries, followed by a string of yeses and uh-huhs until finally she said his daughter wanted to speak to him.

"My hitch is going to be up next month," Heather said, "and I've decided to get out."

"Out of the Army?"

"Yes."

"And toss away a promising career?"

"Daddy, you hate the Army!"

"Why didn't you just tell me?" He scowled at Becky, although he was so damned happy he thought he might cry.

"I thought something was wrong. Besides, I had to ask Mom a question—I've got to break this off before it breaks me."

They said good-bye and when Becky had gotten hers in and hung up, he asked what Heather's question was. "She wondered if it might be all right if she approached you about joining the firm."

"All right?" He couldn't believe what he was hearing. "Why didn't she ask me?"

"Children sometimes have trouble understanding their parents."

"I'm, I'm—" Sherm was genuinely speechless.

"I told her it might be better if she apply elsewhere."

"You didn't!"

"I didn't." Becky opened her arms and took him in. They hugged a good long time, letting the emotion drain in sighs and tears and gentle caresses. "Well," she said at last, "this certainly is good news." She flashed her famous smile again. "Good omen, eh?"

22

Planchettes

Becky left him in front of the jail. She walked off swinging her mother's blue umbrella with the pink and yellow roses, spectacular in her silk hibiscus-splashed island dress as she crossed the plaza toward the sandstone jumble of shops where she hoped to find something for Heather. As she passed the fountain erected in memory of yet another Estaban, Alfonso, a movement caught the corner of Sherm's vision, someone in uniform sauntering down the walk at the far end. A kid on a skateboard whizzed past.

NO SKATEBOARDS ALLOWED, the signs at all the entrances read, yet the cop let the kid pass, didn't even try to slow him, never took his eyes off Becky, and his hand was on his holster strap. Sherm looked back to Becky just as she entered the labyrinth of shops. The cop was leaving the plaza at the other end.

God, he'd almost frozen with paranoia when he should've been feeling good about having an old lady foxy enough to rivet a young cop's attention.

Just then Miles showed up, appearing more puzzled than usual over his partner's antics. "Let's go," Sherm said, "and see what's muddled our client's thinking."

After check-in, they were led to a room adjacent to the one where they'd met with Bruner on the previous visit. There were the same bolted-down desks, necessary, the deputy explained, because a regular chair had on one occasion been used as a weapon. Further, the sheriff had purchased surplus desks from the school district at a great saving to the taxpayer. Sherm wondered how much the taxpayer would save on a fleet of Mercedes. He asked the deputy if they could have a pitcher of water and three glasses.

The room was Spartan but considerably homier than its neighbor, with a painted bookcase containing paperbacks, copies of *Sports Illustrated*, and a Motorola TV. A faded Ray Manley photograph of a saguaro sunset hung on one wall. On another, burlap curtains covered a section of concrete block painted institutional green. No windows, just a barred door through which Bruner entered on his own, waving a "See you, Roy," to his guard. Relaxed and smiling, he slipped easily into the desk and joked about the sunset.

The paradox of Bruner's transformation got to Sherm. Now that the man had confessed he didn't look guilty. Could confession be that good for the soul, or was Kline the better priest? The nervous eyes were steady now and blue. The stringy hair was clean and combed smooth. He'd put on weight and smiled when he said, "I see your eye's gettin' better," and asked what they wanted.

For a moment Sherm was tempted to answer his stupid question by saying they'd come just to see how he was getting along. Now that he'd confessed, all he would need was an expression sincere and sorrowful enough to evoke sufficient pity in Scorchy Tabor's leatherneck soul to persuade him not to throw the switch.

"Raymond, we don't believe a confession of guilt is in your best interest," Miles said softly.

Bruner spun off a quick, light laugh. "Didn't the sheriff tell you I was nuts, whacko, temporarily insane? And don't they lock crazy people in nice, safe places with lots of other crazy people? Like John Hinkley?"

"Is that what Kline says?" The right words stressed; Miles's incredulity implying the lie that Bruner had been conned.

The eyes narrowed, the blue fading to gray, darker, almost black, then only black, pupils ricocheting into the corners, toward the barred door, centering on Sherm. "Kline promised."

"*Promised?*" Sherm brought his hands together on the table in front of him. *Praying for Raymond's immortal soul, old priest?*

"Do you have this in writing?" Miles asked.

Like a lizard's, Bruner's head twisted toward the voice. "It's all on the tape, the whole thing, the promise, the confession—" His attention snapped back to the old priest. "Everything . . ." His voice trailed off.

Yes, Raymond, that's right Raymond. You just realized, didn't you, Raymond, that you are sitting right where you are because of a tape. Sherm had to say it aloud, "We've an idea what they can do with tape, don't we?"

"Fuck—" Bruner coughed, cleared his throat, a "fuckin' sheriff," and several deep breaths. "I should've listened to the cons. Cons know. They know who you can trust." Bruner was gathering himself in. "They said, 'Trust Sherman'—but it's too late."

"It's not too late, Raymond." Sherm poured two glasses of water, handed one to Bruner and, just loud enough to be heard, said, "You may as well tell us; we know about your niece. We know all about her—ah, problem."

The rumble of thunder sounded as though it were coming from a deep cavern.

"You know?"

A nod, then a statement, not a question: "You said you'd gone to Vegas to join your sister Wilma with the Mothers of the Moon. You knew about electronics and could help out."

Bruner put his glass on the floor beside the desk and repeated the part about how he did maintenance mostly, occasionally helping with repairs. Sylvia's brother was in charge and showed him only enough so he'd know what had to be replaced if something went haywire. "I never knew what was going on inside those black boxes any more than in the Army I knew what made missiles work."

The persuasive brother convinced him that security was necessary to prevent theft of the secrets to what had become, according to show papers, the hottest attraction in Vegas. So Bruner went along.

"It seemed like the whole fuckin' world was in line, waitin' two, three hours to see Sylvia in her chrome chair. There's a synthesizer, lasers, breeze machine, and a picture on the ceiling showin' Elysian. Four Mexicans painted it in two days, a bunch of naked women. The one with the silver bow and arrows looks like Sylvia, except she's muscular like a female weight lifter.

"Once a whole Japan Air Lines Seven-forty-seven hit the line at once, five hundred gooks passin' up slots and craps, payin' ten bucks a head. The MOMs were makin' tons of bucks from tourists, then her brother blew it on a TV miniseries about Sylvia."

It had taken millions to make, Bruner explained, yet the production had that same tawdry comic book quality as the ceiling painting. Even independents rejected it, so the Mothers footed the cost of playing theaters where it lost even more.

"They were at rock bottom when Dorothy died." Here Bruner faltered, staring at the barred door, at the unlit window beyond.

It was raining. They could hear it. He was rubbing his fingers one at a time.

"Tell us the rest," the old priest said quietly.

"I . . . I never told you about Wilma."

"Not yet."

Lights flickered. Bruner looked at his fingers. "When we were kids, this crazy old lady who sat us hauled over her Ouija board and there was my name bein' spelled out and I wasn't pushin' the gizmo you put your fingers on and Wilma said she wasn't either. The gizmo was moving from letter to letter telling things I didn't think nobody knew. The old sitter let us borrow the Ouija and Wilma and me would play with it up in the attic. I must've been pretty fuckin' dumb. I can remember it spellin' out dirty kid stuff about me wantin' to pull down Dorothy's pants. Wilma was a rotten kid who grew up rotten. Then she saw her name in Sylvia's tent and come and got me, and I figured she'd changed.

"When Wilma and me flew down for Dorothy's funeral she got a call from the Mothers saying Shelly had a special message from Sylvia. As smart as Shelly was, she still went up to Vegas. She'd seen her mother die and maybe wasn't thinkin' too straight either. The special message was the same old 'mother's happy in Elysian' bullshit; but like with me and maybe Wilma, it contained things only Shelly would've known, like the fact that Dorothy was drunk when she got hit.

"Then I got to puttin' two and two together. The Mothers were broke—shit, heavily in debt when along come Shelly with so much money she couldn't count it, just in time. Only she didn't want to save them. As much as she got taken in by the Mothers, her real interest was still her job.

"Wilma went to work on her, introduced her to some real sleaze, all the time actin' like she'd changed, bein' one of the Mothers and all. A lot of them was whores before, and Wilma stayed one. When I asked my whore sister what she was doin', she wouldn't say; so I told her if it had anything to do with Shelly's money she'd better think again 'cause most of it was tied up in the company and Shelly wanted to keep it just where it was. Wilma said I was missing the picture, got pissed, and told me to go fuck myself. I got worried. Not about Wilma; she could do the same to herself. About Shelly." Bruner slowly turned, scratching his wrist. "This is where that scum bag come in."

Wilma's campaign to bail out the floundering Mothers

with her niece's money began with a bold move to get the shy girl out of her cocoon. Letting Bart Robin know he was dealing with a genuine heiress assured the very best "dates." Even Mr. Robin, an admitted bisexual, took a turn, and it wasn't long before the introvert who'd gotten her Master of Science degree by the time she was twenty-one was known up and down the Strip as a high roller.

But Wilma was losing her niece to Las Vegas.

A plan was developed to prevent her from tossing all her inheritance onto the green felt tables, a plan which would also generate money for MOM.

MOM's base was too small, they reasoned. One town was not enough; Sylvia's word had to be heard far and wide, but the paralyzed mute could not leave Las Vegas. A better alternative existed, the expanding network of cable TV. They would expand with it, with the resources of Shelly Eagan to help them along.

Unfortunately for everyone, Bruner's niece had fallen for Edward Creedmore, one of Bart Robin's most promiscuous escorts.

"When she come back 'cause of AZTECH, the perverted asshole followed Shelly here, with Knight suckin' right behind, their idea bein' this was 'virgin' territory, but not for long. They tried to set up another escort service, only one of the first rabbits out of the hutch blew the whistle so they closed and got themselves an adult shop. Their luck stayed bad. They thought they was gettin' a good deal but the guy had sold out to them 'cause of the new antiporn law.

"Knight's no dummy though. He figured out the hedges against the law."

With Shelly's help, Creedmore, now known as McCreedy, started his own little enterprise, a home porno tape exchange, and paid Bruner to hold, deliver, and pick up the tapes.

"It wasn't just pay; I didn't want Shelly gettin' busted for McCreedy's filthy shit. I mean, she'd turned out like Wilma only she wasn't stupid and I knew someday she'd come out of it."

Bruner poured himself some water, put the glass on the desk where it started to slide, then returned it to the floor.

"Roy said he heard you got shot down in Korea. I was in Nam and got shot at a few too fuckin' many times. Mostly I was scared shitless, but when it came time I won me some medals and picked up some metal." He ran his finger along the watermark on the desk. "I'm no more scared of that shit than the next dude, but there is somethin'—" His finger came up and pointed at Sherm.

"I bullshitted you. I went to the house like I said, only I didn't leave without seein' Shelly. After knockin' on the back door, I went around to the car in front and she was standin' in the doorway, stinkin' of perfume and decked out like a whore in a silky robe slit to her crotch so I could see the pink stockings and fancy garter belt. She invited me in and like an asshole I went. When I asked her what was up, she made a dirty remark, then dug that crummy snapshot out of the drawer in the hallway, the one of her on the rock. She told me she was a movie actress and wanted to know if I liked the photo. I said it was okay, which seemed to make her happy. She hauled me to the kitchen, opened the Frigidaire, and showed me she'd bought my favorite beer. I popped one and asked why the urgent call to come over. She said sometimes girls had 'urgencies.' It was her word but I knew what she meant. I also knew who I was, so I kinda went along like it was a joke. Sometimes we kidded like that. Shelly laughed and said that wasn't why she called. She had a secret, a big secret, but first I had to come back to the bedroom to look at the new stuff that come with the cable terminal.

"That's where it was, in the bedroom, all kinds of electronic shit. Before I could take it all in, she says let me show you how it operates, throws off her robe, takes the remote controller, flops on the bed, and zooms in on herself. She's carryin' things too far. I want to slap her bare ass and get the hell out; then she takes something small, like a mandala, from the equipment stand, and puts it on her tongue, then picks it off and palms it. She turns to push a button or somethin', and all the screens light up with a scene in the woods showin' Shelly with a man dressed up like a goat or somethin'. Weird shit. It really turns me off so I decide to get the hell out and she's cussin' worse than Wilma ever did, and screamin' I'll never learn her secret." Bruner drew in a deep breath. "That was the last time I seen her.

"Like I said, when I was a kid I believed in all kinds of shit, even Ouija boards. But the truth is, I never really got over it and what really scares me is what they can do after I'm dead. Yeah, it sounds stupid, I know; but there's no fuckin' way Wilma could've found me in Denver. Those crazy broads got connections—first I thought maybe it was the Elysian bullshit, but now—well, I ain't so sure."

Slowly now: "You liked your niece, didn't you?"

"Not a lot, but I never disliked her. She had a sheltered life, not even boyfriends, and I guess McCreedy made her a little crazy. Especially after livin' with Dorothy."

"What about Dorothy?"

"A boozer, which is why Jerry, her husband, left. Booze got her killed too." Bruner rubbed his hands together. "She was hit in the middle of the night checkin' her mailbox, which shows how drunk she was. A car, probably another drunk, hit her and kept on. She never came to."

Sherm made a mental note to check the accident report. "Did Shelly see it happen?"

"No, they'd been arguin' and after, Shelly felt real bad about not stoppin' her somehow."

"Did they argue often?"

"Only when Dorothy was drinkin', which I guess got to be most of the time."

"Dorothy played a lot of cards, didn't she?"

"Most evenings she could hardly talk, much less concentrate, but Jerry was real good at bridge and taught Shelly how to play. After he was gone she got someone from where she worked to come to the house to teach her. The lessons didn't last long, I guess 'cause Dorothy was creatin' so many problems."

"Was this woman's name Majida Ammar?"

"Sounds right."

"Did Shelly have any other friends?"

"One I know of, a girl, but I never seen her and I ain't sure they were what I'd call friends. Shelly was smart, but in a lot of ways she was like a little kid; you know, keepin' secrets. She wouldn't even tell me the friend's name when I asked, though McCreedy knew. He talked about her a couple of times and called her Sarah."

"Sarah Jones?"

Bruner shook his head. "It wouldn't of meant nothin' anyway. None of those fuckers go by their right names."

Was *Sarah Jones*, Sherm wondered, another aka?

"You said MOM has connections. The tabloids suggested a mob connection, possibly through prostitution."

"No way." Bruner screwed up his face. "The rest are, you know, like reformed smokers."

"So they'd take a dim view of what Shelly was up to—with McCreedy and maybe this Sarah Jones, right?"

"Real dim."

"Dim enough to punish Shelly?"

"Not directly, with violence; maybe somehow."

"On the other hand, Wilma's letter indicates they were pleased with your work."

"I been thinkin' about that letter. Wilma never writes. Shit, she barely can. It might've been part of the setup."

"When Shelly tried to entice you in the bedroom, was she wearing the mandala around her waist?"

"It was hangin' from the bedpost."

"Was there ever a cable broadcast?"

"One, a test. There were a couple of bugs. Shelly said they'd start regular broadcasts in the fall." Bruner examined his hands. "I'm all mixed up on this, Mr. Sherman. For a while I thought we'd fucked up, with the porn and all, then I wasn't so sure. When they took me through that door at the courthouse I was sure I was dead, but when all hell broke loose, someone or somethin' got in the way and saved my ass."

"Do you have your mandala now?"

"Yeah, I told the cops it was a religious medal." Bruner reached in his pocket and handed Sherm the token, about the size of a thin silver dollar.

"What are these markings?"

"Numbers written in a secret language. Everyone has different ones. Those are mine."

Sherm handed the charm back. "About the hell that broke loose at the courthouse: The rifle that fired the shot that was supposed to blow us all to hell was found at McCreedy's. Do you have any idea how it got there?"

"McCreedy learned I was Army and was always tryin' to talk to me about ordnance. The asshole spent a year in the Guard and thought he was some kind of fuckin' soldier of fortune. He bragged he and Knight had a gun deal once, all of which impressed the shit outta Shelly." Bruner smiled ever so slightly. "I guess he got his; but I'll tell you, he wasn't so fuckin' dumb he'd blow himself up."

"Do you think he placed the explosives in the statue?"

"That scum bag would've sold anything for a price, but he was a supplier, not a doer. It wasn't Knight either. He's the kind who pays to have his dirty work done."

"Like storing contraband tapes?"

"Yeah, and you know, McCreedy was always deliverin' and pickin' them up. Maybe he and Shelly were makin' copies or somethin'. I wish I knew."

Sherm turned to his partner. "Miles, do you have any questions?"

"A couple. First, is it possible your niece and McCreedy were producing pornographic materials?"

"With that scum bag anything was possible."

"Second, could they have been transmitting pornographic materials over cable?"

Bruner shook his head. "Too risky. If they were caught, they'd be arrested by the state for breakin' the antiporn law." Bruner laughed. "And by the FBI for violatin' the copyright."

Sherm untangled himself from the desk and thanked Bruner for a very productive session.

They held up in the foyer. The large pool of water that had formed on the plaza was being pelted by a steady tattoo of rain that showed no sign of letup. Sherm suggested a cab. Miles looked at him. "Have you ever caught a cab in this town?"

Never, Sherm realized, though he was fairly certain he'd seen checkered and yellow vehicles cruising the streets. Surely they were cabs. Then he remembered Becky mentioning she'd gotten Maurice a cab from the hospital back to his shop.

"Your cable TV question was an interesting one."

"Romero's info on the FBI and scrambler has been bugging me."

"Suppose they were checking on copyright violations?"

Miles laughed, then: "It's called a planchette."

"What is?"

"The gizmo used on an Ouija board."

23

An Evening of Bridge

A downpour straight out of tropical Baja, the radio said, the kind that sometimes sits over the basin for days, filling washes, arroyos, and the sandy indistinguishable riverbeds. And it was a driving time that, given the best conditions, usually drove Sherm raving mad, rush hour on a day that would have alarmed Noah; yet Becky plowed the rivered streets as if she were driving a Mississippi River barge, taking in Sherm's summary of Bruner's story with no more outward concern than she showed the predawn morning on the Piedra Parkway that she drove a hundred miles in fifty-eight minutes.

It would be interesting, they agreed, to hear Knight's version.

They were ten minutes late arriving at Knight's home, a low-slung, rambling affair entered through an atrium with a three-foot plaster copy of Michelangelo's David centered on a pedestal in a pool of blue tinted water. The actual entrance was beyond, through a double carved-mahogany door. Inside, the low ceilings and heavy squared-off blocks were so white the place would have seemed as sterile as a hospital if not for plants of all sorts. Knight, oblivious to the bleakly beautiful place he called home (though he'd commented on Becky's umbrella as he folded it) was intent on a descriptive buildup of the person who was to be his partner: Gloria this and Gloria that, not significantly altering the *Gloria* Sherm had put together in his mind, someone not unlike the well-groomed middle-aged women who frequented the bridge club.

He couldn't have been less right.

Gloria Woodward slunk into view murmuring, "No relation to Joanne"—holding out a slender arm, hand limp and white gloved—"though it would be marvelous to share a bedroom with Paul Newman." The platinum sweep of hair had been combed to veil a third of a carefully made-up face somewhat over thirty. Two slender straps held up a white satin evening gown cut across the front like bib overalls and slit to above the knees, meant to be slinky but up close Gloria's thinness, exaggerated by the projection of shoulder blades and hips and by overlarge hands and feet, produced a general impression of bony angularity. Her bra-less breasts, like a pair of lemons, generated ripples in the satin sheen as she moved with the practiced deliberateness of a Forties movie star. Gloria Woodward had attempted to create an image of Joan Crawford with Veronica Lake hair. The result was someone who might be seen at a *Rocky Horror Picture Show*. She seemed rather pleasant though, as she bemoaned the "terribly awful" shooting and fussed over Sherm's wounds, confident his black eye would be only a memory in a day or two.

"I'll bet everyone is starved!" Knight flipped his right hand, gesturing toward the open doors that led out to his rain-washed gazebo, white in the lights where it perched on an extension of patio that jutted beyond the natural line of the cliff. On an ordinary night, it offered an unobstructed view of the city lights spread below. But the rain had snuffed out the lights and this night the gazebo was like an alien lander clinging to the edge of the far side of the moon. "It's quite dry underneath," Knight remarked as Kevin, a muscular young man in tight fitting white shirt and designer jeans, held the umbrellas and escorted them the few feet from beneath the patio overhang to the gazebo where they seated themselves at the white wrought iron table. Knight was correct. Even though the rain was steady, there was no wind and it streamed off the eave, wrapping them in beaded translucence.

Dinner was already on the table in covered silver bowls. Gloria informed them that Barry himself had prepared the mix of gourmet and routine: quiche and a lettuce salad followed by Ragout a la Deutch with steamed cabbage and cooked carrots, ending with a dessert indeed special, French vanilla ice cream mixed with ground, fresh roasted coffee beans topped with whipped cream and maraschino cherries, a treat that prompted a special toast to the chef.

A long day lay behind, a big meal, and now the young man in the tight designers was serving after-dinner Kahluas which Knight suggested they take inside where the cards wouldn't stick together. The game room was an area twice the Shermans' living and dining rooms combined. It was indeed a game room, complete with billiard table, Ping-Pong, darts, three TVs, a VCR programmed to project onto a giant screen, another for discs, the third hooked up to an Atari computer game console. Two air chairs and a fluffy couch faced the big screen, each adorned with a different Siamese that immediately vacated its place. Against the near wall were an arcade Space Invaders, pinball, dollar slot, and pachinko machines. A liquor cabinet and wet bar with glasses hanging upside down underneath and a French phone on top was positioned within easy reach of the poker table. A stained-glass Coca-Cola lamp was centered above and two decks lay flat on the green felt alongside a pad and a gold Cross pen.

Dinner had made Sherm so groggy he was certain his play would disappoint the host; however, had he been playing in a coma he would've done better than Knight, whose knowledge of bidding evidently hadn't progressed beyond suit ranking. He passed when he should've opened and bid like crazy whenever he held five or more cards in a suit. Across the table, Becky somehow maintained her stony-eyed stare at the cards fanned out in her own hand, quietly doubling whenever Knight was declarer. Sherm felt embarrassment for the hapless Knight, apparently oblivious to his shoddy performance. His partner, Gloria, exercised a fair degree of tolerance for one who obviously knew the game. Her bidding was accurate, her play competent, and whenever Knight would bomb she would say that one simply couldn't expect perfect results when competing against a tournament pair. Sherm who could've easily detested this phony celluloid blond, instead found himself admiring her tolerance. The more lopsided the score, the more reckless Knight became and the less perturbed Gloria seemed to be, even when he audaciously redoubled Becky's double and went down twenty-two hundred. This was beyond the pale of human restraint. At the bridge club such a performance would've ended in battery.

"It's been a long time since college," Knight finally admitted. "Sorry, Gloria."

"Don't fret; you know I never take anything seriously."

"I do, unfortunately." In the manner of a losing gambler, Knight shuffled the cards slowly, making certain they were really mixing and not winding up in the same unlucky sequence. "Which is probably why I turned down an opportunity to enter law school. In the courtroom there is always a losing side and I simply cannot stand losing, which is also why I have gravitated to games I win at." He waved toward the other tables. "Such as billiards, darts, Ping-Pong, poker—" His hand came down soundly on the felt. "Could you imagine me defending some common thug and losing? Why I would throw a tantrum right there in front of the judge and jury and get disbarred or worse! I really don't know how, Mr. S., you defend criminals you know are guilty."

"Lawyers do other work besides practice criminal law."

"But that is the real game. For example, take poor Raymond, an exasperation, you must admit. When I read of his arrest and the circumstances I knew instantly he was innocent, yet I seriously considered *not* telling anyone. Can you believe? I even read the editorials with a sort of secret glee, imagining the delightful possibility of producing a video of Raymond's electrocution. My mind literally went berserk. I conjured an image of him being shocked with a phalluslike rod capable of inflicting a terminal electro-orgasm, whatever that could be—a horrible thought, but I'm sure by now you must know what a wretched person Raymond sometimes is. Fortunately my perversity passed. The point is, I knew he was innocent when the newspapers had practically electrocuted him. To quote the sheriff—what's his name, Tom Jones or something?"

"Kline."

"Sheriff Tom let the cat out of the bag by saying they had irrefutable evidence proving poor Raymond's guilt. Now, I ask, what juror will be able to overcome something irrefutable?"

"We hope to select jurors who've not read the paper."

"Oh, good luck, this *irrefutable* business has been in the papers, on television, in national magazines. Sheriff Tom is probably right now cruising the bars writing *irrefutable* on rest room walls."

A throaty laugh slipped from Gloria.

"Anyway it's hopeless now that Raymond has confessed." Knight spread his hands and sighed. "Would any of you like a drink, perhaps some excellent brandy?"

"Nothing for us, thank you," Becky answered without consultation.

"Scotch," Gloria said. Knight opened the cabinet, fixed two on the rocks, handed Gloria hers, sipped his, and resumed shuffling. "You're going to wear off the spots," Gloria warned.

"Hmmm." Knight checked the face sides of the cards. "None missing yet."

"Maybe we should call this off," Becky said.

"Would you mind?" Knight looked at each of them. "This has really become a rout."

They were relieved to get it over with. Playing against people like Knight bred sloppy habits, which they could ill afford tomorrow. Besides, it was getting late and there were things to talk about.

"I really didn't think I would forget so much. I hope it's not old age creeping up." He grinned nervously, stealing a glance at his watch. "I know it's difficult to fathom but in college I was really good."

"Weren't we all," Gloria said.

"*Really.* I was one of those professional students who majored in games, especially sports. You know, those sweating magnificent bodies and all. I was more than somewhat a pain for my mother, which is why, I suppose, I finally settled on her solution and took a degree I could put to use, business." Knight sighed. "Some business . . . I first entered pornography with a great deal of trepidation. Though never overly concerned with its moral aspects, I nevertheless feared the opposing forces, law and order versus organized crime, would crush me in the middle; however, I have been bothered by no one in particular—except, of course, the moron majority."

Knight sipped from his scotch. "None of the Sensa-Vision's neighbors, thank goodness, so much as come near the shop—except for an occasional grubby boy whose curiosity is generously rewarded by a threatening gesture with a Vibo Love Aid. Yet it is ironic what has happened as a result of the morons blowing their self-righteous whistles. Our modest profit-making venture has become a gold mine and should—barring implementation of a *total* police state—lead to a better product. We're already seeing this in the Mythos gourmet fare, *ragout* rather than the common hot dog variety being dished out by the grunt and sweat pornographer—which leads to a question I've been dying to ask, Mr. S.—" Knight picked up the deck and began flipping through the cards. "I suppose I'm a little disappointed you haven't mentioned the tape. I've never seen such a . . . *zero* reaction, or is it simply reluctance?"

Sherm fished the tape out of his pocket. "I'm afraid there's been a mistake, Barry." He handed it to Knight. "This seems to belong to the hot dog variety."

"Hot dog?" Knight flipped the tape over. "This is what I gave you?" Sherm nodded. "Oh, my, how could I? No, you're quite right, this is definitely hot dog. Which means the correct *Nymphs* must be in the other pocket of whatever I was wearing. What *was* I wearing?"

"Your tan corduroy," Becky said.

"You remembered?" Knight looked pleased that she had.

"It was much too hot for corduroy."

"Oh . . ." Knight got up. "It's hanging in the closet just inside the next room."

Sherm raised his hand, signaling Knight not to bother. "There are other matters, about Bruner."

"Of course." Knight put the cassette on the table, settled into his chair, and drew a card from the deck. "I'm surprised you haven't asked me more about Raymond."

The trey of clubs.

"Not quite the bottom card, nevertheless appropriate." He sighed. "When Raymond first came to me I would have described him in a word: *wretched*. He had a harried insect look, as though a big hand was ready to swoop in and cup him in eternal darkness. He struck me as sort of a religious nut, you might say, although religious seems inaccurate. I was taken aback by his appearance, thinking him perhaps a vanguard of the moron majority. He skirted his purpose in obscure, roundabout ways. I half expected *Watchtowers* to come tumbling out of his valise; but no, my missionary friend turned out to be an emissary from his niece, you might say a pathetic, peripatetic pornographer."

Knight paused to enjoy his alliteration.

"Still, I was hesitant to even consider his proposal. There are channels of acquisition usually adhered to if one wishes to remain healthy. I was certain whatever this fly had to offer would be inferior stuff, but Raymond was persistent and since I am not one to force confrontation, I allowed him to show a sample."

"Barry," Sherm interrupted, "I think it only fair to tell you that this afternoon Bruner told us about Rabinowitz and Robin."

Knight squared the deck and placed it in the center of the table. "Then I must keep my story straight, mustn't I?"

Gloria eyed Sherm cautiously with a look that had nothing to do with the present topic.

Knight moved to pick up the cassette, choosing instead his drink.

"You didn't come to play bridge . . ."

"We weren't invited to."

Knight's hand trembled and for the first time his demeanor revealed something beyond the hedonistic insensitivity that had, until then, been the mark of his persona. He was clearly troubled.

"Mr. S., I desperately need a good lawyer."

"Maybe you'd better tell me why."

"*Desperately*, Mr. S., desperately! And believe me, I cannot tell you anything without the assurance of confidentiality guaranteed in a lawyer-client relationship."

This wasn't exactly a confessional, Sherm noted, glancing from Gloria to Becky.

"Gloria is my confidante, Mr. S., and I trust your wife implicitly."

Sherm rubbed his chin. "On one condition."

"Which is?"

"You stop calling me Mr. S."

Knight cupped Sherm's hand with both of his, shaking it as though dispensing holy water.

"Thank you, thank you; you don't know what a relief—"

"Tell us, why so desperate?"

"Because someone murdered Ms. E. and it wasn't her uncle and it wasn't Edward. We three really were together. This same person also tried to kill all of you at the courthouse, and someone you don't know about: me! You see, before Edward was murdered, he phoned me to meet him at his apartment. He said we had to discuss the cable agreement and to be sure to arrive at exactly eleven—which is the real reason, you see, why I came to your house early. More than a little suspicious of having to be anywhere at exactly any time, I chose instead to park and see what, if anything, was going on. When the explosion occurred, I knew my suspicion was well grounded. As with Raymond, I'd been set up." Knight wagged his head. "I feel very fortunate to be alive."

Sherm tapped the cassette. "What was this really about?"

"For me everything has become a game. Even murder. I gave you this as my little clue." Knight picked up the tape.

"You know who murdered Bruner's niece?"

"No, Mr. S.—ah, what should I call you?"

"Sherm is fine."

"Sherm sounds so, so blunt; but very well. No, Sherm, I do not know the name of the perpetrator of violence in this peculiar drama, but I am aware of Ms. E.'s experiments and thought it would be amusing to drop you a clue, like in an old-time mystery novel."

"The young girl seducing the old man was supposed to be analogous to Shelly Eagan's attempt at seduction?"

"As close as I could come. Raymond told me about her putting the make on him when he came to the shop that night. My clue worked?"

"Not one bit."

The pornographer's momentary elation dissolved to a pout. "I apologize for being stupid."

"And dangerous." This gamesmanship could've gotten them all killed. "Especially if the mob is involved."

"Oh, I'm sure they're not. I mean, they're big, rough, hairy men, but they always warn you first. I was simply lured to Edward's place where—" Knight made an explosive *puff* with his fingers.

The blood was pooling in the wrong end of his body, so Sherm pushed his chair away from the table, stood, and walked over to the dart board.

"Was Shelly Eagan in the real *Nymphs* tape?"

"She and her alter ego."

"Alter ego?"

"I call her that, Sarah Jones."

In the cross-examination that followed, Barry Knight's game room testimony revealed a young woman who'd been more than a friend to Shelly Eagan. Not that their love had anything to do with commitment or even sex; rather their relationship, as Knight described, was an affair of the alter ego, an almost narcissistic involvement with another so nearly alike that people often mistook them one for the other.

Sarah had been an employee at Robin's, a female escort primarily for other females, and had met Shelly through Raymond's sister.

"Wilma, I believe her name is, a high pucky-up in a quasi-religious sect. Really a disgruntled band of bawds, no longer able to ply their trade against the rather stiff Las Vegas competition. I've heard them referred to as the 'bull-dyke brigade.'"

Gloria failed to stifle a somewhat vociferous giggle, which Knight appeared to appreciate before continuing.

"I must admit to a muddle here. Apparently Sarah and Wilma knew each other, most likely in the Biblical sense as well, and when Wilma's sister died, the funeral provided a basis for Sarah to meet Shelly, probably in more ways than one. Ms. E. was a regular client of the Robin agency. It was always arranged she should go out with a man, but Sarah became the pot at the end of the rainbow. As I said before, they were lovers who were not in love. Sex to them was much the same as it is to me, another game; so much so, they began videotaping their activities. Edward became their favorite foil, a sex object really. Of course there were others. On one occasion, Edward told me, each of them had three men of three separate ethnic backgrounds. I won't go into detail—"

"Please don't," Becky piped up.

"Are you saying," Sherm asked, "that Sarah corrupted Shelly and the two of them corrupted McCreedy?"

"I wouldn't use the word *corrupt*, and if I did, I would say Edward was quite already that way when the three of them, plus whoever else, got together."

"So what was going on here, in this town?"

"As you must know, there was a plan to pick up Moon Mother propaganda with a satellite dish to retransmit over community cable TV and someone, quite possibly Ms. E. herself, came up with a scheme to tap the outlet for their taped X-rated activities. Ms. E. had the money and technical backing of her company's—"

"I'm not sure I get this," Sherm interrupted. "The new state anti-porn law makes the transmission of obscene matter a felony. And the wording is specific concerning X-rated cable."

"Absolutely! The stroke of brilliance was the fabrication of a system which permitted simultaneous telecasting on the same channel. Only those with proper receiving and descrambling adapters could receive the X-rated portion. Other viewers would pick up only the Mothers' show. My task was to provide subscribers. We tested the system the night before Shelly was murdered." Knight pointed to the big TV screen. "Six subscribers and myself watched in this very room."

"Which could account for the sheriff's sudden interest in X-rated tapes."

"Ah, but he will never find the ones that count." Knight explained that the coup de grace was copying their tapes onto waferlike laser discs.

"Even if John Law finds the discs he will have no way of converting them into sound images on a TV screen without both the transmission and receiving descrambling devices."

"Was this Shelly's invention?"

"I understand not, rather this system was already in use by the military. AZTECH is heavily into military contracts. I suspect Ms. E.'s ex-roomy had something to do with the invention. I understand she's quite brilliant."

"Sarah didn't live with Shelly?"

"For some time. Then a day or so prior to the murder, Ms. E. told Sarah she would have to find another place to stay for a few days, that the old roomy, the one who left when Sarah arrived, had decided to come back. Sarah moved in with us, furious with Ms. E. She described the woman as an absolute prig—not her actual word; however, my impression was that this was a proper lady who could not tolerate Sarah and moved out because of her."

"Do you know her name?"

"I was never told." Knight turned to Gloria. "Were you?"

"No, Shelly wouldn't even tell Sarah. It was one of her little secrets."

"Ms. E. could be very childish sometimes by pretending to know things we mortals are incapable of understanding. She never believed the Mothers' malarkey; however, she was intrigued by their so-called miracles, I think as a challenge to her superior intellect. On our only date she confided that the Mothers found Raymond in Denver simply by calling up his VA records on their computer."

"Shelly was into, I believe Sarah called it, hacking," Gloria added.

"Ms. E. once told Sarah that if ignorance was bliss, her aunt and uncle were saints. I don't think she held the Bruner clan in much esteem, especially for their blind acceptance of these so-called miracles. On the other hand . . ."

At Knight's request, Gloria told them about the night Shelly was murdered.

"Sarah was here with me watching the Channel Five news. I find this chubasco thing terrifying, to say the least. The point is, we were waiting for the weather, which comes on at about quarter after, when we received a phone call. I listened, heard it was Shelly and decided to let the answering machine take it and return her call in the morning. We'd had a number of drinks to calm our nerves during the storm, which at one point I thought would blow away Barry's gazebo, so I completely forgot about the call. Sarah, in fact, remembered and checked it first thing after retrieving the morning newspaper from the driveway.

"I've never seen anyone so devastated. It was as though she herself had been struck dead. I pried the phone from her grasp and rewound the tape." Gloria took a deep breath. "Brace yourself for this, Sherm. Shelly's message to us was that she was going to be murdered by her uncle."

Gloria's obvious anticipation of their reaction turned to surprise. "Well, the point is, I would've laughed it off, called it all a big joke; but there it was, bannered in the morning paper: AZTECH HEIRESS MURDERED, and underneath, that the suspect in custody was Raymond."

Puzzled, Gloria asked if this didn't strike either of them as rather strange.

"In this case," Sherm answered, "we've ceased being surprised."

"We had a similar phone call," Becky explained.

"I woke up Barry and told him." Gloria turned to Knight. He took up the story. "On Fridays I work till closing—tonight excepted. This is our busiest and rowdiest time; and Earl, no thanks to his addiction, is barely able to dispense tokens after ten. At any rate, last Friday I arrived home somewhere around two, much too exhausted to be fooling with the answering machine. When Gloria told me about the call, my immediate reaction was 'not now, Gloria,' certain she was up to some sort of *exceedingly* belated April Fool's thing, which of course she wasn't."

Gloria swished her ice and watched what was left turn in the glass. "Sarah was totally stunned. Saturday and Sunday she moved as though in a trance; then Monday morning after reading the paper about the hearing she came out of her funk. She told us you were Bruner's appointed attorney and seemed almost happy about it. Then she called McCreedy, I guess for the gun she used at the courthouse. You know the rest."

"Not really." Sherm removed a pair of brass weighted darts from the segmented cork. "For starters, who was she really after?"

"Barry and I discussed that." Gloria looked at Knight, who nodded for her to continue. "We know why she wanted to kill Bruner. She probably wanted to kill you too; but we don't know why, except that it had something to do with her parents."

"Did McCreedy fire the other shot?"

"Edward was at the shop." Knight hesitated before continuing. "In fact, he was the one who changed channels so we could see Raymond being brought to the courthouse. However, from his remark, 'Be sure to tape this,' I realized afterward that he knew what she planned."

Sherm stepped to the line and drew a bead on the center circle. The dart dipped abruptly, glanced off the backboard, fell, and struck in the carpet.

"Could McCreedy have accidentally blown himself up?"

"Though he claimed otherwise, Edward knew nothing about munitions, not even how to market them. We purchased guns nobody wanted. Can you imagine single shot *survival* rifles?"

"The twenty-two Hornet."

"We must have a storage shed filled with them."

"But McCreedy could've provided the Hornet to the person who did?"

"And the explosives, yes—which probably accounts for poor Edward's demise."

The next dart held, high and just inside the outer ring.

"Could he have sold them to someone in MOM?"

"Edward would have sold to anybody; but no, the Mothers really are not fanatical. I'm certain they would take legal rather than violent action." Knight let out a long breath. "Which brings us precisely to the crux of the matter. We have absolutely no inkling as to the identity of the other assassin, and neither, we believe, does anyone else. Sherm, I'm caught between the rock and a very hard place. That someone, be it whoever, is still loose and I want out of this, Sherm, all the way out, and I want you to represent me."

Questions were forming in Sherm's mind but they seemed all to have been answered except the crucial one; then the muffled beat of rain on the foam roof was cracked by the jangle of the phone.

Knight reacted as though lightning had come through the wires. "What do you mean, *bombed?*" His hand started shaking. "Yes, yes, I'll be down." He dropped the phone back onto its cradle, and in a wavering voice told them it was Earl calling from the beauty shop, that the Sensa-Vision had been bombed.

"Was anyone hurt?" Becky asked.

"I don't know. Earl didn't say. He said he didn't know what he should do, so he called me."

Sherm got the shop's address and dialed 9-1-1. They'd already received a call.

Their evening of bridge closed in chaos, with Knight and Gloria charging off in her Volvo, leaving the Buick far behind, just as the core of the massive storm that had been stalking them all evening struck as though on cue. A gusher, a Niagara, hurricane and crystal pellets of hail, yellow electricity, and in the midst of all this it came to him like the crack of doom. He shouted above the roar of Mercury's maelstrom so loud and fiercely it caused the ever implacable Becky to swerve.

"What's wrong, sweetie?"

"The Monroe Decision!"

24

Cybernetic Models

Sherm carried his wake-up coffee to the glass door. The overflowing gutter had dumped two months' accumulation of mesquite beans onto the deck and the dreary landscape beyond was bathed in a gray mist. It was unusual for chubasco rain to fall with such consistency or so early in the day, yet depressingly appropriate.

The elation that followed his realization that Shelly Eagan's voice had to have been recorded by 9-1-1 the night of her mother's accident evaporated in the possibility that the mad bomber was still active.

Sherm's call to the command post had been answered while they slept, the answer relayed from Charlie and recorded immediately after a message from Knight.

According to Knight, the porn shop bombing had been an attempt on his life, the explosion centered outside the wall within three feet of the desk he invariably occupied on Friday evenings. This Friday, however, was spent bumbling through bridge hands in hope of snagging himself a lawyer. He'd loaned Earl the Continental so he could deliver the receipts after closing, after securing Earl's solemn promise not to smoke, sniff, pop, or inject anything in the interim. The Continental parked outside the Sensa-Vision, Knight supposed, convinced the bomber that he was at his usual post.

Kline, Charlie reported, thought differently. The state's Attorney General had just flashed the green light to close down all porn exhibitors and the bombing coincided too closely not to make the insurance motive an inescapable conclusion. But Charlie didn't agree with Kline. The bombing had knocked down one wall and torn up some furniture. Why not something simpler, less suspicious, and more destructive, say a cigarette left in a wastebasket? A fire would have consumed the building and its contents. As it was, they'd taken Knight into custody for possession of contraband and the pornographer had wasted his one phone call on Sherm's answering machine.

As Knight's counsel he should have posted bond, but after mulling over the bombing, Sherm decided to wait until Monday. If Knight's skin was in jeopardy, the best place for him was in jail. If not, well, maybe it was best for the Shermans to have Barry Knight in jail.

The message from the command post ended with the note that they'd located the other 9-1-1 tape and to call Charlie.

This time it was not his answering machine. "Do you know what the hell time it is?" Charlie growled.

"The yellow pages say Ace Investigations is open twenty-four hours."

"We get paid for twenty-four; we work four."

"Sounds like misleading advertising."

"So I'm open, so what?"

"So my machine says you found the tape and want me to call."

"Yeah, you knew Knight's shop was bombed?"

"I was at his house when it happened."

"You one of them kind?"

"Them kind of what?"

"Never mind—Donegan's preliminary comparison of the two nine-one-ones shows some similarities and he's pretty sure they were partially synthesized. He can't say exactly how, so he wants authorization to use one of AZTECH's supercomputers."

"He'll have to arrange that with AZTECH."

"He needs authorization to spend the eight hundred bucks an hour they charge."

"*Eight* hundred?"

"Not cheap but he's sure he can wrap it up in less than an hour. Also, he says he has a better than average chance of figuring how the tape was synthesized. I would've given him the go-ahead myself except there's something neither of you know." Charlie took on a tone of confidentiality. "My highly reliable source says even Glidden is changing his mind about your client's guilt."

Nevertheless, Sherm decided, it would be worth eight hundred dollars to clear the question and maybe come up with a clue to who's behind the bombings.

"Donegan says he can demonstrate the results this P.M."

Sherm turned to call Becky but she was there, taking a packet of tortillas from the freezer. He asked how much time there'd be between bridge sessions. The first ended shortly after three, the second started at seven. Nearly four hours.

Charlie noted that with the bomber still at large, it was pretty stupid of them to be playing in a public card game; but he would, if Sherm insisted, set up the meeting for four o'clock.

"I insist—in my office. See you then." Sherm started for breakfast when the phone rang again. He considered leaving it to the machine but was glad he didn't. Miles was euphoric. Glidden, he said, had tossed in the towel but had to talk to Sherm before making it official. Quickly, he told Miles about the four o'clock meeting and asked him to brief the county attorney on what they knew about Knight and to invite him to the meeting. Miles would, and wished them luck in the tournament.

After relating all that was happening to Becky, Sherm confessed that, although the case appeared to be settling down, he was beginning to feel the tournament jitters.

"It's the coffee," she said. "They'll go away as soon as I rustle us some grits." She opened the pack of flour tortillas, heated two in the microwave on defrost for two minutes, scrambled three eggs in two minutes, fifty seconds, spooned them onto the buttered tortillas, topped the eggs with hot salsa and grated sharp cheese, rolled and heated them another minute for a breakfast dish not quite American, not quite Mexican, uniquely Becky. She suggested he try not to think about the tournament. God knows there was plenty else to think about, and all the omens were certainly good ones, but Sherm just couldn't drive it out of his mind that he was an upstart, that their success had been her doing, that he would make an ass of himself (or worse!) and they would be driven from the forbidden garden of tournament bridge like Adam and Eve from Eden.

"We'll beat their socks off."

"Sure we will," he answered weakly.

If anything, the jitters got worse, nearly doing him in when it became apparent they would be late arriving at the Convention Center. They would have had minutes to spare if a concurrently running cat show had not overflowed the main parking lot and forced them to the back lot along the normally dry riverbed, now nearly bank full. They still might not have cut it so close if they hadn't had to huddle under the umbrella from the lot, over the pedestrian cross ramp, and down the runway to the enormous copper doors. Once inside, they jogged through the complex maze, guided by BRIDGE arrows, to the West Room.

Open to half capacity, the room was jammed with players who glared at them, unmistakably hostile, and Sherm could almost hear them ask, "What are you doing here?"—the very essence of a successful beginning: intimidation.

Having failed to take into account that this was a regional contest, he'd severely underestimated the number of participants. There were two couples from every bridge unit in the Southwest, at least a hundred pairs, which was confirmed when, as the last to register, they became pair 104, an unlucky sounding number.

It was just as well they arrived at kickoff because it left no time for the jitters to get worse. Nevertheless, he was shaking, along with many others. Someone had not noticed the rain's effect on an outside temperature that was 85 degrees rather than the usual 105. The place was like an ice box, especially in section D along the wall where the vents were. Sensibly, or as a consequence of long experience, the ladies all wore sweaters. Sherm was freezing and Becky, who had the foresight to wear a two-piece top, said she was cold. The news of Glidden's apparent surrender had buoyed his hopes; now he wasn't so sure. Their last-second arrival, the unexpected size of the competition, and a temperature certain to numb the brain were bad omens.

The bad ones did not go unfulfilled. On the first hand he

bid four clubs over Becky's three clubs, a weak bid on her part that he really couldn't support, an unnecessary and inexcusable error. Down two, doubled and vulnerable.

Keenly aware he'd started them out with the worst possible score, Sherm began concentrating on what he did best.

Whenever they played well, Becky's precognitive awareness of the bidding potential combined with his capacity for remembering what had already been played gave them their edge over the rest of the field. Time after time, simply looking at the thirteen cards in her hand she could predict accurately the makeup of the other three hands. On his side, he was sometimes able to recall the distribution of all fifty-two cards played in a game days before, a talent, however, in direct proportion to his level of preoccupation at the time. There were also times he couldn't remember a card played on the last trick. This wasn't one of those times. He settled into the groove and stayed there, but it was an uphill struggle. The diabolical computer had done it again. There were no slams and few games. Hand after hand was passed out at the two and three levels. Two spade or three diamond bids did not offer much opportunity to recoup losses; and although he hadn't given up, when the round ended at 3:20 he was certain they'd been knocked out.

"They've all still got their socks on," Sherm observed. "I'm sorry."

Becky urged him not to lose heart; they could still be in it. All they needed was to be in the top half.

He wasn't convinced, suggesting it might be good form to wish the twins luck. They hadn't been opponents in the first round but it took no time to spot them moving through the crowd toward an exit, decked out in their usual black, a regal pair whose only difference in attire were the ruffles on Majida's cuffs and shirt front. The twins were out the door before they could get to them.

Usually the Shermans waited for the scores to be tallied to

see how they'd done. Today, unfortunately, there was a meeting three rainy blocks away.

Simply put, Glidden said, Sherm had been right all along in his contention that there wasn't enough time for all that was supposed to have gone on to have happened.

"We ran it through a dozen or more times as many ways as possible, including the rape occurring after the murder. None of it worked. Our problem in the beginning was underestimating the distances necessarily traversed in order for the tape to be valid. That's a mighty big house. If Bruner had entered the front door, proceeded directly to the bedroom, strangled his niece, run to his car, and proceeded in a direction opposite from the way the patrol car came, he would've had just enough time. This omits the rape and, more certainly, the call to the Sensa-Vision, which at first seemed to be the clincher. The missing silver cord, however, was virtual proof the nine-one-one tape wasn't authentic."

Glidden dismissed a good deal of Knight's story, his new scenario centering on an overzealous, avaricious McCreedy bent on collecting all the marbles himself.

"McCreedy's had a record of shady dealings, dope and gun smuggling, prostitution, you name it. He and Knight came here to set up more of the same but they got stung and had to look for ways around the new porn law. Unwittingly, Miss Eagan, an unattractive, lonely young woman, albeit rich, who'd fallen into this mess when she tried Knight's escort service in Vegas, provided the answer via a TV relay on local cable for the Mothers of the Moon. Very ingenious and equally despicable—which Miss Eagan eventually realized. When she balked, McCreedy raped and killed her, and set Bruner up to take the rap. Later, he put the TNT, which we have purchase records to show was his, inside the Estaban statue and fired the shot that would've effectively ended the case and allowed him to escape undetected. Unfortunately for McCreedy, the time bomb he was working on to amend his poor marksmanship at the courthouse put an end to his plans."

And Knight's bomb?

"Your new client ostensibly invited you to play a game you say he knew practically nothing about because he needed a lawyer. I say, why go to all the trouble; why not just pick up the phone? No, Sherm, you were invited so Knight would have an iron-clad alibi. He needed the insurance to cover his losses."

So where did Sarah Jones fit into the prosecutor's scenario?

"Miss Eagan's only friend it seems. From the evidence, very close friends. We also uncovered the interesting coincidence that you defended her father for the murder of her mother, and that he was killed in prison, which would account for her actions at the courthouse. We did our homework."

Glidden's was a morality play with the coup de grace administered by ironic tricks of fate.

"You'd better stick around for the spectrogram." Sherm checked his watch. Thirty minutes late. Not like Charlie at all.

"Incidentally," Glidden said, "we decided on the Baron."

"Mr. Beech makes good airplanes."

"You'll have to go up with me."

"Anytime," Sherm said. "I've just about made up my mind to resume flying."

"Great!" Glidden turned to Miles, who'd been the silent observer during this gathering. "Bruner's murder charges will be dropped as soon as the paperwork is processed, probably Tuesday, and I don't think there'll be any other charges. We'll go after Knight on the pornography violations."

Charlie's voice preceded him through the doorway. The man who followed instinctively ducked and when he straightened, Aaron Donegan came within an inch of striking his head on the air-conditioning duct. His huge left hand gripped the handle of a large, black plastic case; his right came at Sherm like a destroyer.

"Nice to see you again, Sherm."

Donegan was so tall and the greeting over so quickly, Sherm was reminded of a time his mother took him to school to meet his first grade teacher. It was a wonderful way, he somehow remembered his mother telling his sister, to make Peter feel accepted and wanted. It was a lousy idea. As the teacher's big hand swallowed his tiny one, even at his tender age, he knew all the teacher really wanted was a longer summer vacation. Now he was having some of those same feelings, except that seeing Donegan's humorless countenance triggered an image of a pike contemplating a minnow.

The grim giant said there was absolutely no question that the emergency call to the 9-1-1 number was a tape recording; further, the second part, which mentioned the uncle, had been synthesized. Donegan opened the black case, took out the small portable television set, positioned a number of dials on the console inside the case, inserted cassettes into each of the two tape slots, and allowed the first to play until the words *Nine, one, one* appeared on the screen. Another positioning of controls changed the screen into a display of wavy and jagged lines transposed on a grid.

"What is this thing?" Glidden asked.

"A spectrogram."

"I know *that*. The equipment, what's its name?"

"This is the Portable Voiceprint Two-Thousand Spectrograph," Donegan reported. "As the name implies, it's totally portable and can, in fact, be utilized within the courtroom while a witness is testifying."

"It really doesn't look very portable," Becky observed.

"It is," Charlie said, "if you're seven feet tall."

"Aaron," Sherm broke in, "perhaps it would be helpful to all of us if you'd refresh our memories about voiceprints."

The giant struck a stance one would expect at the lectern.

"Basically, the spectrograph is like a human listener in performing aural identification through the use of a memory process which stores information on the perceptual features of the talker voice: pitch, melodic pattern, rhythm, quality, and respiratory grouping. Of course there are a number of intratalker variables such as changes in the acoustical characteristics because of physiological and/or psychological factors. In the cybernetic model a series of neuromotor impulses are codified and correlated—"

"Whoa!" Sherm held up his hand. "In lay terms, please."

"It means your voice is like a fingerprint," Charlie put in, "and we've got a gadget that'll figure out who the print belongs to."

"The Portable Voiceprint Two Thousand is not only capable of analyzing and matching"—Donegan paused to pat the side of the case—"it can also tell who the voice belongs to if that voice is stored in a memory bank."

"So what are we looking at?"

Pointing a huge finger at the screen, Donegan explained as simply as he could, which was by no means simple, the various lines, what they stood for, their significance; then, by transposing the comparison tape, he showed how the real Eagan voice matched up with the first part of the 9-1-1 tape but not the second. He also pointed out the "spurious tape signal"; and, by replacing one of the tapes, demonstrated the similarities of the "duplicate scalloping at the ends of words" in both the "Eagan" call Sherm received and the second part of the 9-1-1 tape, proof that both were synthesized by the same cybernetic model.

"So who is this cybernetic model?"

"Not necessarily 'who'; it could be an electronic voice synthesizer." The giant turned to Becky. "I was told by Charlie that you play tournament bridge."

"Why yes; do you?"

"Hold on," Sherm interjected. "Are there such things?" Donegan gave him his pike look. "As tournaments?"

"Electronic voice synthesizers?"

"They're available in discount stores, Sherm, programmed to teach a variety of skills, some the size of calculators."

"What I meant was something that doesn't go *bleep-bleep*, a machine that actually imitates voices."

"One of the best is being developed at AZTECH, a synthesizer with a potential exceeding the forty-four English phonemes which so limit our native speech."

"A robot Rich Little?"

Donegan was not amused. "I wouldn't call it that."

"If this synthesizer was used to imitate, say Shelly Eagan, could you tell?"

"If it was in the data bank, the Voiceprint Two Thousand would identify it as the source. Unfortunately, AZTECH's defense contracts have tied up the synthesizer, for the time being at least."

"Do you know why?"

"It's all very classified; however, I worked on a voice 'thing' for the Air Force. All I'm permitted to say is that it had to do with authenticating coded messages." Donegan turned again to Becky. "To answer your question, Mrs. Sherman, I do not play duplicate bridge. I will, however, definitely teach myself when time permits."

Miles asked Donegan how he figured the timing was engineered so it matched the responses from the officer manning the 9-1-1 number.

"Simple." Donegan demonstrated by using the soft-touch pause control on the cassette player. "Which is also the reason there was no background sound. You see, there was no conversation, only statements."

"The control was held depressed until the officer finished, then released to allow the next part to play?"

"Correct."

"Why do you suppose Shelly Eagan made a recording of an attempted break-in? I mean, the first part matches her real voice."

"Mr. Purdy, I know of no scientific method of determining motive, but the voice in the beginning unquestionably matches the caller in the Dorothy Eagan incident."

"According to Knight and his girlfriend, Shelly was involved in the production of X-rated videos that appear to be missing. Could it be, one of the missing videos might contain the same voice sequence as the first part of the nine-one-one tape?"

Could be, Donegan granted; but Glidden was having none of it, saying he thought it unlikely that the victim was an accomplice to her own murder.

Sherm turned on Glidden. "Damn it, Marc, it's too convenient to dump everything on McCreedy. Nobody I've talked to thinks he would've had the guts or the brains. From all indications he was a two-bit hood who liked to play around with things that go *boom*—and what about the call we got at the house from this very same 'cybernetic model'? McCreedy couldn't have placed it because he was already dead."

Nodding thoughtfully, the county attorney got up. "I won't deny there are some loose ends." He extended his hand toward Sherm. "But I'm sure they'll be cleared up."

"Sure they will," Sherm muttered as soon as Glidden was out of the office.

Donegan's interest had returned to Becky.

"Mrs. Sherman," he said, "an acquaintance of mine is competing in the tournament. Her last name is Ammar."

A flash of surprise passed between Becky and Sherm. "We know the Ammars," she said.

"I believe Jelila and her twin—Najib, his name is—are expert players, professionals practically."

"They've certainly given us a trouncing or two," Becky said. "But you're wrong, Mr. Donegan."

His pike eyes peered at her.

"Ms. Ammar's name is Majida, not Jelila."

"Oh, that. No, I'm certain, Mrs. Sherman. We attended Stanford. Jelila sat in front of me in graduate school and when I spied her at AZTECH, she responded to the name. It's spelled *J-e-l-i-l-a*."

"Well, when she's playing bridge she calls herself Majida, *M-a-j-i-d-a*."

"Majida-Jelila?" Charlie shook his head. "Why not something down-home, like Candy Bear?"

"That was something-or-other's name!" Sherm laughed. "Like you say, the first thing to go." Becky looked at him like he'd already lost it. "The star of the blue classic I told you about."

"Oh, that classic."

"Now there," Charlie said wistfully, "was a cybernetic model."

"These twins," Miles asked, "are they Arabian?"

"Algerian."

"Which may explain the names. They're probably Moslem. A classmate of mine had four: Habib Farouk Ben Bacaar."

Sherm turned to Charlie. "What'd she call herself when Ace interviewed her?"

"She's listed on the report as Majida."

They were waiting for the elevator when Sherm remembered something he'd forgotten. He'd be right back, he said. Becky urged him to hurry or they wouldn't have time to eat.

215

He went straight for the office closet and, sure enough, it was on the hook where he'd left it God knows how many years back. He shook out the dust, put the trench coat on, and returned to the elevator.

"What on earth is that for?"

"Two purposes," Sherm explained. "First, to keep me from freezing to death; second, in case we qualified, for the ultimate in intimidating apparel."

"You're learning the game," Becky said as the elevator door opened.

25
Double Dummy

Stopping at the Saguaro meant walking in the rain two blocks out of their way with the distinct possibility of being held up and late again; so they chose the tournament buffet for whatever was left, fairly certain they hadn't qualified for the second round. By the time they arrived, the players had pretty much cleared themselves and the food out; and in their dismay at the selection of wilted vegetables, lumpy macaroni salad, and soggy chicken, they hadn't noticed that the other late diner was their favorite director.

When it came to meting out bridge justice, he was the one invariably called on, but Lionel really reminded Becky of a jolly Saint Bernard. He stood flat on one foot, the other pointed down, surveying the unwholesome debris of plates, silverware, and cups for space enough to accommodate himself and his three dishes. When Becky called his name and he saw who it was, he broke out his Harpo Marx grin and asked them to join him. Their pleasure, but they would have to clear off a table themselves before they could join anyone. They stacked the dishes on adjacent tables and Sherm kept the pink record that showed all of the hands they'd played, which someone had left behind.

"What a way to live," Lionel said when they were finally seated. "I swear the food was better in the Army."

"I didn't know you were in the Army," Becky said.

"I don't know any man my age who wasn't."

"Our daughter's in the Army," Sherm said, "but she's getting out."

"Good for her." Lionel prepared to launch a frontal assault on the macaroni salad. "I saw you on the news."

"That was us," Becky admitted.

"That must've been something!" During his first mouthful, Lionel noted that the black eye was looking better and, with a slight fork jab in the direction of the pink sheet Sherm had folded and placed beside his cup, remarked that the hands had been so awful it was a wonder anyone qualified.

"We're not sure we did."

"Oh, you qualified." Lionel scooped up another load of macaroni. "I made up tonight's player lists."

Sherm wasn't particularly joyous, feeling as though he were still hanging onto the edge of the lifeboat.

"I'm supposed to be impartial—" The director lowered his voice. "But by golly there are lots of jerks here I'd like to see you beat."

"I hope you've noticed they all still have their socks on."

Lionel wiped his mouth with a paper cocktail napkin. "Don't underestimate yourselves; you have something going for you not many pairs have, balance."

"In the fourth seat," Becky quipped.

"Seriously, half the players are on some sort of ego trip, and so are the other half."

"That doesn't leave many."

"Two." Lionel glanced around. "Play it cool and you guys could win it all."

"We'll try." Sherm unfolded the pink hand record. "When do you receive these?"

Lionel tried a suspicious look but acting was not in his nature. "You want to buy tonight's hands?"

"You have them already?"

"Yup." Lionel rested his fork. "They're in a sealed case locked in the hotel safe. We don't actually get our mitts on the computer sheets used to duplicate the hands till it's time to play."

"Peter thinks we need all the help we can get." Becky glanced at the trench coat draped over the back of an empty chair. "The latest in intimidating apparel."

"I'm naturally curious is all." Which wasn't entirely untrue. Although suspicions concerning the twins' winning ways had been flirting with his thoughts, with the director at his elbow he was grabbing the opportunity to learn those aspects of the game's mechanics he'd been only vaguely familiar with.

"If you think there's hanky-panky going on I can assure you there is; but only in the hotel rooms after the game." Lionel gulped the cold coffee. "As I was saying, the computer hands for each round are not removed from locked storage until just before that round."

"And where do you get them—I mean originally?"

"They're transmitted via satellite to our tournament computer, which prints them out."

"When?"

"Usually in the morning, an hour or so before the first round of each day."

"Something else, are pairs allowed to switch positions? For

example, can a player be east at one table and, when east-west moves, be west at the next?"

"Not really, but why would they want to be?"

"Let's say they're superstitious about the way the bathtub—"

"Peter, let the poor man eat." Becky wagged her finger. "Let this be a lesson, Lionel, never invite a lawyer to your table."

"I'll remember." He glanced at his watch. "I've got to hurry. There are still things to be done." In an impressive flurry of eating, Lionel finished and wished them luck.

When he was gone, Becky said she'd had enough and wouldn't he like to check the results. He would, and after a quick stop at respective rest rooms, they returned to the playing area, where the afternoon's scores were posted on a wall near the director's table. And sure enough, there was pair 104, bottom qualifier in section D, fourth from bottom overall. What was surprising was the performance of the redoubtable twins, who'd outscored them by a mere six points. Fifty-two pairs had qualified and the Shermans occupied an unenviable forty-ninth; yet the Ammars, with only a six point lead, were twenty-one slots ahead in twenty-eighth.

"This means we're still in contention," Becky said. "To stay in it, all we have to do is finish in the top twenty-six—oh good!"

"What's the 'oh good' for?"

"We don't have to play the twins; they're east-west too." She motioned him to follow her to section A, table thirteen.

"Good old lucky thirteen," he muttered as he put on his trench coat. "Pray for a miracle."

Before the evening ended, Sherm found himself very nearly believing in miracles. Or lucky numbers. Or trench coats. Their game was a barn burner, a monster, the World's Fair. They'd speared the sharks in their own waters and couldn't wait to get by themselves to share their elation. No way could they have missed qualifying for the semifinal round, they told each other more than once. And they were right. As Lionel tallied the scores on the computer, it became obvious that this session they were out in front and pulling away, and when their miserable afternoon score was added, they still held a respectable second place finish in their section. When the two sections were totaled they came in third overall. But the amazing bit of information was the names of the first place finishers, Najib and Majida Ammar.

"Incredible!" Sherm made for the table where the yellow second round hand records were stacked, and carried one to where the score sheets were posted. He located the twins in the left hand column and scanned across the sheet showing the first session results. He found board sixteen. The fantastic twins had gone down the same as they had. The rest of the afternoon had progressed as poorly. In fact, the six points they'd beaten them by came on a hand they overbid and should've collected a near-bottom score. In the first round the Ammars played many of the uninspiring hands worse than they did.

Not in the second round. In the second round the twins did well on tricky part score hands, the same kinds they'd played so poorly in the afternoon.

"Look at board nine. They bid game, four hearts, while nearly everyone else made only two." Becky ran her finger down the column. "Here's a three heart bid and a one, but no other fours. Five extra match points right there; what luck!"

"Or like me and the Sunday bridge column." Sherm examined the hand record. West had to go for south's singleton queen to drop on a fake finesse to east's dummy hand, an illogical play because it risked a bottom score if it failed. More important, east should have opened with fourteen high card points and six hearts. West's hand included the three and five of hearts, a five card spade suit headed by the ace-queen, and no points in the three-three minor suits. The only way west could have gotten the bid was by means of an illegal transfer signal or by claiming a psychic bid, which was legal but absurd with this holding. The Ammars were the only pair in either section who bid the heart game the only way it could be made, in the west.

Had Becky seen which one played west?

Majida, she thought; then, no, Sherm was right. At the corner table she was west, but at the last table Becky was certain she'd switched to east.

Like Lionel said, why would they want to?

"When we're east-west," Sherm said, "I'm always east."

"Habit, I think."

"Something else I noticed, when we played north-south during qualifications, was that Majida usually played the impossible hands."

"She's a woman."

"Sexist."

"People could accuse us too. There were at least three boards I lucked out on."

"Here's another, board twenty-two."

Twenty-two looked like another double dummy result. But how? There were thirty-two boards in all, and (as it had been with the Bruner presumption) there simply was not time enough to study 128 hands, 1,664 cards and come up with the certain number of hands that could be double-dummied to advantage, then memorize them.

"This isn't the first time we've seen remarkable improvement in their second session play." Sherm rubbed his chin, trying to figure out from what Lionel had told them how the hands could've been studied between sessions.

"You know what they say about twins and ESP."

"Yeah, one peek's worth a thousand ESPs."

"That's not how it goes; and look how long it's taken us to figure out these two hands with the scores posted and a hand record in our laps. There just wouldn't be time between rounds to double-dummy, unless . . ."

"Unless what?"

"Unless Majida has some sort of photographic memory. Mr. Donegan might know."

"He didn't even get her name right." Sherm stepped back, bumping into someone. Lionel.

"I see the trench coat worked." He winked. "See you tomorrow, and good luck with the game."

Against the power of the twins, Sherm knew, they would need all they could get. Still, he couldn't get the word out of his mind: *game*.

Game.

Bridge was a game, just a game, all a game. So why was it so important to him, to them, to everyone?

And what about everything else that had happened: murder, rape, bombings, mixed identities, a call from a dead girl? Was all of this a game, just a game, all a game?

Double dummy . . . double dummy . . . double . . .

Could someone, somebody, something be seeing all the hands at once?

26

The Colorado Plateau

Filthy liquid whirlpool of green algae and formless debris, and suddenly they're squeezing through the canyon, the sides of the boat inches from the red sandstone on either side; and it is horribly cold, and he knows he will never be picked out of the water in time, that the Game is indeed over, for he is being dragged down, the CO_2 out of his Mae West, then the sound of paddle blades whacking the bare ass of Mother Luck, and looking up he sees Mickey Rooney grinning from under the shamrock green tophat, and in the hatch opening someone he knows is calling down, and even above the sound of the helicopter blades he hears, "Hang on, we'll save you. We'll save you, Dad—"; and when he awakens he's on a cot in a tent on the Colorado Plateau, and he knows it is snowing, and Becky will be along shortly to take him home because this has happened before; and finally he really is awake.

A dream within a dream, the law of seriality, events ubiquitous and continuous, the acausal at work, the game repeating itself.

Numbers, everywhere numbers: cards, computers, telephones . . .

It was barely daylight and he needed all the sleep he could get to be sharp and able to handle the . . . numbers.

You're up there, aren't you, you little son of a bitch, somewhere in the attic of the mind, hiding in a clutter of broken furniture and discarded toys? You, you numerical bastard, pushing us around like you were a—what did Miles say it was called, a planchette?

He tried to go back to sleep, but when he closed his eyes Vic was waiting and sleep was not possible, so he got up so as not to disturb Becky and hit the road.

It was cool and color was beginning to tint the high terrain, a touch of rust up near Finger Rock, the piñon thicket that had been an inkblot taking on green. Soon there would be no hiding places for ghosts—except in the head, where they already were.

Ridding the mind of ghosts was not easy. About all one could do was work his Pac-Man through the maze of life gobbling as many as possible, or avoid them completely; except that those chubascos of the brain, dreams, kept bringing them back. So here he was, again running from the ghost and the guilt he would never escape.

Who encouraged Vic to take flying lessons, insisted it would build his confidence, make him independent, teach him to think when the going got rough? Who claimed flying was a better prep than the classroom for the courtroom? Sherm knew *who*. And he knew who never should've handed the keys over, that it was an irresponsible act, that his boy had never soloed over so great a distance and never over such hostile terrain.

Still, Vic was an excellent pilot and the Skyhawk was new. An excellent pilot in a new airplane with the best in radio-navigation equipment, was that irresponsible?

Yet he was lost over the . . .

A year, one year spent in searching the . . . searching from the air and seeing all of the . . . forests and canyons of the . . . combing the wilderness on foot—

Shoes pattering against macadam, on and on and on to the . . . Sherm slowed. If he kept this pace he would burn himself out and there was a long way to go, a long way to the . . . a long way to unblock the circuits, to release the thoughts, to face up to what really happened, to release the guilt, to the . . .

"Damn!" Sherm cried out. "Get rid of this ghost!"

To the *Colorado Plateau*:

It started off as his fault. He'd built a case no mortal could handle in the time he allowed and when it came time to go skiing he was still tied up in court. It was their condo in Telluride so it didn't matter whether or not they made a particular schedule. Sherm simply picked up the phone and called Riley, the manager, and said they would be a week late. Riley said the snow wasn't much anyway, that they were running additional buses from the north side to get people back to town. You could get down via The Plunge, Riley chuckled, if you didn't mind a few rocks toward the bottom. No thanks, Sherm replied. For The Plunge he needed plenty of snow to cushion his falls. Vic didn't, and although he didn't complain, Sherm could see the disappointment. Christmas vacation had come at the end of the first semester of law school and he'd been working like a very busy beaver, looking forward to this ski trip probably more than any they'd taken. Now it was being delayed by a crummy case that should've been over in a week.

His client was not only guilty of murdering his wife, he was outright proud he'd done so. On the stand he said she'd made too many people miserable too long and deserved exactly what she got, three point-blank blasts from his Browning automatic shotgun. Yet the case dragged on, the young assistant county attorney striving to keep his own name in the news as long as possible. "Where else can I advertise?" he'd had the guts to say, to which Sherm replied that if he didn't end the case soon he was going to get plenty of free publicity as the victim of another homicide.

While Vic maintained radio silence about the delay, Becky was not so kind. She actually nagged, telling him he should bring in one of the firm's younger partners, that the only reason he was hanging on was because he, not the prosecutor, was on an ego trip. Sherm argued that she was not only being unfair but patently stupid. Why on earth would anyone wish to have his name linked with the hopeless defense of a self-confessed murderer? Which was exactly why he wouldn't turn it over to anyone else; his personal ethic wouldn't permit it.

Calling Becky stupid *was* stupid. It hurt her deeply and launched their worst fight ever. It began vocally but soon progressed to silent rage. To make matters worse, even though he was aware of the insult, he misinterpreted her silence, which angered him and made him think of his family—all except Heather who was off in New York State skiing with her friends from Wells—as the spoiled rich who pout whenever they don't get their way. At one point Becky's icy anger became so intense Sherm briefly commiserated with his client.

In this spirit the trip began.

Except for occasional radio chatter, the flight to Montrose and the seventy-mile drive to Telluride were indeed quiet, and it was only after skiing that he finally admitted it was stupid of him not to have planned for a time-bumper in case the trial lasted longer than expected. He went so far as to offer Vic fatherly advice for when he became an attorney, not to follow his father's example, to always allow time for his family. Vic responded by saying he didn't think he'd ever get married—which drew a "now see what you've done" from Becky.

That Vic was with them at all was a last minute concession on his part. Because Christmas vacation ended in the middle of the week, he would have to report back to school on Thursday. That gave him a maximum of two days skiing. Fly up Sunday, ski Monday and Tuesday, back on Wednesday, to school on Thursday. Selfishly, Sherm first tried to persuade Vic to ditch Thursday and Friday. Two days, he argued, wouldn't hurt anything—which he knew wasn't true. In law school every day counted. Missing two could mean flunking out. Then the brilliant plan hit him. Vic could solo back home Wednesday, and—what time were classes out Friday? Ten o'clock. Good, that gave Vic time to get back up Friday. Sherm would drive him to the airport and pick him up. If they kept to their schedule they would have all day Saturday and half of Sunday on the slopes—and to be sure to bring his books so he could get in some studying on the way home.

Vic said he'd think about it, but it was easy to see the boy was tickled pink at the prospect of flying all by his lonesome over all that beautiful country. On the other hand, Becky openly questioned the wisdom of allowing anyone to go off by themselves over such a desolate land, especially in winter when one was always reading about airplanes icing up and crashing. So when it came time for Vic's departure from Telluride, as much as she probably would have enjoyed being away from her husband alone in the condominium at that particular time in their lives, Becky rode along to make sure they checked the weather. They left before sunup to catch the smooth early morning flying, not noticing until she brought it to their attention that there were no stars out. A gray, snowy sheet of middle clouds had moved in overnight and not too far to the north there was a cold front, an ugly snow-packed wall of clouds no person in a light plane in his right mind would fly through. Fortunately, Vic was headed south.

They called Grand Junction Flight Service for the enroute weather. It looked pretty good if he left right away. Some light snow over the Colorado Plateau, good visibility and ceilings except in the vicinity of Tucson. There would be low clouds approaching home, possibly light rain showers. Stay away from the light rain, Sherm warned as Vic completed his preflight, the aircraft's skin will be like a metal ice tray out of the freezer. Water hits it and *ptew* it turns to glaze ice.

"And airplanes don't fly well carrying a load of ice," Becky added.

Vic had laughed, for this was an adventure he wouldn't let a pair of quarreling old fogies spoil. Not even his mother's nervousness dampened his spirits. He told her to be careful not to break any legs, that if she did, two was the limit. And Becky instructed her son to be sure to call as soon as he landed and Vic answered with the last words he would speak face-to-face with either of them, "Sure Mom, close out my flight plan with FAA *and* Mrs. Peter Sherman."

Becky was nervous before he took off, but once the airplane was in the air and she could see him in the clear underneath the clouds as he went out of sight over the hills, she relaxed and was even downright friendly for the first time in over a week as they talked over coffee and cookies from the airport vending machines. Her good humor lasted the twenty-seven miles to the 62 turnoff, fading rapidly as they started up the Dallas Divide and the snow that had begun in spits and spurts thickened so that by the summit, driving was like trying to hold onto a live trout and Sherm thought he'd have to pull over and put on chains. Once over the top it slackened and he didn't need chains after all. He saw out of the corner of his eye Becky dipping into her valium bottle. It didn't help.

"Look," he said, trying to calm her, "Vic's well down the road by now, past Tuba City, I'll bet. He's a good pilot, experienced in mountain flying. Shoot, I remember the time—"

"Shut up, will you!"

It kept on snowing all the way to Telluride and the road got so bad Sherm finally had to put on chains, a job he hated, made worse by the fact that there never was a chain invented that fit quite right, and the absence of snow clothing, which he'd left in the condo. When he got back into the car Becky was glaring at him as though stopping to put on chains had been the wrong thing to do; but it wasn't chains that brought on the scowl. "You never should have let him get in that airplane and take off," she hissed.

She resumed her role of silent sentinel and Sherm gave up trying to communicate. It would be useless, he knew, until they were back in the condo and got the phone call that her son had landed safely. She knew what time to expect the call. She'd made a point of writing down Vic's ETA and added to it, ten minutes for taxiing in, another ten for postflight and tie down, a final ten to get to the telephone, thirty minutes in all.

Vic's ETA passed. The thirty minutes came and went. "Nobody can be that precise," Sherm said. "There could've been headwinds he hadn't counted on—" Becky wasn't glaring any more. Her worst fears were coming true with each tick of the clock: thirty-five, forty, fifty minutes. Nearly an hour and no word. Outside, the storm had reached blizzard proportions. Sherm pitched another log onto the fire. He went to the window: complete whiteout; what powder tomorrow! He turned, believing what he was about to say would make her think about something else. He knew Vic was all right; he just hadn't gotten to the phone, maybe met a good-looking girl at the airport and forgot. Or maybe he had to circle. There were low clouds in the vicinity and maybe a lot of inbound flights held him up. A million things could've kept him from making the call; so Sherm, trying to help out, said, "Tomorrow we'll have the greatest powder in the history of skiing."

"You self-serving—call home right now!"

As he reached for the phone it was an hour and five minutes past Vic's ETA and before he picked it up, it rang. "Sherman here." The operator wanted to know if he would accept charges and he said yes, by all means. But the caller wasn't Vic. It was a much older sounding man who asked if this was Peter Sherman, father of Victor Sherman, and his heart leapt into his throat: *the call in the night from the state trooper, the sheriff's deputy, the cop downtown, the call in the middle of the night.*

"Who the hell is this?" he shouted.

"Oh, my God," Becky choked.

"This is David Sheffield, Flight Service controller. I'm sorry this took so long but we've got a bushel of weather down this way and I just couldn't call sooner."

"What happened?"

"Your son had to land at an Air Force auxiliary strip short of destination. That was about the only place he could get into without going IFR. After he got down he radioed a request for us to give you a ring to let you know everything is okay."

"Everything's all right?"

"Yes. He's going to sack out in the plane overnight and take off at first light, weather permitting. He said to tell you he took on fuel at Winslow so he has plenty. Sounds like you got a good pilot there, Mr. Sherman."

"Thank you, thank you for calling." Sherm let out a long sigh of relief. "And yes, Vic is very good."

As it turned out, the blizzard at Telluride wasn't associated with the cold front to the north so much as with moisture being pumped into the Southwest by a disturbance off Baja, the same weather that forced Vic to land at the auxiliary field.

The next morning he called from school and talked to his mother. He'd gotten home okay and was really excited to hear about the blizzard, hoping it would clear up and they'd have the runway shoveled out by his Friday ETA. He looked forward to taking The Plunge with his dad and at least once, the three of them together would ski See Forever. Becky told Sherm all of this going up on the Coonskin chair lift after an early lunch. By then the blizzard had abated considerably. You couldn't see forever but you could see the person in front of you.

They were on the slopes all afternoon and by evening the battle was over. If not lovers, they were at least friends again. They had a fine rack of lamb at a fine old wild West-type restaurant, a good bottle of light red wine, and a bracing walk back to the condo.

Vic's call awoke them early. The sun had barely come up. Sherm rubbed a clear patch in the ice so he could see out. Mist was rising from the stream, the only space not humped with great mounds of fresh snow. The good news lay overhead. He could see Venus low on the valley horizon in the cleft between the steep mountainsides. The sky was absolutely cloudless. CAVU: ceiling and visibility unlimited. Perfect flying weather. That was good news, Vic said, but his heart wasn't in the statement. He liked challenge. It was adventurous to fly through sleet and hail and dark of night. It was boring to bore holes in a limitless sky, droning on hour after hour—except that the sky between there and here was over some of the least boring land on earth, the Colorado Plateau, and Vic loved every square meter of its kaleidoscopic desert, brooding mountains, and gaping canyons. And today would be a perfect day to see it all.

"This school gives you so much work," Vic said, "that I won't be doing much socializing. Fact is, I'm bringing along enough books to keep me up all night—but complaining isn't the reason for this call." He said they would have to pick him up at Cortez. The airport was farther south, more out on the open plain away from the mountain effect, and received less snow. They were still shoveling at Montrose and he didn't want to arrive and not be able to land.

Cortez meant a shorter flight and slightly longer drive, which also included a higher mountain pass. It also meant making arrangements for the car. All of this could be handled. He told Vic the skiing was nothing short of fantastic. Vic said he'd wear his long underwear to class so he wouldn't waste time once he got there and maybe he could get in a couple of runs before the lifts closed down. Maybe, Sherm said, he could bribe a lift operator into running just a bit longer. He didn't have to worry about Vic getting lost on the mountain; he knew it better than most people know the inside of their car. Vic gave him his tentative ETA and said he would see him later. "We'll take The Plunge, Dad, and this time I'll wait for you."

Vic never got the chance. Something happened out there they were never able to find out about; nor could they even guess at with any degree of certainty. It wasn't the weather.

231

Later they would learn about the Twin Comanche that had iced up and crashed trying to do what Vic had wisely avoided on his trip home, one of those once-a-winter desert storms when you can't see the mountains for two days. He'd handled that.

What Vic didn't handle (for whatever reason) was one of those perfect days when the sky is so blue when you look up you think you're at the edge of outer space, when the air is so crisp it almost squeaks and your shoes do squeak when you walk on snow, a day as can only exist in the imagination of a poet or in the Colorado Rockies. It was the kind of weather that lifts the spirits so high only the greatest of calamities can bring them down.

The ride to Cortez was a little slick but who cared: our vibrant, incredible boy is flying to ski with us, to go up the many lifts to the summit of the world to *See Forever* as we ski down. Sherm didn't even mind taking off the chains when they hit the bare macadam just outside Cortez. He unsnapped them with a flair, clapped his hands together and said to himself what a goddamn beautiful day! And Becky, in spite of her only son being up in an environment hostile to the wingless, seemed about to bubble over. It was the weather, of course, and something else too. This trip was marking the end to a war that had raged the better part of two weeks, the worst they'd ever gone through, and now it was over. Peace was declared, which was enough to make anyone bubble.

Becky kept her spirits even when the plane was a little late, and she still showed no outward concern after the same length of time after his ETA that she'd nearly gone into hysteria over two nights before. When he was an hour late, Sherm called Flight Service.

What he heard sank his heart.

Vic had landed at Winslow, taken on fuel, and was off ten minutes ahead of schedule. He called in a position report, Victor-210 at Round Rock Intersection, and notified FAA he would be detouring to the west of his intended course to take a look at Monument Valley, and to go ahead and close out his flight plan. That was the last call anyone was sure he made.

Sherm went back to the car where Becky was sitting, still quite cool. Vic was probably sight-seeing, she said, without him even telling her what he knew. It was too beautiful a day not to. Sherm glanced at his watch. How many hours of fuel left? Plenty if he filled his tanks. And maybe Vic *was* sight-seeing. Sure sounded like it. He told Becky what the controller said. "See, I told you." She was busy with her eternal, infernal knitting. "Vic'll show up any minute."

But the hourglass ran out.

Even now, with the sound of his feet pad-padding on the foothill macadam he could feel what he'd felt that day on the Colorado Plateau and for a long time afterward; a great pressure against his chest as though there were something wadded up, waiting to be spit out.

Becky had let it out all at once, an hour-long weeping jag; then it was pretty much over and there were "arrangements" to be made, Heather to be called back from Wells. Poor Heather, she adored her brother. Indeed she did. She didn't let up the whole time she was around, and after returning to college she wrote that it would be a long time before she would be able to face home without Vic, then the telephone call that she'd decided to join the Army.

"For Christ's sake, why the Army?"

"Because they offered me a commission and I accepted it."

In spite of his prediction that Heather wouldn't last a week, she'd lasted five years. When she came back would she still be afraid?

Of what? Reminders? Memories? A ghost?

Nonsense, Heather was too much like her father to be haunted by ghosts. She knew there was always an explanation, a rationale, a causal relationship between perception and perceiver—

Bullshit, wasn't it a ghost that kept you like a madman up there on the Colorado Plateau, kept you after all reasonable time limits had passed. Expecting what? To find Vic like some sort of airborne Robinson Crusoe shacked up in a wickiup fucking away the winter? Maybe you thought he'd crashed into a cave where he was warm and well-fed. Is that what you were thinking when you were up there on the Colorado Plateau and the newspapers (lunatic themselves) were making you some sort of a hero? Did you think he might've crashed into Lake Powell and taken up residence on a small island tucked away in a sandstone canyon where he could live on fish caught on lures fashioned from fragments of the plane's skin? Hadn't the both of you lain awake nights in your sleeping bags by campfires talking about survival? Hadn't you even talked about the men who cannibalized each other in the Andes and hadn't Vic given you a list of reasons why what they did was stupid? Hadn't he done that? So he could've been alive out there somewhere, alive and healthy, waiting for someone to come along and take him home. God, you had that feeling. You weren't looking for a ghost; Vic was alive.

When the FAA began its search, Sherm tagged along, cajoling them, praising them, swearing at them, doing anything he could to keep them in the air searching. He told them about Vic's survival know-how, and once when one of the pilots commented that the temperature had gotten down to thirty-six below on the Plateau the night before, Sherm recalled Vic's remark about long underwear. The pilot responded with a look Sherm couldn't understand at the time.

When the FAA pulled out, he leased an entire flying service and hired pilots from other airports in and around the Plateau, those who'd accept his money. Many wouldn't. They knew he was wasting his time and they didn't want to take advantage of a man when he was down. And he asked everyone who planned to fly over the region to keep an eye out for a red and white Cessna Skyhawk.

Where could it be, in the snow? In the snow! After the spring thaw, there he'd be, kept alive by his survival know-how, and they'd say he kept his life by his own hand. Get it, *kept* his life?

Sherm was not mad yet because he was aware what he was doing was.

Spring came and the snow ran off as water or evaporated; then summer, bone-bleaching, brain-baking summer that had over the eons so dried the land that even the wind could sculpture stone into bridges. And when summer had turned to fall and the season was swinging back to the time of year Vic was lost, even then Sherm persisted. True madness indeed.

He threw away nearly everything they'd saved for: vacation condo, certificates, bonds, real estate investments; every piece of change he could get his hands on, even the bit Becky had put into insurance from teaching while he was finishing law school.

Everything went into the search.

There were days when light planes blanketed the Plateau and days later when the same aircraft would be out covering the same ground. The pilots (he knew even then) were shaking their heads behind his back while the press was breathing unwarranted confidence into his escapade, calling him a "true-life tragic American figure"; and even as the stories became single column additions to the classifieds, they gave the impression that somehow this man could succeed. To fail would be unthinkable after such persistence. And when he succeeded, the reporters assured him, they would be there and his story would pay well. So he didn't worry when he began cashing in his life insurance policies; it would all work out.

What worked out was that Becky finally put a stop to his madness.

It was a very cold night in the Kaibab Forest on the North Rim of the Grand Canyon and, since he could not afford much else, he was living alone in a tent, a bearded, unwashed recluse. Each day he would go out alone, tramping through the forest, expecting any moment to spot the aluminum that had once been their Skyhawk there in the woods with a lean-to nearby, a smoldering campfire, and maybe one of those big Kaibab bucks strung up in a tree, half butchered. And Vic would step out of the lean-to, a beard halfway to his balls and give his dad a big grin, laughing, maybe crying a little, asking if he was ready to take The Plunge.

When Becky showed up, Sherm argued that Vic had always been an adventurous soul, that it was not inconceivable he might have altered course just to fly down the canyon, right?

Wrong.

For nearly a year Becky had been trying to hold things together while he kept throwing them away, though at first she'd blamed herself for his actions because of the way she'd placed the burden of guilt on him even before the accident, so when it happened it all came down at once like an avalanche. She realized this and understood, but enough was enough, she said as they shivered in the Kaibab night; it was time to go home.

So they started out, driving as far as the Wahweap Lodge on Lake Powell that first night. And the next morning he said there was one more thing he needed to do. Vic once bet he could fly a plane under Rainbow Bridge. It was December and cold and Sherm hired a fifty-foot tour boat to take the two of them to the great stone arch where he looked down into the green water, seeing a reflection of himself, the bridge, and a stone slab that seemed to slide into eternity, and he felt saddened, and Becky cried, and it was a waste of time because it was December and cold and there were only two of them.

They stayed for Christmas and watched as the Indian girls painted the windows that looked out from the restaurant over the lake, water paintings of Santa Clauses and Christmas trees, snowflakes and holly, candles and toys—and Sherm remembered a little boy wanting a train for Christmas—and the carols on the Muzak made Becky cry, so the day after Christmas they left in a snowstorm that looked as though it would never end.

The Colorado Plateau had swallowed his son and he knew he would never be the same again. It'd taken too much out of him, deprived him of that part of his sanity most reasonable, for there were no reasons, not even a clue. The experience had left him considerably older but no wiser. For a long time he cared about nothing and no one. He read and jogged, and sometimes late at night would listen to cassettes Vic recorded in high school. He didn't work and when he did go back it was only to counsel. Three years went by before he took his first case. He was a long time coming back (if indeed he'd yet arrived) and was afraid some of the madness still hung on.

The experience had taken much of him, yet it had also given him a slight reprieve. Up on the Colorado Plateau he'd grown lean and tough. Now he wasn't so lean and not nearly as tough, but he wasn't falling apart either. Now he did a lot of jogging. He wanted to keep as lean and tough as he could. He'd given up those activities that used to keep him that way: tennis, skiing, backpacking, all the things he and Vic did together. They'd never jogged; there were too many other things to do.

Lean and tough . . . lean and tough . . . feet against the macadam . . . legs pumping . . . lean and tough—

Now he had the feeling he got every once in a while that

he was training for something big, a heavyweight match, but the only thing he could think of was back on the Colorado Plateau, the old madness. So here he was alone on the street training for something he wasn't sure of, unless it was the battle against fatness and flab, feebleness and senility. Against dying? Or was he out here running away from something, a dream, a lost son—

Not *lost*. There was no bearded, laughing young man about to step out of a lean-to on the Colorado Plateau, no young man at all, no son. He wasn't lost; he was dead.

Sherm pulled up, that awful pressure in his chest again. He wobbled to the side of the road, looking around. Where was he? How long had he been running?

How many minutes of fuel were left?

He sank to the boulder alongside the road, slowly raising his hands to cover his face. The damned thing was coming up and he could feel himself taking the plunge again; then he heard the throaty midengine growl and looked up to see the Fiat coming over the rise.

She stopped the car across from where he was sitting, got out and came over, stooping in front of him. His hands were on his knees and she patted them.

"I heard you call out Vic's name." She looked down. "I thought it might be better if you jogged it off."

"So why did you come after me?"

"I got worried." She slumped to the rock beside him. "It's after six."

"After six? I've been out here two hours?"

"You're miles from home."

"How'd you find me?"

"Old *shortest* distance. Are you up to handling the rest of today?"

"I don't know."

She got out her handkerchief and shared it. "Sweetie, call it luck or whatever, this is our first time in a major tournament that we have a chance to win, but we have to be sharp; so what say we head home and go back to bed for a couple of hours?"

"Yeah, sure."

"And we need to talk about Vic."

"I'm not sure."

"We've got to, Sherm." Becky bit her lip. "We . . . we've never even held . . . held a memorial service."

"We will," Sherm said finally, "as soon as Heather's home."

27

Flying Fenders

Until Becky reminded him, he'd forgotten that the Sunday tournament started earlier so the out-of-towners could arrive home before time to get up for work; and in his haste to shower and dress in an absolute minimum of time, he made an unfortunate choice of dark brown slacks, a pre-Beau purchase now severely matted with the familiar white hair of their favorite feline companion. He searched for the miracle brush when it would've been quicker to change pants, running them so late Becky said they wouldn't have time to stop for gas, so they'd have to take the Fiat. He grabbed his lucky trench coat. She looked like an Irish princess; he felt like a shag rug. Bad omen, but not the only one.

Becky was forced to pick the back lot again, square in the

middle of a model air show. It was raining and no airplanes were flying, but the director or whatever he was, came bounding over to the X1/9 with the notice that they would have to park elsewhere.

"We paid two bucks to park," Becky declared, "and we're not about to go looking"—she held up her watch—"when we have two minutes to make our game."

The ex-intimidator backed off. "Okay, but if your car is damaged, don't blame us."

Sherm would've as soon stayed to watch the SBD, P-47, F-16, two Pitts, and others that resembled only what they were supposed to be, radio-controlled models. The actions and volume of their pilots, huddled under a red, white, and blue drooping awning in the company of several cases of Coors, gave every indication that if it rained much longer, this would be *some* air meet.

With regret, he spread the trench coat over the both of them and they dashed. On time but no need for coats, trench or otherwise. Lionel was on the PA explaining that the air-conditioning would soon be in operation. Steaming, Sherm thought, was preferable to freezing and might even be a good omen. The ladies could put on sweaters but they would never remove their blouses.

What followed was the feeling Sherm got playing against blackjack dealers who bust hand after hand; and winning, he knew, was the second best feeling in the world. Even when the cards went sour and the Shermans were out of the bidding, it didn't matter; their defense was as flawless as their play. They were winning when the twins arrived at their table, Najib and Majida, who, except for a nod of recognition, were as darkly unresponsive as their black tuxedos. In icy, aloof silence they stared into their private nowhere, their mere presence lowering the temperature a good five degrees. It was intimidation and it was working.

Sherm rustled his trench coat but couldn't bring himself to

put it on, then began to fidget, picking at the bear hair clinging to his thighs as though it were growing there, dropping it half an arm's length away so it wouldn't come floating back like metal filings to a magnet. He'd managed to free himself of several clumps of the stuff before he noticed the hair had been drawn into another magnetic field, Majida's sharply creased, spotlessly black, left trouser leg.

For an instant Sherm considered saying something, but the game was beginning and he didn't wish to have the director called on him for whatever infraction was certain to occur if he opened his mouth. Besides, it gave him satisfaction to think of this automaton picking at her pants between rounds in a hopeless attempt to restore impeccability. The thought so pleased Sherm that he chuckled aloud, causing Najib to glance sharply in his direction and Becky to look at him with a puzzled expression. When he laughed a second time, Majida called the director.

Lionel listened patiently to the charge that it was not Sherm's turn to bid, therefore he should not have made the sounds he did. This time Becky laughed and said they were being ridiculous. Lionel's eyes indicated he agreed; nevertheless, he quoted the rule which barred Sherm from one round of bidding. As a result, the hand was passed out. The remaining two boards were played by the twins. The first had been the Shermans', so the result was bad. The second two looked to be average. After the play, Majida said she hoped Becky understood.

"I hope you understand you're an asshole," Becky replied.

Majida raised her eyebrows but said nothing, undoubtedly having heard this before.

The next pair were two blue-haired ladies who, in the few minutes before the boards arrived, revealed their names (Gladys and Peggy), that both were retired elementary school teachers, they loved Olivia Newton-John, thought Richard

Pryor was smutty, and wasn't it wonderful what the sheriff was doing?

The last got Sherm's attention. He asked *what*.

"Closing down the pornography places."

The blue-haired pair continued chatting off and on while administering the Shermans their first drubbing of the day, playing as though it were second nature, finishing before the other players, probably so they could chat without distraction. During this chitchat period, Sherm learned they were the runners-up from the Sunny Valley Bridge Center, that Denise and Beverly, the first placers, had already been eliminated, but that they were doing just fine, in fact could've won the session. Then one of them recognized him and was about to launch an enormous fuss over the issue of crime in the streets when a rather sharp rap flexed the windows high on the opposite wall.

Sherm thought it was probably a sonic boom.

A few minutes and several subjects later, the door by the director's table burst open and in flew another blue-haired lady who immediately planted her feet to search out the audience, then—spotting Gladys and Peggy—did a quick, high-heeled jog to their table, babbling in a high-pitched voice from several tables away about them never believing what happened.

Lionel barely caught up with her at the table, and holding his hands, palms out toward her, tried in his most diplomatic way to explain that this was a very important tournament, that many players had not yet finished, and she must hold down her voice. Lionel bowed, pulled an extra chair to the table, and held it for her. When she was seated, he put his finger to his mouth; then, with his big grin spreading, he turned and whispered so only Sherm and Becky could hear that she should not refer to other players as assholes. Becky blushed at being caught, but reminded him that Majida really was.

"I know," Lionel said, leaving.

"It was horrifying," the new arrival continued unabated. "I was never so scared in my—"

"This is Denise," Gladys said.

"She was knocked out yesterday," Peggy added.

"Better luck next year," Sherm said.

Becky asked what was so horrifying.

"An explosion!" Denise twisted in the general direction of the back parking lot.

"One of the model airplanes exploded?"

"No, no, a car. A little yellow car was blown all to pieces."

As they stood at the edge of the lot gaping at the scattered remnants of their X1/9, neither of them had ever felt so completely bewildered. A crowd had gathered, a few complaining because the area had been cordoned off by police who'd arrived immediately from the main station a block away. The complainers, mostly bridge players with dinner reservations that had to be driven to, couldn't get to their cars. In all there weren't twenty at their end of the back lot and only two near enough to have been damaged by the blast.

One of the officers came over to ask if anyone knew who the vehicle belonged to.

"It was ours," Becky said.

The officer began asking questions just as Kline came roaring in, lights flashing, siren winding down. He jumped out, apparently recognized the pieces, and when he'd spotted Sherm, came straight over, adjusting his gun belt while his other hand slid along the leading edge of his Stetson, saluting his fans. The sheriff was smiling but Sherm could tell he was angry.

"What the hell happened this time?"

"I believe we lost a car."

"You're lucky, damned lucky." Kline turned to survey the

wreckage, talking over his shoulder, "I'm beginning to believe you ought to be locked up for the safety and well-being of society."

"How about after the game?"

Kline spun around. "Game?"

"Bridge. We're in the tournament finals."

"After this, you want to—" Without another word, Kline made clear his view of Sherm's sanity.

"Tom, you're looking at me like I'm crazy. I'm not, but I was and this craziness I had is gone. At least I think it's gone. And you might say this game we're playing is a sort of coming-out party." Becky squeezed his hand. "It's our chance to prove we've still got our heads screwed on tighter than most people. We may not win but we'll sure give it a run; besides, I gave my solemn oath on a stack of Charlie Goren bridge books that we'd play come hell or high water."

Kline removed his hat and waved it across the scene of the wreckage. "There's your hell, and we sure as hell have high water." The river beyond was bank-full. "Every dry crossing in the county is running water, half are flooded, and I've got every spare deputy on barricades to keep the citizens from drowning themselves. This could be our hundred year flood."

"Unless it washes away the Convention Center, we're playing."

"If you're still around." Kline put his hat back on. "This bomber's missed twice and I wouldn't think the third time's necessarily charmed."

The city cop who'd questioned them trotted up with the news that they had the guy who detonated the bomb, but not the one who planted it.

"It was accidental." He pointed to the tall fellow surrounded by police and other pilots. "He said when it stopped raining he turned on his remote control and *kaboom*, just like that he was nicked by a piece of the car."

"A remote control detonator?"

"On the same frequency as the model plane."

"Try this," Sherm said, not believing a word of what he was about to say. "McCreedy planted the bomb but didn't live to set it off and today it was, purely by accident."

Kline wasn't buying. "The Friday night bomb was also remotely detonated and I don't think they hold model airplane meets in the dark, in porn shop parking lots."

"Okay, but whoever planted this bomb won't know it went off accidentally."

"He will now." Kline nodded toward the invasion of TV vehicles. "We've got to place you in protective custody; otherwise we're liable—"

"Hold on, have you forgotten the Miranda Decision?"

"Miranda? Are you all right? You're not being arrested or even charged—"

"Not that Miranda. The Mexican Mafia case. Mike Miranda and the right of the individual to reject the state's protection even under the most life-threatening circumstances."

Kline eyed him suspiciously.

"Las Vegas, 1983. Miranda refused the witness protection program, told the police bodyguards to get lost. They arrested him; he won in court."

"What happened to Miranda?"

"Murdered."

Kline threw up his hands in despair. "If you want to get murdered, go ahead."

"Come on, sweetie, we don't want to miss lunch." Becky took Sherm's arm. "Provided we don't get knocked off in the interim, would you care to join us, Sheriff?"

"I would if it weren't for the high water."

As they started off, Becky turned. "We will need a ride home, Sheriff, if you can spring a car, a Mercedes maybe?"

"You'll have one," Kline promised.

245

On their way they checked in at the director's table to see how they'd done. Lionel's face was etched with concern.

"We didn't do well?" Becky asked anxiously.

"I heard about your car."

"It wasn't a very lucky car," Sherm said.

"This is really awful. You were doing so well."

"How well?"

First north-south in their section, second overall right behind the blue-haired ladies from the Sunny Valley Bridge Center. The twins, they learned to their intense satisfaction, had come in eighth, practically out of the running.

28

Bear Hair

Their walk from the Convention Center had been through the gloomy shadow of a cloud that threatened to burst at any moment so there was no need to wait for the eyes to adjust to the interior darkness of the Saguaro Club. Charlie lifted his hand to wave them to the booth, tipped his cane and, in the process of rescuing it, sent the plastic RESERVED marker clattering onto the tile.

"Damn," he growled, "I hear they tried to bomb you again."

"News travels fast."

Flo, Charlie said, saw it on TV.

They slid into the booth, Becky first to the center of the crescent with Sherm and Charlie on either side.

"I tried to talk you out of that damned card game."

"We're glad you didn't." Becky put on her famous smile. "We made the final round."

"Yeah, and you nearly made the big final in the sky." Charlie's was a very disgusted face. "If there wasn't a lady present I'd say something real pertinent."

"Feel free," Sherm said. "My wife got nabbed for calling a player a dirty name."

"Asshole," Becky added. "Which she was being."

Where was the Jolly Grim Giant, Sherm asked.

"Donegan'll be along as soon as he's exhausted his quarter." Their spectrographic analyst, Charlie explained, was a video game junkie, and he was about to elaborate when the giant himself loomed over the cactus garden and plodded to the table.

Before Donegan could start in on the bombing, Becky asked which game he played.

"Gravitar, fifty-five minutes on a single quarter."

"Is that doing well?"

"I have a good chance of winning the machine."

"Yeah," Charlie muttered, "competition's all twelve years old."

"We used to play the home version," Becky turned to Sherm. "We were quite addicted, weren't we?"

"Gravitar was pretty tough, which I guess is why Atari sold it only to club members. However, my wife was particularly addicted to Megamania."

"I got as far as the fourth wave of radial tires."

"Yar's Revenge was my favorite."

"Sherm became attached to the little fly."

"Radial tires?" Charlie looked from Becky to Sherm, eyebrows ascending. "Little fly?"

"The little fly eats the shields—never mind."

Becky rescued him. "Isn't it too bad video games went *kersplat?*"

247

"They're making a comeback," Donegan said. "And I see some incredible applications coming out of the work at AZTECH."

"He spent his Sunday morning there," Charlie said.

"My other recreation: work. There was no way I could wait until Monday to take advantage of the opportunity to try out some of their new stuff."

Sherm must've shown his shock. Donegan laughed.

"No, Sherm, not at eight hundred an hour. We struck up a reciprocal agreement; they use my Voiceprint Two thousand, I use their unclassified equipment for the same length of time. I'm really impressed how much they're in the forefront of some very exciting technology. By the way, how did your tournament go?"

"Second overall," Becky proudly announced.

"Congratulations!"

She waved off his handshake as bad luck since they hadn't won yet.

"Good luck, though you may not need it so much now that the Ammars are out."

"How did you know that?" Becky asked.

Before he could answer, Sherm advised caution. A couple of blue-haired ladies were still in there and the twins weren't really out of it. "Eighth place isn't good but it isn't out either."

"There must be some mistake," Donegan said. "I talked to Jelila at AZTECH."

"You mean Majida."

"Yes, Mrs. Sherman, you were absolutely correct. It is as Miles Purdy suggested. Miss Ammar does have two names and has decided for now to be called Majida."

"What time was this?" Sherm asked.

"Let me see, I signed in—eleven-thirty, give or take five minutes."

Sherm hadn't noticed her being late for bridge. He asked

what she was wearing. A white lab smock. Under the smock? Donegan shrugged; couldn't tell. Any mention of the game? No, he didn't want to embarrass her.

Sherm rubbed his chin. "Must be a hell of a driver; AZTECH's fifteen miles north of here."

"Not much traffic on Sundays," Becky said just as Flo arrived.

The waitress apologized for the delay, said she was sure sorry their car got blown up, and took the orders. When she was gone, Becky asked Donegan if he thought Majida might have a photographic memory.

"Somewhat absentminded, I'd say. The first time I saw her here she acted as though she had forgotten who I was, although it could have been preoccupation with her work. I'm sure it had to be."

"I'm *sure*," Charlie put in.

"Yes, my size, I know; which is what I was thinking at the time." Donegan appeared mildly amused at the thought. "When I recalled the employment problems she was having because of her citizenship—rather lack of it—I was surprised to see her working."

"For security reasons?"

"Especially at a company like AZTECH which is active in SDI and so many other defense projects. You see, all security clearances require what they call a complete background investigation, which is practically impossible if you're from a country like Algeria."

"Maybe she's into unclassified work."

"Quite the opposite. Today, I couldn't see what she was working on because of the scope attached to the viewing screen, but I did notice she was using the new AZTECH Micro Laser Discs I've been reading about, so I asked if I could peek. She said, 'No, this project is classified.'"

Somewhere in Sherm's circuitry a weak *clang* registered. "These are video discs?"

"Much more. They can be used with computers in the interactive mode for practically unlimited applications."

Which meant nothing to Sherm. "How 'micro' are these discs?"

"Silver dollar size and thin like a card."

"Card as in ace of spades?"

"Correct."

"These discs then represent a new technology? By that I mean, do they make existing stuff obsolete?"

"Not at all. AZTECH's discs come with an adapter that plugs into your present set and is no larger than a home video game cartridge. You are, of course, limited by your hardware."

"In other words—"

"Peter—"

"I know, I'm cross-examining. Habit, I'm afraid—ah, here comes the food."

It was fortunate the meal arrived when it did or they might not have eaten. As it was, they had to rush to make it. Charlie offered to pick up the tab and walked them to the door where he took Sherm aside, touched the bulge in his jacket and said if he wanted him to, he'd trail along to keep an eye out. Sherm thanked his friend but said no, it was best Charlie not get shot again.

The detective shoved him on his way, wishing them good luck with the cards.

As they entered this final arena, Sherm knew that every fiber of concentration would have to center on the task of winning; yet he found himself too easily distracted. He was pleased to note Majida sitting west and wondered if Lionel had arranged for them not to play against each other. Seeing her also brought on a tinge of amused satisfaction at the thought of her picking at the bear hair stuck forever to her black pants; then he saw that it had not been futility at all. The hair was gone.

After their conversation at the Saguaro, he should've figured out what had happened to the hair; instead he was distracted by its disappearance, so much so that on the first hand he jumped Becky's mildly encouraging three heart response to his strong opening to a small slam she had to play. Down two for a certain bottom score. Bad, but with twenty-five boards to play, not the end of the world.

And play they did. With each hand he sensed improvement, not the world's fair of the evening before, rather a slow whittling away at the opposition a match point or two at a time. And, as the points accumulated, the disappointment in Becky's eyes changed to hope, the white flashing whenever she glanced his way, that famous smile reined but ready. They could almost taste it: winning.

A grim silence hung over the blue-haired pair from the Sunny Valley Bridge Center and there were unspoken accusations in each partner's eyes. They played quickly and this time carelessly, and when two boards were put to rest the one named Gladys said in response to no question and to no one in particular, "We *were* in first place."

"That's ah . . . nice," Sherm mumbled, knowing damn well it wasn't.

Gladys tossed her head back. "It *was* nice."

Peggy lit a cigarette. "It wasn't my fault; it was those people in black."

Becky initialed the score card. "The twins?"

"Yes," Gladys said, returning. "They managed to shake up my partner so, she made the stupidist play."

"What about your little beauty?" Peggy snapped back.

Luckily, the announcement to move for the last round got them away from the ladies before they started taking it out on them. While they waited for the E-W seats at the last table to be vacated, Becky wondered if they'd ever speak to each other again.

"They'll be playing together by Wednesday, I'd bet."

"The wonderful world of bridge."

"Yeah, I think I'm about ready to go back to playing with the little fly."

"And radial tires?"

"Them also."

"What do you think"—she squeezed his hand—"about this game?"

"W-I-N-N-I-N-G."

"Don't say it."

"I didn't; I spelled it."

"I'm holding my breath," she whispered, letting go of his hand. "And crossing my toes."

He knew what she meant. Many things could go wrong; one did.

The Ammars' win so unnerved him that he failed to comprehend the obvious; then Majida's gratuitous little speech about how upset they must've been after someone bombed their car, ignited the spark that would light the fire that would burn away the cloud. The spark was something Charlie said a long time ago: "Never investigate your own mother's murder," meaning there is no way you can see through your emotions.

Good advice then, good advice now:

> First, Donegan is somewhat of a genius.
> Second, geniuses do not make dumb mistakes.
> Third, he was right the first time about her name.
> Fourth, there is no way Majida Ammar could've been at AZTECH at 11:30 and here to play at noon.
> Fifth, there is a way the second round bridge hands could have been studied.
> Lastly, it's absolutely impossible to rid one's black trousers of bear hair between bridge sessions.

Sherm grabbed Becky's hand and marched to the director's table to file an official protest. Lionel asked on what grounds. "Gross improprieties." He didn't explain. "Call the Ammars and the five of us will discuss it." He looked about and pointed to a vacated, though cluttered, corner of the big room. "Over there."

Lionel held up his hands as he had with Denise. "I know how the bomb must have upset you—"

"I'm serious about this, Lionel. They cheated!"

"Shhhh." Lionel flexed his hands as though he wanted to close them over Sherm's mouth. "Hold your voice down, *please*."

When they were safely out of earshot of the crowd around the director's table, he whispered, "Do you know, if you file a protest that doesn't hold water, both of you could be expelled from the ACBL?" Lionel's gravity suggested that this was the worst punishment he could imagine. "I know you had a little run-in this afternoon." They finally stopped in an area strewn with two sessions of drinks, snacks, and cigarettes, far enough from everyone so no one could overhear. "I understand your disappointment; they are assholes. Nevertheless, unless you have very, very, *very* concrete evidence, there is no way we can accuse the twins without—"

"They're not twins, Lionel."

"What, what's that got to do—"

"Triplets."

"What do you mean, triplets?"

"Call them over, Lionel."

Lionel wagged his head but raised his hand to boom his request: "The Ammars please, over here!" And even before they arrived, Sherm could see in those cold Algerian eyes that she knew they'd been found out. Lionel lowered his voice and came right to the point. "The Shermans have informed me they wish to file an official protest—" Najib opened his mouth to say something but the director's hand came up fast, a signal to listen, not talk. "These things tend to become very messy—"

"Jelila?" Sherm asked quietly.

"Majida!" Najib exclaimed.

This time Jelila's hand silenced her brother. "No, no more of this." She looked at Lionel. "What must we do?"

"Well, ah . . ." Lionel placed his hands flat on the battered card table. "Ah . . ." He turned to Sherm.

"May I suggest that if there was an unauthorized substitution on your team, you plead ignorance of the rule and withdraw at this time."

"Done." Jelila took her brother's arm. "We must go, Najib."

Clearly wishing to protest, Najib drifted as in a trance but said nothing as they moved through the battlefield of tables, trash, and chairs, glancing back only once as they were leaving.

Lionel congratulated them and, as they returned to the director's table, tried to piece together what had transpired.

"Unbelievable, but what made you suspect them in the first place?"

"My wife says I have a suspicious nature." He motioned toward a nearby coffee urn. "Let's see if there's any left."

There was, and while they were sipping what amounted to dregs, Sherm recounted how he'd reached his solution.

"On more than one occasion I noticed that, while most players stick around to see how they scored in the first round, the Ammars always bugged out without checking anything. Now I see that they needed time to drive to where they could make the switch and discuss their upcoming strategy without being seen or overheard. I also noticed that during the second session they never played north-south. North and south players of course remain stationary. Another item, meaningless until now, was that during the east-west move from one table to the next, they frequently changed positions.

Jelila, who'd been west, might, for example, switch to east. Now I see why. She was placing herself in the seat that required an unusual line of play to make the best score.

"The cat hair was the clincher."

"Good old bear," Becky noted brightly.

"You're suggesting this Jelila knew what cards would be in each of the hands before she saw them?" Lionel demonstrated his dismay that such a breach in security could occur.

"No, this is not possible, unless—your questions concerning the computer hands were not pointless, were they?"

"Not pointless."

"How on earth?"

"While Majida and Najib played the first round, Jelila, who is Majida's identical twin—or should I say triplet, identical triplet?"

Sherm put down his Styrofoam cup and looked to Becky, who made her "heaven only knows" gesture.

"Anyway, while her brother and sister play in the first session, Jelila sits at an AZTECH computer studying the second session hands that she's hacked while they were being transmitted via satellite. No need to memorize all twenty-seven; just those where an unusual line of play wins the most tricks for their side. These could be offensive or defensive tricks. Once the best line of play is determined, she must make certain she's properly positioned east-west to either play the hand or make the killing defensive lead. This is why they frequently switched positions, to put Jelila in the best seat."

"I'd better write this down just in case someone decides on an inquiry. You never know." Lionel ripped a sheet of blank computer paper from a nearby machine and asked to borrow Sherm's pen. "So let's see if I've got this. The Ammar brother and one sister play the first session while a second sister steals the computer hands and studies them for the best possible scoring plays; then during the break between sessions the sisters, who are identical twins or triplets or whatever,

255

switch identities so the one who has seen and studied the hands plays them during the second session."

"I think you've got it."

"Amazing."

"The absolute ultimate in double-dummying," Becky said.

Both amazed and amused by the antics of the Algerians, Lionel suddenly put on a very serious face and asked if Sherm wanted to file charges.

"I'll leave this one to the ACBL, thank you."

"We've had a trying day," Becky added.

"Understatement of the year."

Sherm glanced at his watch. "Well, Cinderella, it's near pumpkin-turning time."

Becky nodded toward the far exit, temporarily filled with their burly friend, Romero. "Our carriage waits," she said.

"Oh," Lionel said, "the photographer." He waved over the man with the Polaroid who snapped a quick picture, took their names and club affiliation, checked spellings, and wished them luck in future outings.

On their way home Becky told Romero about the bear hair and good old Beau solving another one.

"He didn't exactly *solve* it," Sherm said.

"Sure he did."

Becky gently squeezed his hand, smiling. But the grip hardened and the smile faded with the passing of each arc lamp.

"There's still the big one to solve, isn't there?" she whispered.

"Yes." Sherm agreed humbly. The euphoria was gone, replaced by the specter of a thousand scattered pieces of the little yellow car that once was Vic's.

29

The Hundred-Year Flood

A question dropped, innocuous and out of the night: Had Romero noticed anything in the Eagan house that resembled a video game cartridge?

Several, to go with the old Atari 2600. He'd played Asteroids, he was embarrassed to admit, a game all his kids beat him at.

No, the ones Sherm meant only *resembled* game cartridges. Sherm asked if they could drop by 1220 Rio Verde.

Too late, Romero answered. Kline had called off the house sitter, returned all the stuff they'd taken to the lab, and told Bruner's sister she could go ahead and settle the estate.

"She's flying in this morning." Romero put his finger to the digital dash display: 12:38 A.M. "If this rain lets up." He was hunched over, trying to see under the wiper blades. "It don't look good. The old geezer with the zoo next door got plans for a big wood boat."

With a startling suddenness they were out of the downpour into sprinkles that followed them to their doorstep. Romero had them stay in the car until he'd checked the house. "All clear," he said, "except for a vicious cat." He apologized for not being able to stay. The department was really short-handed because of flooding, but if they used the beeper he'd be there *muy pronto*.

Becky was first into the house and first to fuss over her bear. She told him how indispensable he was in the war

257

against cheaters and for his reward he could have all the special tuna he wanted.

When he was fed and the fuss subsided, it was 1:02; yet, except for Beau, who'd buried his nose in a leather shoe, the household was wide-awake. It could have been due to the high generated by winning but it wasn't.

Too late . . . too late . . .

Sherm unlocked the sliding door and stepped out onto the deck. The sprinkles had stopped and the chubasco had drifted south into the mountains of Mexico where its lightning, like a fiery heartbeat, enlivened the distant horizon. As he touched the railing a sudden commotion lifted his own heartbeat, a small flapping shadow that rose through the branches, an elf owl abandoning the mesquite for the safety of its home in the saguaro.

Becky rubbed against him, Beau purring in her arms.

"Mr. McCreedy's dead; Mr. Knight's in jail, so who can it be?"

"Wilma Bruner," Sherm answered instinctively. "But why? Why would she want to do away with us? What is left for us to learn that isn't already known?"

"Maybe we've still got it turned around," Becky said. "Maybe this TV porno scheme was really hers and she doesn't know we know about it and doesn't want us to find out."

"Maybe even bigger; MOM has great financial pains, which local cable couldn't possibly alleviate."

"But a little sideline maybe could?"

"Definitely could."

What they were saying sounded okay, but Sherm knew they were being illogical as hell. The sheriff's department most certainly had amassed more information than their small investigation could have garnered. Kline would know about the scheme, yet the bomb was not meant for him; which also meant there was a bit of information, a specific bit that only the Shermans knew, and the bomber would also know they knew.

And what in the hell could that be?

"I wish we could take another look at that house before Wilma Bruner takes over."

Did he still have the lockbox key? He did, and they still had a car with enough gas to get to 1220 Rio Verde and back.

"Let's go for it," Becky said, using a phrase rather of Vic's generation—particularly Vic's, and the steeper, more moguled the run, the more emphatic: *Plant your poles and push off; go for it, Dad!*

But Sherm held off. Tonight they'd be attempting runs they'd never been on before, and he felt too tired and too old to be taking any "plunges" at this hour.

Becky sensed his reluctance and said she was feeling a little like Pandora herself.

"Yeah." He drew in a deep breath of rainy air and pushed himself away from the railing. "So let's go raise the lid to see what comes flying out."

While Becky brought the car around, Sherm took a pair of Mini-Mag flashlights from the office desk and opened the cedar chest. He lifted the old H & R from under Vic's tattered blanket, loaded, and shoved it under his belt. He locked the front door and looked up at the sliver of moon. A good sign; they'd had enough chubasco for one summer.

More than enough. Twelve-twenty Rio Verde was on the edge of washing away. Much of its sixteen acres of creosote and beer cans already had. As they pulled past the drooping gate into the driveway, their headlights caught an angry surge of brown current tearing at the crumbling bank of the wash only a few feet beyond the mailbox. Uprooted plants and trash, aluminum cans, a plastic garbage bag somehow inflated, a pack rat on a chunk of firewood. Water was backed into the carport and when they got out of their car, a river that hadn't existed the week before roared like a passing freight.

The key worked and they entered to find the house without power. Sherm cursed. Even if they located what they were looking for, they couldn't check it out. And they found it where it'd been all along, in the cards.

They dropped to their knees, putting down the flashlights to beam a cross of light, and placed the tiny laser disc at the intersection of the cross.

"Innocuous, isn't it?"

"Yet lethal. Three dead and almost how many more?" Sherm rubbed his chin. "Why do you suppose Wilma Bruner hid it in a deck of cards?"

"What better place? No one would be opening the box searching for evidence and if they did, they probably wouldn't see it or recognize it for what it is. She knew she'd inherit the house, so it was only a matter of time."

"But why hide it at all when it can be so easily disposed of?"

"Look at it," Becky said. "Practically indestructible. She couldn't risk someone finding it. And who knows what might be on there that she doesn't want destroyed."

"We've got to find the adapter."

They found it in a box of old eight tracks, black plastic, rectangular, but smaller than a regular eight track, with a pronged connector recessed in one end, a slit in the other into which the disc fit perfectly.

Wrapped up, or so Sherm thought.

Becky lifted the opened card box as though it held some special significance and turned it to catch the light.

"Bridge cards."

She placed the disc on the pack. "We've still got this wrong, sweetie." She flipped over the disc. "They gave up much too easily." She opened the pack and slid the disc inside. "Wilma's letter—she was practically illiterate. This is the work of a genius who knows all about laser discs, someone who has the wherewithal to synthesize voices and alter information in computers, a person who enjoys complex games and knows where the decks are kept because she came here to give Miss Eagan bridge lessons."

With the suddenness of a summer thunderstorm it came pouring in, yet all he could utter was that same magic word that had won them the tournament: "Jelila?"

"The first time Mr. Donegan accidentally ran into her—" Becky's face was a mask of light and shadow in the aura of flashlights. "Don't you think he must've told her who he was working for and don't you think she must've realized you would eventually piece together her association with AZTECH and Miss Eagan, the cheating at bridge, and the rest?"

"I think she displayed an enormous amount of overconfidence. I'm not sure why she'd kill the Eagan girl in the first place."

"Think about it," Becky whispered. "Jelila works in a company with a big defense contract, in a lab where they develop the stuff, even though she's not a citizen, remember? But because she's an identical twin she can work as a so-to-speak nonperson. What would happen if just that was found out? Prosecution, prison, and deportation back to God knows what? Everything is at stake: her true identity, her job, maybe even her life. And motive, what motive, Shelly Eagan left practically everything to the research lab!"

Every reason in the world to kill.

"I don't know, bombs and young women aren't usually associated one with the other."

"She grew up where terrorism practically began—Algeria!" Becky dropped her voice to a bare whisper. "Don't you see?"

"I get the picture, but why are you whispering?"

"I don't know."

Sherm dusted off his knees and helped his wife to her feet. "Well," he said, "that's not quite all of it, but close enough."

"I wonder—" Becky began, breaking off when a headlight beam coming through the front window splashed across the wall.

"Oh, shit," Sherm whispered, "that must be Wilma Bruner."

"Tell her we're checking on the flood damage."

He opened the front door and put the light on the visitor getting out of the Porsche. She was dressed in black and one hand was out of sight inside a black leather handbag. She was not Wilma.

Sherm jerked the revolver from his belt.

"In this bag, Mr. Sherman," Jelila said coldly, "I have a remote control detonator and a bomb. My finger is on the switch." She stepped into the headlights. "Please give me your handgun and spare us all."

A gust of wild, improbable action assaulted his reason—like shielding Becky from the blast with his body; then reason took over and he handed her the revolver.

"Thank you." She held it firm in her cold white hand. "I presume you've located the disc and adapter, so may I have them also, please."

With a sideways jerk of his head he indicated they were inside.

"Inside then."

Becky gave her the pack. Jelila rattled the box. "I thought I'd found the perfect hiding place." She put down her handbag and examined the disc with Becky's flashlight. "Very damaging evidence, Mr. Sherman, but you didn't get to view it, did you?" Keeping the revolver leveled and steady, she held up the disc. "If you had, you would have witnessed the final struggle of a depraved whore being freed from her life of debauchery."

"You strangled Shelly Eagan."

Jelila laughed quietly as she nodded. "With the silver cord symbolic of her foolish cult."

"Miss Ammar, why not give it up?"

"Give up? You fool, Sherman, you don't appreciate what is at stake, do you? Just like that Eagan pig, jeopardizing our magnificent work with her disgusting smut, you fail to grasp the divine significance of our endeavor or that those who impede it must be removed, even if it means eliminating a plaza filled with people."

He wouldn't look, he decided, just take the three or four steps; then it would be in his hands. So, without further thought, Sherm took those steps, unbelievably restrained, and too easily got the purse in his hands, feeling for the shape through the leather.

Jelila laughed aloud. "You *are* a fool. There is no bomb."

Only a flashlight.

"Though I do have one in the back of the car, generously supplied by that rotting scab, McCreedy, but you came out before I could get to it." She slipped the disc and adapter into her purse and tucked it under her arm. "So now you have a choice of being shot or blown up. Which will it be?"

"Neither," Sherm said more dispassionately than he would've thought possible. And, with a great deal more confidence than experience dictated, he drew in a deep breath and dove as he had toward the gun emplacements guarding the bridges at Sinanju, hearing the *click, click* of the trigger, the firing pin catching the corner of the cylinder, not striking the shell casing, misfiring.

He jerked the barrel down and to one side as a round fired and there was another sound, like a finger snapping. Jelila cried out, grasping her finger, staggering backward, stumbling out the door, off the step, into the headlights. Sherm lunged but she spun away and he slipped in the mud and came down, his cheek smashing against something hard, momentarily stunned as the Porsche jerked backward nearly running him over, then forward into his sights but the revolver misfired again. She was getting away as he struggled to his feet and tossed the useless weapon into the darkness where it plopped to a final watery grave.

She didn't make it. Lights flashed out of nowhere, a patrol car at the gate blocking the driveway. She swerved, took out the mailbox, and the last they saw of Jelila Ammar that night was the blinking of her taillights as they were snuffed out by the Rio Verde River in its hundred-year flood.

Early the next morning a police helicopter found her alive, clinging to the tangled branches of a flood-swept mesquite.

30

In Memoriam

Whether it was a hundred- or a fifty-year flood was the sort of nondebate the *Desert Star* seemed addicted to; so three weeks after the fact, with the Rio Verde as dry as ever, the subject kept cropping up in the Metro section. The other ongoing story belonged to Jelila Ammar.

Never missing an opportunity, Sheriff Kline had taken credit for her capture, explaining in a seemingly endless string of interviews how the returned household goods were used to bait the killer back to the scene of the crime. Convinced from the beginning that the setup in Shelly Eagan's bedroom indicated something had been videotaped, possibly the murder itself, yet unable to uncover any tapes to support their suspicion, Kline and company decided to bug the terminal and make it available to their prime suspect in hopes of catching her in the act of making an illegal transmission. He didn't name the suspect, however.

Everyone's prime suspect, Wilma Bruner, really had wanted to set up a local cable outlet for the Mothers of the Moon, but the technical aspects were more than she or her cohorts could handle.

AZTECH, in a magnanimous gesture that made no mention of the enormous technical loss certain to occur if they fired the remaining two Ammars, pardoned the erring Algerians for hacking bridge hands, pointing out that although there should be one, no computer fraud statute existed in this state. Forgiven, but unhumbled, the pair returned to the bridge club amid a chorus of protests from players who wanted the Moslems' fingers chopped off. In what they decided afterward would be their final game of the year, the Shermans were soundly beaten by the Algerians, this time Sherm thought honestly. The occasion for Becky and Sherm's decision to temporarily absent themselves from the wonderful world of duplicate bridge was the return home of their only daughter.

Heather, a bit heavier than Sherm remembered, but still looking very good, arrived on a jumbo jet with two pieces of luggage, the shoulder bag she carried off and a pet carrier they picked up from the conveyor.

The wiry Abyssinian she'd named Mouzer took all of ten seconds to make herself at home. Beau was, of course, bent completely out of shape, retreating frequently to his under-bed hideout rather than confront the affectionate interloper. Mouzer took over the house and Heather took over the new RX-7. Commiserating with the bear, Sherm told him that's the way things were; you get a little rusty around the edges and they toss you out.

No one was being tossed out, Becky chided. "We have a new friend until Heather finds a place of her own; and two cars with only one licensed driver—one of which Heather may as well drive, also until she finds one of her own."

Heather, Sherm grumbled, didn't seem to be in a hell of a hurry. He ached to get his hands on the wheel of his new rotary bandit, forcing himself to be content, for the time being, as a passenger each day his autobahn-initiated daughter barreled them to work.

They kept busy preparing Knight's case. Heather had arranged the plea bargaining with a fair certainty of getting off with a fine and probation or less in exchange for Knight turning state's witness in the Jelila Ammar trial. The new antipornography law had fallen into limbo and would probably be declared unconstitutional when it came before the high court. Also, the way they'd botched up the charges, it was possible Knight would get off free.

The plan to pawn Pauline Lundquist off became unnecessary. In the last of her tape-recorded one-sided conversations she informed Sherm that she'd gone to Vegas for a "quickie." Three days later Terri said a Mrs. Dornbusch had called to say hello, Pauline Dornbusch.

Terri also sprang some news she'd promised Charlie she wouldn't tell, especially to Sherm. Charlie was thinking about remarriage.

"Who's the victim?"

"You won't believe—Margot."

"Margot, the assistant county attorney?"

"The same."

Charlie, Sherm said, was going to have to change his opinion about lawyers. When he called his detective friend to find out if congratulations were in order, Charlie asked how he'd like a fat lip to go with his black eye.

The new black eye bothered Sherm a lot more and a lot longer than the first. He was afraid it might never go away. The fall he'd taken the night of the flood had lacerated the skin and chipped a bone in his cheek. Becky was almost certain it would and Heather suggested he blacken the other so he didn't look so off balance. He didn't much enjoy this shiner but felt very lucky that things hadn't gone a whole lot worse. The trap that accidentally snagged Jelila had nearly got them both snagged. Kline had planned to spring the trap after Wilma moved in and the deputy who arrived was on a routine patrol check when he saw Jelila's headlights. If he hadn't, or if she hadn't seen his, things might've turned out terribly different. Sherm would take the black eye.

As the case against Jelila Ammar was being prepared, Glidden called on the Shermans to go over their testimony, expressing concern that Sherm might feel uncomfortable in the witness box, "On the other end of the stick, you might say."

"You'll be lucky if he doesn't cross-examine the cross-examiner," Becky said.

Sherm promised he wouldn't if Glidden promised to keep it short.

Glidden said he would and before he left, told Sherm that Jelila Ammar wanted to talk to him.

Most unusual and not very good practice, but he couldn't resist; so he went to where they'd sequestered her in a private corner of the women's jail, not really a cell, rather a room he might've expected in a girls' dorm, except the locks were on the outside and bars covered the window.

Cozy by any standard, the cell was probably a result of Tom Kline's concept of how women should be interned. But the real centerpiece was the woman herself. In black silk pajamas, the kind that achieve sensuality by covering in such a way as to accentuate form, rather than revealing, the tournament automaton had become a Mediterranean temptress.

She motioned him to take the padded chair, seating herself on the edge of the bed. "I'm so glad you're here, Peter."

"Miss Ammar—"

"Don't you like the name Jelila?"

"I like it," he said.

"I could seduce you."

"You tried to murder me."

"Aren't they practically the same?"

"What did you want to talk about?"

"To explain." She bowed her head, the nun's veil closing over her face as she told him that it had never been him; the rest yes, but not him. Circumstance was to blame.

"When I first saw Aaron at the lab I knew it was only a matter of time before you found out that Eagan's call had been synthesized."

She lifted her head, those penetrating eyes storming into his.

"We grew up with violence, Peter, in Algeria."

Her parents had manufactured bombs in their kitchen and one day while the triplets were in school one went off. The handsome children were split up and sent to Moslem foster homes, Majida and Najib to America, Jelila to Iran. Later, when Jelila came to the United States as a graduate student, they were reunited. All three had turned out remarkably alike, each with degrees in computer sciences. Unfortunately for Jelila, she was not a U.S. citizen and could not get a job. When the Ammars learned of their sister's plight they went to Shelly Eagan with their bizarre scheme.

"Eagan certainly recognized the benefits of having three for the price of two, but I think the real reason she accepted our plan was because she'd become enamored with my sister and me. Having two made one of us available, the other a silent partner working overtime shifts and earning amounts which added to our already considerable salaries.

"It was quite amusing, actually. Eagan couldn't tell us

apart so we played the same game we had played as children so successfully that our father couldn't tell who was Majida and who was Jelila. They loved the game, as did Eagan, so much so she invited one of us, not specifying which, to move in with her for security reasons, she said, so that Majida and Jelila would never be seen together, thus revealing their subterfuge."

Curiously, Jelila's narrative had slipped into the third person.

"Fortunately for Eagan, she'd taken after her brilliant father who also taught her bridge; however, she knew little of the game's intricacies until tutored. Indeed, it was a sight to see the four of them playing at the same table, a sight that drove Shelly's pitiful, alcoholic mother to the limits of distraction, never quite sure she wasn't seeing double, or triple.

"Bridge was one game; hacking was another. Eagan was an intelligent but plain girl who became easily bored, so they spent many nights at the lab breaking into various computer networks. They kept records and occasionally would come across another hacker and exchange information. Eventually they gained access to almost any program they wished, perusing them at will.

"Another game they invented they called 'Conversations.' After recording familiar voices from TV network programs, they would see who could put together the most amusing conversation with the synthesizer. It was all very innocent and quite safe—until the night Eagan, who was at the end of her rope with her drunken mother, synthesized her father."

Jelila assumed the male baritone. "'Dorothy,' her father's voice said, 'sober up or I'm gonna come back and kick your ass.'"

At this Jelila laughed.

"Unfortunately, they had discussed their work at the house and when they returned from the lab that night, Mother—in her typical drunken rage—said she'd personally put an end to the Ammars' deception. Biting her lip until it bled, Shelly cried out that she wasn't going to take any more shit, which set mother to screaming all sorts of obscene accusations. In the midst of this screaming she mercifully passed out.

"'This is the end of me,' Jelila said. 'They will send me to prison, then back to my country where I will surely be executed for defecting.'

"They both looked at the heaving, gurgling lump passed out on the rug and, without speaking, carried it to the car, drove it to the gate, and propped it up against the front bumper. They sat in the car for several minutes in silent debate before Jelila reached over and placed the shift lever in low gear. When the car moved, Eagan's foot was on the gas pedal.

"This execution was the catalyst, I suppose, for what followed. While Jelila looked after the house, Eagan went to Las Vegas at her aunt's request and when she returned, she returned with Jones, a thoroughly depraved whore only slightly less despicable than the slimy eel who slithered in behind, McCreedy. When they began exploiting AZTECH's marvelous technological creations for their private perversions, Jelila moved to her own apartment.

"Eagan would bring Jones to the lab and the two of them would play their licentious version of Conversations, using the telephone to perform obscene pranks, in one instance synthesizing the sheriff's voice to send a TV crew into the desert to film a nonexistent murder/rape victim—which provided, ironically, the model for what was to come.

"In spite of Jelila's warnings that their abominations could not go unpunished, they increased their level of debauchery until virtually no despicable act was left unrecorded.

"Eagan had become drunk on carnal excesses and threatened Jelila to either 'shape up or definitely ship out.'

"Realizing that Eagan's lust had driven her beyond reason, Jelila pretended to shape up by suggesting they record a rape fantasy together. The slavering pig fell for the ruse, set up the cameras, and followed Jelila's insane script to the letter, except that it ended with her silver cord wrapped around her throat. Eagan died so easily Jelila could scarcely believe she'd killed her."

Jelila took the cord, trusting its disappearance and the letter's presence would cast suspicion on Wilma and her cult; but it was a mistake, she admitted, not to have taken the disc, which she didn't want on her person if she was picked up, especially at the AZTECH lab where it could be viewed.

The idea to frame Bruner came from Wilma's letter and Jelila's belief that he was part of the debauchery. After strangling Shelly she went straight to the lab, synthesized the message to Jones and the last part of the emergency call. After editing and combining the 9-1-1 tape, she placed both tapes in the telephone answering machine and made the calls.

"A perfect crime—until Aaron. McCreedy supplied the munitions after Jelila promised that she and Majida would perform depraved acts, his kind of payoff. But he is the one who paid. Also Jones. Jelila hadn't meant to shoot her but it was right that she did."

Jelila leaned forward, arms crossed on the black silk-clad thighs, intense now.

"Jelila has never been prouder of anything she's done than she is of executing those festering scabs. Her only regret is that she twice missed the other scab, Knight, once when he responded to her synthesized call but did not enter McCreedy's apartment, a second time because he was not where he was supposed to be."

Sherm waited for more, then: "Is that what you wanted to tell me, that they deserved to die?"

"Yes."

"Nothing more?"

"My lawyer is an incompetent pig." She hesitated asking, but it didn't matter.

"The state's star witness could hardly be expected to represent the accused, do you think?"

"I'm not stupid, Peter."

"I'm well aware you're not, but there is one thing you haven't mentioned that makes me wonder."

"Which is?"

"Your Shelly Eagan call to our house provided a comparison tape that virtually proved the nine-one-one call was phony."

"I made no such call."

Still playing the game? "In Donegan's words, the cybernetic models were identical. 'Fess up, Jelila."

"My name is Majida."

It was a precaution taken in the beginning, a double switch. They knew if they were ever caught, a way out would be if the wrong one was arraigned. And this, she explained, was not simply a matter of switching names. Majida was innocent, utterly innocent of anything beyond bridge hacking. Jelila had crawled out of the rolling Rio Verde a mile downstream and made her way home. There, she convinced Majida that if she didn't plant herself on that mesquite in the middle of the river her sister would certainly die in the electric chair.

In spite of everything, Sherm felt immense admiration for the brilliance of this young woman. Her claim of the switched identity was most certainly a lie, but what a stroke! A case of mistaken identity could go on forever, especially when the other one also claimed to be Majida.

Poor Glidden.

"I can't possibly defend you, Miss Ammar; however, I can recommend another Sherman. My daughter, Heather, is an attorney and if she wishes me to, I will be pleased to assist." He got up to leave. "Think about it."

"I will."

* * *

Heather hoped whichever Ammar she was wouldn't think about it too long. She was sitting on the floor in her bikini, grappling with the Atari joystick positioned between her V'd legs. His twenty-nine-year-old ex-Army captain, ex-member of the Judge Advocate General's staff, NATO, had become engrossed in a video road race, zipping around cars and negotiating curves at dangerously high speeds.

"I hope you don't drive the Mazda like that."

"Daddy—" She shot between two slower cars. "I've never had an accident, even on the autobahn."

"Let's keep it that way."

"You should drive—" Checkered flag. She turned and smiled. "You should drive on the autobahn sometime."

"I have enough trouble with streets." He smiled back. "You know, even if this Ammar, whichever-one-she-is, hires you, your chances of winning are nil. You know Glidden has a video laser disc recording of the murder."

And wasn't there also a recording, Becky reminded him, proving Mr. Bruner did it? She was busy by the sliding door doing an 'action watercolor,' she called it, of the cat who nabbed the nefarious Algerians. Sherm tried to argue but was ignored. The bear, for his part, had become used to the hyperactive Abyssinian, who was always scratching the glass to get out.

"May I also point out that Ms. Ammar confessed to us twice."

"Didn't Mr. Bruner confess?"

Indeed he had—and he'd paid them a last visit at the house before he left town. He wanted to meet his benefactor, he said, now that he had something he could give her. Bruner asked them out to his car where he got out the gifts.

273

"One of the deputies, big Mexican fellow, said you liked these things."

Two Grey Hills, Ganado Red, Burnt Water, Wide Ruins, and a Daisy Touglechee!

Flabbergasted, Becky tried not to accept them. "Mr. Bruner, do you know what Navajo rugs are worth?"

"They'd be worth nothin' to me if I'd been electrocuted." No way would he take them back and Becky, so happy she almost cried, hugged the rigid little man until he was embarrassed. These were the most beautiful gifts she'd ever received, she said.

They were also reminders of the Colorado Plateau and an unfulfilled commitment.

The best place to hold the service, they decided, was right at home. There should be a stone with a simple inscription, a priest would probably handle it best, and the mourners would be restricted to those who'd known and loved Vic. Heather saw to it the old friends were notified. Becky took care of the adults. Not a large group, a sincere one. They would hold the service early while it was still cool, and afterward gather by the pool for coffee, juice, rolls, and remembrance.

On the appointed morning Sherm got up with the sun and put down the stone on a knoll above the wash behind the house where Vic found the best obsidian arrowhead either of them had ever seen:

IN MEMORY OF OUR LOVING SON
VICTOR SHERMAN
1960–1982

All by himself he got through that, but no more. He slumped to the knoll and for a long time wept for his golden boy, and all the other young men lost in this vulnerable age.

Finally he struggled to his feet and drew himself up straight, wiped his eyes and looked up.

Behind Finger Rock the sky was a fierce blue, the mountains as though etched by the Great Finger itself, and in the canyons the trees, a denser green, were thicker and cooler looking. And below the mountain, up on Ridge Road, the new gazebo looked grown over.

Sherm went back up the path to the pool where he finished setting up the tables and chairs. When he finished, he placed his hands flat on the cap block of the wall he and his dead son had built and knew now he would get through it.

Not many showed up, perhaps fewer than a dozen. They'd put the service off too long and the young had scattered with the winds of fortune; but the number didn't disturb him so much as not knowing who they were, particularly the sad-eyed fellow who looked as though the world had been lost to him. The priest kept mercifully to his ritual, though the final words, "forever in Paradise," nearly did it. Two girls cried; the bearded fellow sobbed without shame; and Becky and Heather wept in each other's arms again and for the last time. The rest were appropriately sad, but time with its new friends and new situations had lessened the impact.

After the flowers were placed, Sherm said a few words, encouraging them to come whenever they wanted and to tell others who might not have been able to be there today, that they should feel free to visit also. Becky said there would be refreshments by the pool and time for becoming reacquainted.

The bearded fellow turned out to be Larry, Vic's inseparable boyhood chum. They talked about football and fishing and Indian Guides.

"'Pals forever,'" Larry said.

"That was it, wasn't it . . ." Sherm nodded sadly; the Indian Guide motto.

Larry said his father had died.

In the days that followed others did show up. Some came to the door; a few were escorted to the stone by someone who'd attended the service. One morning Sherm was in the kitchen getting a glass of water when he looked out and saw a solitary figure kneeling on the knoll. She was wearing black and her hair hung like a nun's veil about her face. Taken by the resemblance to the Ammar women, he went to get Becky. When they returned, the girl in black was gone. On the stone was a bunch of daisies and a rosary. They never learned who she was.

Epilogue

Majida's story exploded across the front pages and the irony involving the two Shermans was mentioned in each: father testifying against, daughter defending. There was no mention of electrocution.

Sherm tossed the paper on the floor, causing the Abyssinian to jump.

"What was that for?" Becky asked.

"I think I've just decided that for me this case is over."

"About time."

"But I won't renege on my promise to help out."

"That's good," Heather said. "For me it's just a beginning."

"For you maybe; for me it's over and I, for one, am glad."

"Wasn't it fun?" Becky asked.

"Fun?" Sherm looked at his wife as though she'd lost her mind. "A boggler, yes; fun, never. And I hope I never have another like it."

Becky gave him her famous smile. "But, sweetie, aren't all of your cases like that?"